THE FORGOTTEN DAUGHTER

The Ashmead Heirs, Book Three

Caroline Warfield

Dragonblade Publishing, Inc. is an imprint of Kathryn Le Veque Novels, Inc.

P.O. Box 7968

La Verne CA 91750

ceo@dragonbladepublishing.com

Produced in the United States of America

First Edition January 2022
Print Edition

ARE YOU SIGNED UP FOR DRAGONBLADE'S BLOG?

You'll get the latest news and information on exclusive giveaways, exclusive excerpts, coming releases, sales, free books, cover reveals and more.

Check out our complete list of authors, too!

No spam, no junk. That's a promise!

Sign Up Here

www.dragonbladepublishing.com

Dearest Reader;

Thank you for your support of a small press. At Dragonblade Publishing, we strive to bring you the highest quality Historical Romance from some of the best authors in the business. Without your support, there is no 'us', so we sincerely hope you adore these stories and find some new favorite authors along the way.

Happy Reading!

CEO, Dragonblade Publishing

Dedication

To my beloved. Never underestimate the quiet ones!

Quiet minds cannot be perplexed or frightened but go on in fortune or misfortune at their own private pace, like a clock during a thunderstorm.
(Robert Louis Stevenson, *The Strange Case of Dr. Jekyll and Mr. Hyde*)

The hero is commonly the simplest and obscurest of men.
(Henry David Thoreau)

Additional Dragonblade books by Author Caroline Warfield

The Ashmead Heirs Series
The Wayward Son (Book 1)
The Defiant Daughter (Book 2)
The Forgotten Daughter (Book 3)

CHAPTER ONE

The Road from Manchester to Ashmead, May 1818

G RIPPING A RETICULE containing proof of her parentage, Fanny considered that Mam may have been right to try to shield her from the circumstances of her birth. But here she sat in a coach of the royal mail, rocking back and forth as it careened down the road, on her way to confront the Earl of Clarion and her future. Frances Hancock— Fanny to those who cared—had always known she was a bastard. Her mother's husband had made sure of that. She hadn't known her father was an earl until her mother had died.

Her stepfather, Horace Rundle, no use to anyone and half-crazed on gin, had croaked in the gutter outside the Happy Cock public house ten months after Mam had passed. It had taken Fanny another month, six visits from credit collectors, and damage to the remaining inventory in the back of the shop to fully accept the degree to which the reprobate had bled her grandfather's drapery store dry. She and her two younger siblings stood on the brink of homelessness and hunger. Fanny knew she had to find this earl and demand his aid, no matter how many dire predictions Mam had uttered over the years.

Never one to sink under troubles, Fanny had gone to work immediately. The information she'd found scribbled on a scrap in her mother's sewing box identified the man as the Earl of Clarion. She'd visited the reading room of the Royal Manchester Institution and learned his primary estate lay near the village of Ashmead. And so it was to Ashmead that she aimed herself like an arrow of righteousness.

Anxious about the coming conversation, she kept her mind busy and at ease by spinning plots for another book, for Fanny Hancock was a writer. As she often did, she entertained herself by studying her fellow passengers and trying to decide what sort of characters they might make in one of her books.

She scrutinized the man across from her from under lowered eyelids. Tall, irritable, and whip thin, his collar button looked fit to choke him. Useless as a hero. He might, she thought, serve as a cruel and moralistic director of a charity school if she had room for one in her current book. She may have to save him for later. She closed her eyes and tried to envision the hero. Neither of the other two passengers, a portly businessman and an elderly woman on her way to visit her daughter, would do. There had been a rather good-looking gentleman demanding service, with a thoroughly haughty voice, at the last change of horses. She had taken note of his golden hair, broad shoulders, and air of command. Yes, she could use that. But this time, she planned to make the hero an earl. Even if Clarion refused to help her, he might serve as inspiration. Perhaps this book would sell, and God knew they needed the money. The last three had not.

The final change went smoothly enough, and Fanny actually slept. She awoke with a start when the coach stopped in Ashmead to make its mail drop, one so brief that she had little time to clamber out. She almost didn't make it. The driver tossed her portmanteau from the top and pulled the coach out with a shower of road dirt, leaving her standing in front of another inn, alone, blinking sleep away. The Willow and the Rose appeared respectable; some they had passed hadn't. She dusted herself off, picked up her portmanteau, and entered.

An elderly gentleman with a friendly face took her coin and handed her a key. Though she saw concern—and curiosity—in his eyes, he had the courtesy not to comment on her age, criticize her solitary state, or ask about her business in Ashmead. Perhaps her book needed a kindly innkeeper. Fanny certainly needed kindness and would, she suspected, need it even more before she finished her task.

She paid for one night, telling him vaguely that she wasn't sure how long her business would take. She failed to mention she had no money for additional nights. No money for her return fare, either. She counted on the earl providing that much at least. The mail was more expensive than the stagecoaches but much faster. She'd left Wil, who was only twelve, in charge of Amy and the store. She couldn't stay away more than a day or two.

As the innkeeper led her to her room, the clock in the entranceway caught her attention. Not quite noon on a Sunday morning. She had time. She chucked her portmanteau and was soon out the front door. Ashmead seemed peculiarly quiet, but she supposed many were at church.

Will the earl be at services?

She wanted to find him home, but then, she hoped he wasn't so much of a heathen that he would fail to take responsibility. A man who impregnated an innocent, as her mother had been, and abandoned her probably lacked a moral compass. Fanny planned to force him to find one.

She walked right and then right again at the first intersection, following the directions the young woman in the public room had given her. Crossing the bridge as directed, she trudged uphill toward Clarion Hall, back straight, an inferno in her heart, determined to make war if necessary to get help, for Wil and Amy's sake.

ELI BENSON SMILED from his pew at Saint Morwenna's Church in Ashmead on a sunny Sunday in May, a man at peace with his world. He beamed at the congregation in the old Saxon church, several of whom he'd had cause to assist in the previous year. It had been difficult, and his accomplishments were a source of pride. He had much for which to be grateful.

Several years before, the previous earl had shocked Ashmead with a scandalous will in which he'd stripped his son and heir, Eli's employer, of everything not covered by the entail. The rest he'd left in specific bequests to his by-blows, listing each of his illegitimate children and their mothers by name.

The bequests had enriched some, embarrassed others, and complicated the lives of many. He'd impoverished his son, left his only legitimate daughter (whom he labeled "defiant") nothing at all, and humiliated his wife. The widowed countess had refused to accept the insult. She and her accomplices had compounded the earl's mischief by ruthlessly defrauding both the estate and the would-be heirs.

Eli's brother Sir Robert Benson, former soldier and veteran of Waterloo, along with the new Earl of Clarion, had uncovered the mess. With heroic efforts, they had identified the perpetrators, confronted would-be kidnappers, and captured a murderer, but it had fallen to Eli to sort out the details.

Serving as the Earl of Clarion's land steward and solicitor—the combining of duties itself a cost-cutting measure necessitated by the straitened circumstances of the estate—Eli had dug into the complex and convoluted mix of petty spite and fraud while stabilizing the finances of the current earl. He took pride in a job done to his satisfaction and, if he might say so, remarkable in its speed and thoroughness.

He may not have been the hero of the saga, but he'd certainly facilitated happy endings for many.

Alice Wilcox, the tailor's daughter, had gotten five pounds and a pearl necklace. It had been taken as an insult by Tailor Wilcox, who'd promptly put mother and daughter out. Charley Granger, who'd always known he was a bastard, had gotten the title to three of

Ashmead's shop buildings that had been paying rent to the earl. He'd sold them for a pittance, skipped town soon after, and died in a bar fight in Liverpool, the money gone. Little Willy Hammond had gotten fifty pounds, the sum pocketed by Walter Hammond, the father raising him. A schoolteacher three towns over had gotten a valuable racehorse. Twelve others had gotten different commercial property, cash, trinkets, the odd bits of furniture. One had gotten a rocky farm in Scotland. Eli's brother Rob (half-brother as it turned out) had gotten the prime piece of property, one of the earldom's minor estates. Every blasted one had gotten the earl's green eyes and auburn hair—Caulfield family traits. The whole town had pretended to miss it until the will had come out and then they couldn't.

The minister's booming voice reached the end of the sermon, and the congregation rose. Eli opened his hymn book to "God Our Help in Ages Past," caught sight of Prudence Granger, Charley's mother, in her much-patched Sunday gown, and cast a prayer of thanks heavenward. If they hadn't uncovered the fruits of dishonest dealing, Eli would not have been able to help her. He wouldn't have had a job at all.

Conveying property to heirs should have been a simple affair. The widowed countess and her minions had set out to rob every one of them, creating fraudulent copies of the will, skimming funds, substituting cheap jewelry, and so on.

The Grangers had been given false information about the property Charley had inherited and had sold it well below its value to a company that had eventually led back to the countess. The sharp increase in rents had hurt everyone in Ashmead. The teacher had gotten a broken-down nag, while the prime stock had been sold and the proceeds pocketed. The honest value had been repaid. Alice's pearls had proven to be fake; she and her mother had been on the brink of starvation until the new earl (or Eli, truth be told) had found Alice a teaching position on the other side of Nottingham. She was now married. And so it went. Eli's efforts had put it all to rights, even a modest amount for Prudence Granger as Charley's heir.

Eli's voice rose on the final notes of the song. He was humbly aware his accomplishments rested on the heroism of others and on luck. The countess, Eli had discovered, had amassed a tidy amount embezzled from the estate for many years before the notorious will. Those funds and the fundamental decency of the current earl had provided Eli with the tools he needed to rectify the fraud. Without that, he had no idea what they would have done. He had even made progress in stabilizing the earl's own finances.

Walter Hammond, Willy's papa, greeted him effusively in the churchyard as he always did. The Reverend Mr. Arthur Styles shook Eli's hand; the vicar's respect always warmed his heart. Eli declined the regular invitation to dinner at the vicarage, anxious to be back at his place at Clarion Hall. The goodwill of the people of Ashmead over the entire affair had fallen on Eli for the most part, the earl being in London much of the year and a distant figure in any case.

Paul Farley, the physician, rode with Eli back through the village, and they chatted amiably, professional man to professional man, until they reached The Willow and the Rose, the inn that had been Eli's childhood home, where they parted company. Good memories and bonds of family drew Eli to join Farley in the dining room, but he had reports to write and a career to consider. He rode on.

He tipped his face to the sun as he traveled across the bridge and started uphill to the hall. The last of the heirs had been found and given just compensation. He looked forward to a year as steward without the tedious paperwork that had plagued him in previous months, grateful for the opportunities given to him by the earl. A career as a land steward brought prestige and compensation greater than Eli might otherwise have been able to contemplate. There was much to learn, and Eli planned to make the best of it. He looked forward to a quiet afternoon.

The sight that greeted him boded ill for that hope. John, the first footman, who served as a sort of underbutler when the senior staff went off to London with the earl, stood on the front steps of the hall in heated conversation with a slip of a girl.

Eli dismounted instead of riding around to the stables and climbed up to investigate. The girl, a bit of a thing, didn't come up to John's shoulder, but she confronted him with a straight back and commanding voice. Though slender, she had the look of someone used to hard work. She wore a plain, rather rumpled gown. He suspected she had been traveling for some time. An unadorned straw bonnet covered her head.

"Is there a problem here, John?"

"Aye, Mr. Benson. I was explaining to this person—"

"I demand to see the earl," the chit said at the same time. Face to face, Eli judged her to be fifteen or so. She had cheek for one so young.

"May I ask your business with the earl?" Eli studied her closely. Her face had character. He'd give her that. Perhaps she was older than she first appeared.

"Who are you?" she asked, fire flashing from her eyes. Her very attractive green eyes... *Oh no.*

"Show some respect, girl," John said. "This is Mr. Benson, the steward. I've been telling you—Mr. Benson will see to whatever it is. The earl isn't here."

"Steward, is it? Then you'll have to help me." Disappointment inched across her face, driving the determination to the side but not away. She glared up at the footman.

"I'll deal with this, John. Please care for my horse," Eli said.

She bounded past John, into the foyer, where she came to an abrupt halt, wide eyes taking in the magnificence that was Clarion Hall's entrance: the parquet floors, the marble mantle, the gleaming banister curving upward beside carpeted stairs...

She spun toward Eli, that fire raging in her eyes. "The earl will help me. He has to."

She pulled the ribbon on her bonnet and took it off, shaking her head and loosening a fall of hair. Glorious auburn hair… *Oh no.*

Eli's peace had just been upended by a problem—one cursed with Caulfield hair and Caulfield eyes. One encased in the dainty body of a beautiful young woman with the heart of a warrior.

Damn.

CHAPTER TWO

F ANNY EYED MR. Benson while he spoke softly to the servant, shut the massive double doors, and turned to peer at her, hands behind his back. Realization dawned that she had just been closed into an unfamiliar house—a great palace of a house—and was alone with a stranger. She might be putting herself in danger, but she didn't feel threatened.

She found his hair a plain brown and his eyes predictably brown as well. Attractive enough, this one, but no hero. He might do for the feckless younger brother or hero's best friend.

"If you would follow me, perhaps we can hear your story, and you can tell me why you need the earl so urgently." Up close, the earl's man had a peaceful manner, graceful hands, and an expression bright with intelligence. He didn't wait for a reply. When he gestured to a hallway to the left of the stairs, she followed him past rooms closed behind ornate doors and fancy woodwork. She imagined each of the spaces to be as opulent as the entrance.

He led her deeper into the house, and a frisson of alarm crept up her back. Mam would not approve of this entire escapade. Fanny glanced at Mr. Benson's back. Slender. Taller than Fanny, but most men were. Not as tall as that giant footman. They turned a corner.

He might be a villain, one who uses charm to lure maidens to... But no, not this one.

A huge desk, all dark wood and carved edges, dominated the room he led her to. Books lined most of the walls, floor to ceiling. She glanced up at him.

"This is the earl's own study," Mr. Benson said. "If you make yourself comfortable, I'll be a moment."

Study? The reading room at the Royal Manchester isn't much larger. At a loss, Fanny looked around her. She set her bonnet on a side table by the door but clutched her reticule in her hand. She did not sit in any of the massive leather chairs that would likely make her look even more like a child if she sank into one. She didn't want the man looming over her when he returned. *If he returns…*

He did, and a young woman carrying a tray followed. At Benson's orders, she placed the tray with porcelain cups, a teapot, cream, and sugar on a small table in front of the window, flanked by two of those overbearing chairs.

"I thought tea wouldn't go amiss. Shall we sit, Miss… But I didn't get your name. My manners have forsaken me," he said.

"I am Miss Frances Hancock. I didn't come for tea." She glanced at the maid.

"This is Sally, Miss Hancock."

The little maid dipped a curtsey. "I'll stay nearby, Miss. Don't you fret." She took a seat on a stool by the door.

Chaperonage. As if I'm a lady instead of a store clerk. The courtesy warmed her heart until it occurred to her the girl may have been called to protect Mr. Benson from false accusations just as well.

"That settled, shall we sit? I could use tea if you don't mind." He sat in one of the chairs by the window.

At least he isn't looming over you, or behind that gigantic desk. Fanny sat on the matching leather chair, perched on the edge, hands primly in her lap, still clutching her bag. She was afraid to sink back for fear the chair would swallow her.

He poured a cup of tea and put it on her side of the table before pouring one for himself. "Now, Miss Hancock, tell me why you came here."

"I need help. The earl is my father. My natural father. He must take responsibility." *There. I said it.* She lifted her chin. She felt shame burn up her neck, but she refused to let it shake her. The circumstances of her birth were her father's shame, not hers. Oddly, Mr. Benson didn't look shocked.

"What makes you think that's the case?"

She reached into her reticule and pulled out the paper she had found in her mother's sewing basket. She handed it to Benson. She knew the words by heart. *Darling Fanny. I never wanted to tell you who your father was. Never wanted you to know the evil man, but...*

He read it, winced, and read it again. When he looked up at her, compassion simmered in his eyes. Warm brown eyes, she noted. Definitely a best friend type.

"I'm afraid you're wrong about one thing," he said.

When she opened her mouth to object, he raised a hand to stop her.

"The current earl is not your father. That person would be the previous earl, dead these five years."

Dead? How can I confront him? How can I tell him what I think of a man who charms and violates a young woman? Fanny had no doubt that was what had happened. *How can I tell him only a bounder would refuse to support his offspring, that...* But Benson was still talking.

"...left out of the will, I'm afraid."

"What will?" Hope soared and crashed down again. He'd said "left out."

Benson spun a fantastical tale about the earl, how he'd listed children fathered by many women, leaving a bequest to each. If Fanny had been tempted to think him generous, she remembered he'd ignored her—and her mother—her entire life. Besides, he had apparently cut out his legitimate children. What kind of man did that?

She'd known she had been sired by a man who was disgusting, irresponsible, and selfish. To that list she now added spiteful.

Resentment didn't distract her from her purpose. "Are you certain my name is not there or my mother's? Complicated things, wills," she said.

"I wish I could say otherwise, but I assure you I know every line of that will. I've been through it dozens of times, ensuring justice to the heirs. I fear, Miss Hancock, you were forgotten." His sorrowful expression didn't soften his words.

Forgotten. Ignored your entire life and forgotten. She bit her lower lip to keep her flood of grief under control and peered around the study. The desk alone would sell for enough to feed Wil and Amy for a long time. She sat up straight and lifted her chin once more.

"Perhaps so. But the estate still has an obligation to help me," she insisted, grateful her voice didn't break.

⪢⪢⪢⪡⪡⪡

ELI THOUGHT FOR a moment that the woman might collapse under the weight of disappointment, but Miss Hancock was made of sterner stuff. A jolt of utterly inappropriate attraction scrambled his wits momentarily. *She's only...* He wasn't sure now how old she was. Probably not fifteen now that he looked at her. Looked entirely too closely. Whatever her age, he owed her respect.

His respect, however, was of no consequence, no matter how much he admired her backbone—and other assets. "Unfortunately, I know of no legal obligation of the Clarion estate to assist you."

He sipped his tea, silently urging her to do the same, and considered the appropriateness of offering her something stronger. He glanced at Sally, who dutifully sat with her hands folded and directed her gaze at her lap.

Miss Hancock took the hint and lifted her cup, but her hand shook, and she put it down. "You seem to believe me that the earl is—was—my father."

"Your mother's note might hold up in court. Your appearance likely would, at least in this county, but I don't need proof."

"My appearance?"

"The Caulfield family has distinctive eyes and hair. The old earl bequeathed that to his natural children without exception, in my experience. You have them. So yes, Miss Hancock, I believe you. That doesn't change your position, however. The earl didn't acknowledge you, and he didn't include you in his will. That frees the Clarion estate from any legal obligation."

This time, he feared she would fall apart, so tightly wound did she appear. Eli's growing belief that the estate had a moral obligation was personal, one he had no authority to act on. It would take him some time to see what could be squeezed from the already stressed estate, and it would be no help unless David Caulfield, the current earl, agreed with him.

"I will notify the current earl about your visit and your request. I'm afraid that's the best I can do," he said.

"How long will that take?" she asked. Eli could swear he heard her mutter what sounded like "fernstubble" before her jaw clamped tight.

"The earl is in London. If I send an urgent packet, we may have word in four or five days." As he studied her carefully, a dash of panic crept into her already distressed expression. He mentally reviewed the petty cash situation. Funds set aside for charitable emergencies were meant for Clarion tenants. "Miss Hancock, may I assume your problems are of an immediate nature?"

She swallowed hard. Pride appeared to war with what he suspected was desperation. Desperation won. "My sister and brother are in danger of starvation and eviction, Mr. Benson. Perhaps not immediately, but very soon. I don't know this earl's relationship to the one that sired me, but I assume he is family of some sort. Will he want someone with Caulfield eyes and Caulfield hair, as you call them, put out on the streets?"

That he would not. Bile rose in Eli's own gullet at the thought. *Shrewd threat, Miss Hancock.* "I'll make sure he understands the urgency when I contact him," Eli said, concern for her immediate situation growing. "Is it that your rent is in arrears?"

"We do not rent, Mr. Benson," she said with outraged pride. "My grandfather left my mother a valuable freehold, where we live and do business. Unfortunately, after her death, her husband mortgaged it. The earl—That is, we might manage the rest if he would see to the mortgage."

When he asked the size of the loan, the amount staggered him. Valuable freehold indeed. David Caulfield, the new earl, couldn't manage it from his personal funds, nor could the estate invest in it unless there was promise of significant return. Too many people depended on the estate's prosperity.

Eli swallowed. Hard. "Do you have a place to stay until we hear back from him?"

"I'm staying at The Willow and the Rose. I—I only paid for one night."

Something in her voice told him her situation might be worse than he thought, but the Willow was a problem he could do something about. He bit back a grin lest it give offense. "I will speak to the innkeeper. He will no doubt extend credit for several days."

"But if the earl won't cover it, what will the inn do?" Tension tightened the delicate lines of her face.

"You won't be put out." Confidence rang in his voice, but Miss Hancock gnawed on her lower lip. *Terrified* might be too strong a word for her—*worried* certainly. Eli leaned forward, tempted to take her hand in his. "Trust me, ma'am," he said. "As it happens, I know the innkeeper well. He will help you."

His assurances had little impact; her frown deepened. "I left my sister and brother alone. I only meant to be gone three days. I can't wait several more for this earl." The determined chin rose yet again.

"If I could presume on the estate to loan me fare for the mail coach—or a stage would be less—I need to go home. The earl can reach me with his decision there."

She'd come alone by public coach? Eli's horror gave way to consternation. *Of course she did, you lackwit!* She'd come without return fare, and she'd left two children to fend for themselves. Desperation indeed.

The vision of two children alone and in precarious financial straits curdled his stomach, and he tossed about for a way to help. However tenuous this woman's claim was on the benevolence of the Clarion estate, her siblings had no claim at all. Eli had no idea how to help, but he couldn't leave them on their own.

"For now, Miss Hancock, I suggest we take you back to the Willow. We'll see what can be done. The Bensons will help if Clarion cannot."

CHAPTER THREE

W HAT WOULD A hero do if a lady in need appeared on his doorstep? Lift her gently in his arms and carry her inside? Sally forth, sword in hand, to attack the villain pursuing her? Fanny puzzled over the question as she rode down Clarion Hall's lane in a nice little gig, Mr. Benson at the reins.

Her dream that she might find such a hero at Clarion Hall had died quickly. Eli Benson did not fit any of Fanny's ideas of a hero by any measure. He wasn't particularly tall. His pleasant face had nothing of the tortured hero nor his looks anything of the blond Adonis she pictured for the next book. A hero strode forth with an air of command. Mr. Benson had the competent air of a solicitor. A hero would not, she was certain, sit and consider the legal aspects of the lady's situation or whether she was entitled to his help before acting.

They turned onto the road downhill to the Willow, and Fanny admitted something else. *You, Fanny Hancock, are a shop clerk, not some grand lady.*

Truthfully, she didn't think much of the ladies in most of the novels she read. She tried to give those in her books a bit more backbone, but they still left rescue to the hero. A girl needed dreams. If she was brutally honest, she'd come to Clarion Hall hoping to find a hero who would take her burdens off her shoulders. *That should teach you the futility of dreaming, Fanny-girl.*

The gig hit a rut and lurched to one side. The man next to her easily brought it under control. Yes, *competent* was the word for Eli

Benson. As they bounced on down the hill, toward the Willow, she couldn't help thinking her hero would have whisked the lady away in his well-sprung carriage richly fitted with plush seats, clever pockets for drinks, windows to block out road dust, and a soft blanket to cover her knees. It would be drawn by four white horses, and—

"I'm sorry about that rut. I've been meaning to see about improving this road, though there's little enough traffic on it." Benson's eyes never left their path. He brought the horse and vehicle smoothly onto and across the bridge. Moments later they pulled into the stable yard at the Willow.

The innkeeper she remembered came out with a welcoming smile. "Eli! You've brought our Miss Hancock back to us." He grinned up at Fanny. "I am pleased my son brought you safely."

Son? No wonder he spoke about the innkeeper with confidence. Her solicitor-who-was-not-a hero took her hand, helping her down as if she was a grand lady after all. At his touch, gloved hand to gloved hand, her fingers tingled. The only man who'd ever touched her before was Grandfather.

"Miss Hancock needs our help, Da," he said.

"I thought that might be the case." The old man nodded, his eyes filling with concern. "Come inside and we'll sort it out."

"We may need Emma's help as well," the younger man said, irritating Fanny. She needed assistance, true enough, but not a public spectacle!

"Then it is a blessing your sister came over to inventory the linens this afternoon," the innkeeper said.

Neither gave her room to object nor even speak. "Come along, Miss Hancock. Has my son fed you? I thought not." The old man urged her toward the private dining room, calling an order for tea along the way. "And a well-laden tray, Annie. A wee dram of brandy, too. She looks as if she needs it."

Sun shone through the west-facing windows of the dining room, a cozy space with four tables covered in linen, windows with chintz curtains, and wooden chairs with seat cushions. Fanny's last vague thought before she sat down was that her kindly innkeeper might not be a hero, but he, at least, had that air of command. For the first time, she felt hopeful.

>>>><<<<

ELI TOOK A moment to write an urgent message for the earl and gave it to Alfred, the ostler, to put on the London-bound mail. With the time it would take to scare up and order a post rider on his way, the mail would be just as fast. Satisfied with his effort, he trotted off upstairs to find his sister bottom-up in the fourth-floor linen closet, sorting a bin of towels.

"Emma, we need you downstairs. We have a guest with a problem."

His sister, a plump, cheerful matron three years his senior, blinked up at him, clearing her vision and putting up a hand to fix her hair. "What sort of problem?"

"Technically it is a Clarion problem, but—just come so I don't have to say it all twice."

She glanced at him skeptically and laid her apron and inventory list on the bin. "Since when are Clarion problems the Willow's problems?"

"Since a forgotten heir turned up needing a room at the Willow."

That put a spring in her step. They entered the dining room to see Miss Hancock devouring a cold chicken sandwich. When their father urged another on her, she took it.

"Ah. You found Emma. Good. Let's give this lovely lady time to finish her tea. She'll feel more the thing with nourishment," Da said.

"When did you eat last, Miss Hancock?" Eli asked.

The girl chewed slowly before wiping her mouth with a serviette. He wondered again how old she was.

"I finished the bread and cheese I brought this morning before we passed through Ashbourne."

"Have one of the Chelsea buns. Our cook's are the best in England," Emma urged her. "I'm Emma Corbin by the way. My brother forgets his manners."

"Emma is correct," Eli said. "For once. Miss Hancock, may I make known to you my sister, Emma, and my father, Mr. Robert Benson, your innkeeper. Da and Emma, this is Miss Frances Hancock."

"A Caulfield," Emma murmured.

"Caulfield is the earl's family name, I take it. Is it that obvious?" Miss Hancock asked, blushing prettily.

"Plain as day to anyone in Ashmead," Emma responded. She patted the young woman's hand. "We've become used to it. Perhaps you should tell us your story."

Eli thought for a moment she would refuse.

"I shouldn't have come. My mother didn't want me to, but…"

"Circumstances drove you here, Miss Hancock. If we're going to help, we need to know what they are," Eli told her.

"But I came for the earl…"

"Who is in London, and you need help now," Eli said.

"The Benson family is very good at helping, Miss Hancock," Da assured her.

She glanced from one to the other before letting her shoulders sag. "I have no money, Mr. Benson. I can't even pay for this food."

Her obvious shame tore at Eli. He opened his mouth to reassure her, but she pulled herself together quickly and sat upright. *Ah. The determined chin again. Bravo, Miss Hancock.*

"I am obliged to ask for help, Mr. Benson, but I don't take charity. The earl, or at least the Clarion estate, is under some obligation to me. I'm certain of it and will press my case. If he does as he ought, I will be able to pay back any loan. I already paid for tonight. If you could advance me fare to Manchester tomorrow, I will see to it you are paid back."

"She needs more than that, Da. There are two children dependent on her who are in danger of eviction and worse. The earl may assist, but the need is great and aiding the children is urgent."

She looked mortified that he'd aired her dirty linen to his family. "You have no right—"

"My son means well, Miss Hancock. You wish your privacy respected, understandably, but if your situation is truly that dire, you can count us as friends. I have no doubt the young earl will be, too, once he meets you. Trust us with your story and we'll see how we can help," the old man urged.

Miss Hancock took a sip of tea—for courage, Eli thought.

"Tell us about the children," Emma urged gently.

"They are my brother and sister, children of my mother and her husband. Wil is twelve, and Amy is eight."

"How is it they are alone?" Emma probed.

"Our mother died over a year ago and Rundle—their father—ten months after that."

Emma's face crumpled in distress. "How tragic! He must have loved her very much."

Miss Hancock snorted. "Hardly. He wasn't sober a day after he got his hands on the till. Drowned in his own sick." She must have regretted the impulsive words, for she apologized to Emma immediately.

"He left you destitute?" Da asked gently.

Miss Hancock raised her eyes to the ceiling and appeared to come to a decision. "Holy damson plums," she swore before gazing at Emma directly. "We shouldn't have been destitute. My grandfather left Mam a prosperous drapery business. I knew Rundle was dipping into the till for a while, but Mam looked the other way. After my mother died, he emptied it as often as he could. He spent freely on fancy clothes and newfound cronies. I started hiding the take so I could feed the children. When he died, I was relieved. I thought we'd manage, the ducklings and I, but worse happened."

"Worse?" Emma asked, eyes wet.

Eli already wished the man was still alive so he could knock his lights out. He didn't want to hear worse.

"I found the ledgers and business papers in his bedroom. He had borrowed against the store the day after Mam was buried. It explained how he bought the sporting curricle and horses he boarded at the livery. That stable master came to collect the day of his funeral and the moneylender the day after. They were just the first."

"And so you fear eviction," Eli said.

"I expect it soon. We have the papers demanding payment on the kitchen table," she said. "The livery says they'll take the equipage in lieu of money."

Eli doubted any livery was owed as much in several months as the value of a new curricle and two horses. Every businessman the bounder dealt with would be out to fleece these children. Someone needed to look at agreements, payments, and ledgers.

"You left the children alone?" Da made it a question.

She bit her lip and nodded sadly. "We had no choice. Clarion was the only place to turn, and we didn't have fare for the three of us. Wil is capable, but he's only twelve. I told him to lock up for three days even if it meant turning paying customers away and wait for me."

Eli met Da's eyes, coming to a decision. "I'll need the rest of today to put things in order at the hall, but I'll see you home, Miss Hancock, and have a look at your situation. The earl would expect it." At least he hoped that was so.

Emma's eyes darted among the girl and the men in her family. "Not alone you won't," she said with her older-sister voice. Eli had been dodging it most of his life.

"But I'm perfectly capable—" Fanny began.

"We know you are," Da said, cutting her off. "But Eli is obliged to report your situation to the earl. He will require an investigation into the business details. There's nothing for it. He'll have to go to Manchester."

Trust Da to know how to convince her! Eli watched the old man's words knock the wind right out of Miss Hancock's sails. He could see her mind searching for an answer and finding none.

"My father is correct. I've explained the legalities, Miss Hancock, but I owe it to my employer to document the extent of your situation so we can weigh it against what the estate is capable of contributing." He sounded pompous even to his own ears, but he accepted it as an occupational hazard.

Miss Hancock appeared mulish, but she didn't fight him. "I accept, but Mrs. Corbin needn't worry. I'm not some titled flower with a reputation to protect."

"All women deserve protection," Emma grumbled.

"She'll be perfectly safe with me," Eli snapped. He peered at their guest more closely. Perhaps she was older than he'd first thought. He hesitated only a moment; he knew how to behave like a gentleman no matter how great the temptation. Besides, his interest in Fanny Hancock was strictly estate business. He didn't need his sister interfering. "In any case, my gig only has room for two, and it is faster than that lumbering coach of your husband's. Time matters. That settled, I have work to do. Get a good night's sleep, Miss Hancock. We'll leave early."

He left before anyone could object. He'd see the girl home, take a look at her situation, and be back in his office in four days. Five at most.

CHAPTER FOUR

TRAVELING LONG DISTANCES in a two-wheel gig was a miserable experience. Fanny almost missed the mail coach, although she had to admit the fresh air in her face—and the faint whiff of Eli Benson's woodsy scent—smelled a far sight better than unwashed bodies and the onion sandwich the barber from Sheffield had brought aboard.

It didn't help that she shared the seat with an overbearing man who claimed she had no legal right to help from her father's estate but inserted himself into her life anyway. It was the moneylenders that had gotten his attention, she decided, not the hungry children. Ledger ink must run in his veins. She thanked the angels he didn't chatter, at least. He said nothing at all during the morning, leaving Fanny to plan a scene inside her head in which a young mother, the heroine's sister, and her children were put out to freeze on the side of the road by a cruel earl.

Benson didn't speak at all until they pulled into a posting inn. They'd come thirty miles, he said, and the horse needed to rest.

"You can't mean to stop here for the night. We'll be three or four days on the road at that rate."

"Don't be daft. I'm changing out horses. I'll rent a hack and arrange for Cicero here to board until I pick him up on the way home." He began to unhitch the horse with skill and an economy of movement that didn't surprise her. Benson seemed skilled at everything he did.

Did that wretch just call me daft? "The mail kept on through the night. If we do the same, we can be to Manchester tomorrow morning."

"That we will not do. The roads aren't safe for such as us in the dark. We'll stop for the night and rest ourselves and the horse overnight so he can take us the remainder of the way." He spoke without looking up from his task.

"Where will we stay?" she gasped. The cost and the company both weighed on her.

"Not to worry. I know the better ones. Why don't you have a bite in the public room while I take care of this."

I have no coin in my purse, you nodcock, and unlike your father's inn, this isn't a charitable establishment. He had obviously forgotten, and she wasn't going to ask for money. Her debt—the earl's debt—piled up quickly as it was. "I'm not hungry. The basket the Willow provided has kept me well fed. I will take a walk."

She strode up and down, mentally reworking her story so that it was the earl's coldhearted steward who put the family out. She nibbled her lip, wondering if she ought to change the duke, her hero, to an earl. Or perhaps the villain would be an earl. She returned to find a fresh horse in the traces, and Eli Benson leaning against the gig, sipping a drink. "I thought you were in a hurry," he grumbled, handing her a mug.

The cider tasted close to perfection and cooled her dry mouth.

Benson handed his mug to a grinning ostler, who had been assisting him. He reached for hers. "I put your sandwich on the seat." He gave her mug to the ostler and reached out a hand to help her. "Up you go."

His hand sent a cascade of feminine awareness up her arm to her middle, leaving her uncomfortable with his looming presence. She scooted to the edge of the seat.

Soon they were tooling on down the highway while Fanny nibbled her sandwich.

He broke into her habitual reverie. "Tell me about the store."

"What do you want to know?" she asked.

"What sort of premises do you have?"

She described the size (large for the type of business), location (prime commercial district), and condition (good repair—Fanny saw to that herself). "We live above it. It is home."

"How long have you lived there?" he asked.

"My entire life. Grandpapa built the business. He left it to my mother."

"And Rundle ran it into the ground."

She nodded morosely. "The worm ruined everything."

"How is business?"

"Not as good as in Grandpapa's day. Mam did well enough, but she hadn't the knack for business or customers. I plan—" *But that doesn't matter now.*

Benson shot her a penetrating glance. "I gather your plan is to ask the earl to cover the mortgage outright, and run the store yourself. Tell me what is 'good.' Average monthly take, number of customers? Do you have a lot of repeat business?"

She answered him with the figures. "But Horace ran customers off, turning up in the store reeking of gin. Even the loyal ones thinned out."

His interrogation continued for an hour or more. He had more questions than a six-year-old, but Fanny had answers. She thought she heard respect in his voice after her explanation about relations with suppliers. Eventually he ran out of things to say and they sank back into a silence that didn't feel as welcome as Fanny expected.

The drizzle that descended on them late in the afternoon added to her misery. Benson pulled the hood up, and it helped some. They rode on for another hour or more.

"Sorry, Miss Hancock. I can't control the weather, and I thought you'd want to go as far as we could before dark. The Happy Dutchman up the road is clean and safe. We'll stop there."

The place was cozy and respectable as well. So respectable the innkeeper eyed Fanny dubiously, glancing back and forth between them before leaning toward Benson's ear to hiss, "I've known you for years, Eli Benson, and I've never known you for a fornicator. Assure me that woman is as decent as she seems."

Fanny felt her face burn. *At least you seem decent, Fanny-girl. Buck up. Maybe no one will notice your red face.*

Benson replied, glancing at her once, but he spoke so softly she couldn't make out his words. She could see he was not happy, though. Whatever he said worked. They had two rooms, clean and comfortable, but not so much that they'd be tempted to stay. They were up and on the road at dawn.

The hired nag did his job, and true to his word, Eli Benson pulled up in front of her Grandpapa's store—her store—just after noon.

ELI GAZED UP at a first-rate sign proclaiming "Alfred Hancock, Draper." Old Alfred, her grandfather, may be long in his grave, but the woman hadn't exaggerated. The store sat in a prime location, and the building appeared to be in fine trim. At least it would have if the front window weren't broken. Someone had boarded it up from inside. That would need attention.

Miss Hancock leapt from the gig before Eli could climb down and help her. She tried the door, banged on it with a fist, and called her brother to open up. When the door didn't immediately open, she dipped into her ever-present reticule, searching for the key.

The sound of a lock turning got her attention, and the door slid open an inch or two. "Is that you already, Fanny?" a boy asked.

"Wil, oh, thank God! Are you well?"

The door flew open and a small girl shot past the boy to fling herself into Miss Hancock's arms, sobbing out a story that froze Eli's heart. "Fanny, Fanny, Fanny, bad men threw a brick through the window, and Wil got Grandpapa's gun. He made me hide under the bed."

Why would someone do that? Eli's resolve stiffened. He would have to answer that question if he wanted to protect the place and the people in it.

"When?" Miss Hancock almost choked on the word.

"Last night." The boy stood in the doorway; an antique blunderbuss dangled from his hand, pointing at the floor. "We cleaned up the mess and boarded the window. That fancy table cover display you put out has glass shards embedded in it, but no other stock was damaged." He looked past his sisters, glaring at Eli. "Is this your earl?"

Miss Hancock turned to Eli, one arm around the little girl. "Mr. Benson, this is my brother, Wilber Rundle, and our sister, Amelia. Wil and Amy, this is Eli Benson, the earl's steward—or is it solicitor?"

Eli waved the question away. *Steward, solicitor, man of business, agent, bookkeeper, general factotum…*

Wil frowned. "Solicitor? Money would be better, but we probably need one of those, too."

Blunt talker, this one. Like his sister.

"I'm here to take a look at your situation to see…what can be done." He had begun to say "see to things," but that sounded definite, and he didn't want to foster false hope too soon. To the list that had been forming in his head for two days, he added, "Fix storefront window." As it was, it hurt the property value, which raised the question again. Why?

Eli was never a man given to impulse, but he came to another of his quick but measured decisions. In this case, he judged security more important than propriety. "With your permission, Miss Hancock, I'd like to impose on your hospitality. I had planned to find a hotel nearby, but given what happened, it might be best if I stayed here. I can sleep downstairs in the store until we sort this out." *And he may need more than a day or two to look into the situation.*

Her expression, a muddle of relief and indecision, settled into acceptance. "That may be wise, Mr. Benson. I thank you."

And gossip be damned. His Miss Hancock had deceptive depths of strength. Eli pried his gaze away from the woman, reminded himself he had come to help, not ogle, and lifted her portmanteau from the boot. His valise followed. Wil, a promising lad, leaned the blunderbuss inside the door and took the items from Eli.

Miss Hancock hugged Amy. "Well, ducklings, have you had lunch? I'll see what I can scare up in the pantry."

"There's soup from last night. Wil made it. He used that old ham bone and the last of the beans," Amy said.

Eli added "buy groceries" to his list. "As delightful as that sounds, I need to find a place to board this horse and gig. Can you tell me where the gentleman who plans to take Rundle's curricle does business?" *You may as well get started on the accounting, Benson. The list is growing.*

An hour later he had arranged care for the hack and storage for his gig at Cunningham's Stables a few blocks away. He handed over cash for a week in advance.

"Now, Mr. Cunningham, I have some questions."

The undersized, squint-eyed Irishman peered at him. "'Bout what?"

"I understand you are owed money from the estate of Mr. Horace Rundle. I am his stepdaughter Miss Frances Hancock's man of business. I would like to take a look at any agreement Mr. Rundle signed, your ledger of moneys owed and payments. I'd also like to take a look at the curricle and team to make my estimate."

"Estimate?" Cunningham almost swallowed his tongue.

"Of their value, Mr. Cunningham. Of their value."

Cunningham swore under his breath.

CHAPTER FIVE

B Y THREE O'CLOCK, Fanny wondered what Benson had been up to, gone as long as he was. By four she worried.

Wil grumbled, "I thought that solicitor said he would stay here."

"A hotel would be more comfortable for a professional man like that. Perhaps he changed his mind," Fanny said.

"He left his luggage here," Amy, ever practical, pointed out.

The soup had been thin, but the children seemed satisfied. The empty pantry taunted her with the need to ask for a further advance on the earl's funds—or the Benson family's charity, the earl's being so far a mere wisp of hope.

When a knock at the door sent Wil scrambling to respond and Benson climbed the stairs, overburdened with bundles, Fanny's knees almost failed her. She took one of the parcels with trembling hands, treated to the smell of fresh bread. "Groceries?" she squeaked.

"It sounded like we needed some if you're to keep me fed. I eat a fair bit—a man has to maintain his strength," Benson said.

He talks as if we do him a favor accepting all this.

While Amy rhapsodized over cinnamon buns and Wil stared at the bounty, Fanny added onions, potatoes, apples, carrots, beans, a huge round of cheese, coffee, and some salted meats to the pantry along with some tinned foods.

"Do you think we might have a share of your buns, Mr. Benson?" Amy asked, earning a glare from Wil, who couldn't quite keep the hope from his eyes.

"Well, Miss Amy, if you put on some water for tea, I expect there might be enough for the four of us," Benson said with a smile.

Fanny picked up the two loaves of bread from the table to store them in the bread box and found a container of biscuits under them. She raised a brow at Benson.

He shrugged. "I like sweets."

"That must explain the butterscotch drops I found with the tinned fruit." Fanny tried to appear stern but feared she failed.

The children and the man (who proved to be as enthusiastic about his food as he claimed) made short work of the cinnamon buns and tea. Fanny had to admit she enjoyed them, too.

After Amy cleared the table, Fanny sent the ducklings, who had forgotten their schoolwork entirely while she was gone, off to their rooms. She lifted the fresh chicken, feathers still on, that she had left by the iron stove box next to the fireplace. "This won't keep; I best cook it for dinner tonight," she said. "Since I have a guest with an outsize appetite."

Benson laughed at that. "I hope you know how to pluck it. I wasn't sure an astute businesswoman like yourself had time for learning such skills."

She treated him to a glare, though she suspected he was only half teasing.

"Sit with me first. We have things to discuss."

Puzzled, she wiped her hands and sat in the chair across from him. When he took out a purse heavy with coin and set it on the table, she drew back her head, brows raised. "What is that?"

"Mr. Brendan Q. Cunningham and I came to an agreement that Rundle's two high-steppers and extravagant curricle were worth far more than was owed for stabling. He humbly accepted them in payment and sent you the difference."

"Cunningham? Humble? What did you do to him?"

"Worry not. He is in possession of all his body parts and will make a tidy profit in spite of my efforts to remind him of his conscience."

"He was cheating us!"

Benson nodded. "I suspect he isn't the only one trying to take advantage."

She hefted the coins, peered into the bag, and sighed. "It won't cover the mortgage."

"Not even close. But it's coin in your pocket. Tomorrow morning, I want you to make a list of creditors and their claims. Then we'll inventory your assets. First thing, though, is to fix that window."

"So we can open up."

"Yes," he said, drawing out the word. "Perhaps. But also to maintain the value of the property until we settle this mortgage business. Besides, with the window fixed, the place won't shout 'victims live here' and invite more trouble."

"It will salvage Wil's pride."

"His sister's, too, I suspect," Benson said.

She didn't deny it.

⤜⤜⤜⤜⤜

ELI SET ON the worktable in the center of the store his candle and the bundle of bedding Fanny Hancock had provided and looked around. Bolts of cotton, linen, silk, and wool lined shelves against the back wall. A sort of lectern or pedestal stood in the corner. A quick inspection beneath it yielded paper printed with the store's name and pencils for receipts. He suspected the cashbox would sit on top.

The table in the center had drawers built in. He pulled one out and lifted his candle to peer inside. One held shears and other tools of the trade. The goods within one included fancy lace-hemmed table covers and handkerchiefs. Another held silk scarves and shawls; a third contained hosiery. Hancock's did not, Fanny had explained, deal in tailoring of any kind. He would need her help tallying the value of the inventory.

He dropped onto the chair in the corner, weighted down by the reality that faced him—not the work. No, Eli Benson could balance the goods on hand against the debt easily. Once he had a clear picture, the financial decisions would slip into place.

The reality causing his throat to ache and his heart to sink was of an entirely different nature. Fanny Hancock believed a boost from Clarion would enable her to rescue her grandfather's failing concern and carry on, shouldering the business and the raising of two children. *How am I going to convince her it can't be done?*

The voice in his head, the one that generally kept him focused on the slow and steady tasks, that enabled him to solve knotty and complex problems, chided him. *You don't know that yet. Perhaps…*

Eli sincerely doubted Miss Hancock could save the store on her own, but until he ascertained the full amount of the debt, he couldn't judge whether Clarion could afford what it would take to rescue the business. A small bequest might be throwing good money after bad if it was pouring cash into a doomed business. The mortgage would be one hurdle; cash reserves to restock would be another.

Dealing with Cunningham successfully had been a stroke of luck. Benson couldn't count on more of those. Innocents were ever the prey of the unscrupulous. Fanny Hancock was a peculiar mix of that kind of innocence and hard-nosed common sense. At least he thought she was, but how well did he know her really?

He laid the bedding on the floor next to the table and snuffed out the candle, planning to begin the accounting in the morning. His unruly thoughts kept returning to the woman who slept upstairs. What other options did she have? And how might the Clarion estate assist? They'd found a teaching position for Alice Wilcox, now married to a vicar on the other side of Nottingham. The earl would be well served in finding Fanny Hancock a husband. That solution would be tidy, but for some reason, it didn't please him as much as it ought.

He awoke to banging on the door and a sleepy Wil Hancock stumbling down to answer it. He scrambled to his feet to forestall the lad, pulling up his trousers, but the boy had sense.

"We aren't open," Wil announced through the door, one hand on the stock of the blunderbuss that still leaned against the wall next to the entrance.

"You ain't been open all week, and from the looks of that window, you won't be anytime soon. Cunningham says Miss Fanny came home. I need to talk with her or him that came with her. You lot owe me money. I want it before the bloodsuckers at the bank get to you."

"When we open; not now," Wil said, his eyes pleading with Eli.

Eli strode to the door. "Who makes these demands?" he challenged.

Silence met the sound of what must be—to the noisy debt collector, at least—a stranger's voice. It didn't last.

"Jeremy Cramer, dealer in coal, and that family hasn't paid me since winter."

"You will be heard, Mr. Cramer, but you may have to get in line. We will make ourselves available at three o'clock." *We should be ready by then. I hope.*

"I were here first," Cramer whined through the door.

"Three o'clock, Mr. Cramer. Do be prompt," Eli said with a wink at Wil, who grinned in delight.

Cramer's profane muttering faded. The man walked away. For now.

"How are we going to pay him, Mr. Benson? I know you got some cash out of Cunningham, but Fanny says the mortgage comes first."

"We aren't, at least not immediately. Our first goal is to figure out the whole picture, the size of your father's debt. Then we'll see what may be possible."

>>>><<<<

FANNY UPENDED THE box full of receipts, bills, and messages dunning her to make good on Horace Rundle's debts. Benson wanted a list, and so he would have one. He had taken Wil off to search for glass to repair the window, leaving her to it.

If only every item didn't turn her stomach. She might feel better if she had eaten breakfast, but she hadn't been able to down more than a bite after he'd told her he'd invited Jeremy Cramer to come at three to discuss payment. Her gut knew word would spread and half the neighborhood would descend on her.

Eli Benson is no hero. He's a stubborn man of business. She wished him to the devil. He could join Horace Rundle.

Fanny fiddled with her pencil, unable to decide how to start. She'd rather be writing. *The Duke's Dreadful Debacle* would not write itself and was just as likely to help them financially as sorting this pile of debt.

"Do you need help, Fanny?" Amy, who had eaten a hardy breakfast thanks to Eli Benson's bounty, put a hand on Fanny's shoulder. Her cheer had been the one bright spot on a dreary morning.

Fanny tried to smile at her little sister. "I don't know how to organize this," she admitted.

"Easy. Sort them. Like you taught me. We can do alphabetical, or date, or…"

Fanny gave Amy a smacking kiss. "You are brilliant, of course. Let's do alphabetical by last name. Then date."

At the implication of "us," Amy sat down and picked up the first one. "Sixty-two quid for the tailor?" She gazed up at Fanny, in stunned disbelief. Her sister's heart sank. She'd tried to keep the worst of their father's excess from the ducklings, but here it was spread out before the girl.

Fanny shrugged. "He wanted to look the part of a prosperous

merchant."

"Prince Regent, more like," Amy muttered, head shaking. She picked up the next bill and began to sort by merchant, leaving Fanny lost in thought.

How many suits did the worm have? He can't have destroyed them all with gin. She hadn't gone back inside his room after she'd found the ledgers and mortgage papers. She hadn't checked his clothes press. Benson had said they needed to assess the assets. A fancy suit was an asset, wasn't it? First debts, then assets, he'd said. She stopped tapping her foot and went to work with Amy.

An hour later, they had a dozen piles, from Abbot the greengrocer to Williamson the carter, each sorted by date. Even Amy noticed that the numbers increased with every bill. More tailoring debts surfaced, and so did ones from a fancy modiste never patronized by Fanny or her mother.

"They're back," Amy whispered when noise erupted downstairs.

For a moment, Fanny feared a break-in, but she heard Wil's voice above the low rumble of other sounds. He didn't seem alarmed.

"Why don't you go down and see how the window project is progressing?" she asked.

Amy hopped off happily. Fanny sighed. She told the sneaky bookkeeper taking shape in her mind, the one she threatened to make the minion of the villain in her story, to be quiet and began her list.

Chapter Six

I T DIDN'T TAKE Eli long to clear the damaged glass and old putty, raise the new pane, and anchor it with fresh glazing putty, with the boy's help. The framing hadn't been damaged, easing the repair. Wil absorbed the process with eager curiosity.

"I didn't know solicitors repaired windows," Wil said.

Eli almost laughed out loud. "Most don't. I grew up in a coaching inn. We had to do most things ourselves. Now I'm a steward and put it all to good use." Da had taught him how to repair windows when he'd been Wil's age and a drunken traveler had thrown a chair through the window in the taproom. That man hadn't been welcomed back to the Willow. Eli put a hand on the boy's shoulder. "A man can't have too many useful skills. You never know when you might need them. Now we best get cleaned up if we want to impress the invaders at three."

"Impress them?"

"The secret of success in life is to always look like you know what you're doing. A clean face and a fresh suit help. Even if you aren't exactly sure what you're doing, you can't let parties in negotiation see weakness. Confidence, Wil, is our best weapon today."

Pursed lips overshadowed Wil's nod when he turned away. The boy's skepticism saddened Eli.

That boy learned too early not to trust anyone, even you.

Eli shook it off. He wasn't certain he could do the family much good, and until he had the full picture, he had few ideas.

Rounding the top of the stairs, Fanny, stiff-backed and determined to face her stepfather's debt, caught his eyes and assaulted his heart. Resolute in the face of disaster. *She may be dainty, but her frame is steel.*

»»»«««

THE CLOCK TICKED past two-thirty. Fanny added the suit she held to the asset list and laid the garment down on Horace's bed. She added the bed to the list, too. They wouldn't need it.

Benson's enthusiastic approval of her idea to catalog her stepfather's personal belongings had gratified her more than she found comfortable. *You don't need that man's approval, Fanny-girl. You know your worth.*

Listing assets proved difficult. Two suits had never been worn, but she doubted they were worth the purchase price unless she and Eli had a buyer who stood a scant inch above Fanny and ran to portly. Three others showed signs of wear. She'd included his linen, but she suspected that would only bring pennies from the ragman.

The contents of the box on the top of a chest rocked her back on her heels. The pocket watch had value and... *When did Horace acquire three jeweled stickpins? If the gems are real, they ought to count for something.* But would a jeweler give her what they cost?

She grimaced. *When did you become so greedy?* Wil and Amy deserved keepsakes. He may have been a worm, but he'd been their father. She hardened her heart against the thought. A keepsake would do no good if they went hungry, and taken as a whole, the pile on the bed didn't seem much to build hope on.

"Mr. Benson would like you below stairs, Fanny, when you are ready," Amy called from the door, scanning the items on the bed with avid eyes.

Fanny ushered Amy out in front of her and closed the door with a snap. Benson had been quite clear about appearances. She'd donned one of the gowns she wore in the shop. It would have to do; it was her business uniform, after all. She hurried to wash her face and see to her hair.

>>>>><<<<<

ELI STUDIED FANNY carefully when she entered the shop. Did she know her gown was the same green as her eyes? A simple muslin with a modest neckline and fichu, it flattered her figure just enough to give any man entering the store ideas. What healthy male could resist feasting his eyes on her? She'd done up her hair, too, in a simple bun that showed off the graceful column of her neck. Eli almost regretted insisting she join him in the drama they were about to enact. The distraction would take him off his game. Then again, she might unbalance the debt collectors as well.

How old is the woman, anyway? Hope and his baser instincts raised that question. He mentally increased his estimate. *Nineteen perhaps.* Male interest, unleashed, ratcheted upward.

He blinked his eyes shut and peered at her again. She wore a cap and looked the perfect picture of a competent businesswoman, exactly as he had asked. She also refused to meet his eyes, alerting him to the discomfort his scrutiny caused.

"Perfect," he said, unable to conjure a full sentence.

"What is?"

"Your appearance," he said, his throat tight. "It suits our purposes," he added belatedly lest she mistake his meaning.

When Eli tried to send the children back upstairs, Wil objected vociferously, insisting he was the man of the family and needed to hear what was said.

Eli had no argument for that. "Very well. You may serve as doorman. You will call them in one at a time by name and guard the door."

To Amy, he added, "You may go up or sit on the stairs quietly."

Fanny intervened. "Not one word out of either of you ducklings or back up you go!"

Wil muttered, "I'm not a duckling," but agreed to her terms.

Eli explained what he planned to do. Employing her alphabetical arrangements, they would call them one by one, let them talk, and then compare demands with the documentation. Fanny would take notes.

"How will we pay them?" she asked.

"We won't, of course. Today we're verifying debts and assuring them of payment."

Her brows rose, but she didn't ask him how he planned to do that.

Good thing, Benson, because you have no idea. Yet.

⟫⟫⟪⟪

A CROWD, VISIBLE through the newly restored window, milled around outside the shop when Benson gave the signal to start. Fanny wondered how long they would stay orderly.

"Mr. Abbot," Wil called before admitting the greengrocer. Fanny almost laughed when he shut the door in Jeremy Cramer's face. Some laughter came close to hysteria. She resolved to be careful.

"You know I've always been fair, Miss Fanny," John Abbot began.

"Of course you have," she murmured.

"But I have my own family to feed, and with Rundle gone…" He shrugged.

"Did you bring your records, Mr. Abbot?" Benson's words, firm but respectful, set the tone for the afternoon.

"I brought the tab I keep. You'll see I wrote down payments as well." Benson spread the receipts and bills they'd found and tallied the tab. "Your tab appears to be off. In Miss Hancock's favor."

The Abbots were always kind. Fanny's fingers itched to pay this one off, but Benson had warned her not to. "We thank you for that," she said.

"It was your establishment I visited last night, was it not? I paid cash, you may recall," Benson said.

"Aye. I remember. If'n I'd knew it was for the Rundles, I might have given you a discount," Abbot replied.

"There'll be no further asking for credit, Mr. Abbot, but we can't repay Horace Rundle's past debts until we know the full extent."

Benson suggested they note Fanny's own estimate but that they write the money claimed on the long sheet headed "Horace Rundle's Total Debts Claimed."

Fanny wrote, "Abbot, Greengrocer, £2 2s. 4d."

Abbot, torn between guilt and frustration, turned to go.

"I'll pay you, Mr. Abbot. Don't doubt it," she called after him, ignoring the furrows in Benson's brow.

The next claimant, Jeremy Cramer, gave them more trouble. He kept no records and scoffed at the handful of bills and receipts Fanny had collected. He reeled off a list of deliveries Fanny could only call fanciful.

"I know for a fact you made no deliveries in March. Not to me and not to my late stepfather," she insisted. The old reprobate. The ducklings had shivered in the cold most of March. She vowed to put a greedy merchant into the next book.

"Unfortunately, Mr. Cramer, we can't repay undocumented debt," Benson said firmly. "According to our records, the late Horace Rundle owed you two shillings. At most." Benson held the man's eyes while Cramer huffed and sputtered, unable to come up with a riposte.

"You'll be sorry next winter when there's no coal in your hearth," Cramer spouted at last. He stopped halfway to the door, glanced at the newly repaired window, and glared at Fanny. "There are those that don't hold with cheats and debtors and won't wait for the magistrate to bring charges to get rid of you." He stomped out without an answer.

The threat sent a chill down Fanny's spine, and she shivered. She felt Benson's hand on the small of her back and pulled herself together, standing as tall as she could but unable to look at Benson.

"Mr. Fredericks," Wil called, pulling Fanny out of her numb distraction. She reached for the stack for Fredericks the chandler but pulled back her hand when she heard Wil insisting, "Sorry—Edwards, is it?—but you aren't on my list."

Edwards. Who is Edwards? Fanny searched her memories for any such merchant.

"Don't care. I hold the man's vowels!" someone shouted back. "The debts are legal—and fairly mine."

Vowels? Gambling? Fanny's stomach threatened to rebel. The room began to close in, but Benson's gentle hand on her elbow steadied her.

"May I handle this?" Benson whispered, his gaze searching hers.

Fanny bit her lip. The warmth of his touch shot like an arrow to her heart, giving her strength. Just for a moment.

He strode to the door and had words with the stranger, then returned with a piece of paper promising to pay one R. Edwards thirty-two quid.

"Is this your stepfather's signature?" he asked.

She nodded with dawning horror.

"Then it is owed, but it won't hold up in court. He has no legally witnessed and notarized documentation and so no recourse in the courts, but he could make trouble. He has several of them, Miss Hancock."

She glanced at the window and nodded morosely. "Tell him he is last."

A grin broke Benson's bland, professional expression. "Good answer."

He strolled to the door as if he dealt with gamblers every day, nodded to Wil to open the door, and told Edwards exactly that.

"Last? I'm in line jest like you said. I have a right to my money."

Fanny's heart leapt into her throat when she saw Edwards point a filthy finger at Wil through the open door. "That boy's 'is father's heir, not the wife's bastard. He owes me, and I'll have me money. One way or another."

Fanny strained to hear the rest, but a clamor of voices from the waiting creditors covered whatever was said, and Edwards was shoved aside. Moments later he glared at her through the front window, black eyes spearing her with threat as obvious as if he had spoken the words. He'd be back.

CHAPTER SEVEN

S ITTING AT THE kitchen table, staring at their lists of debts and assets, Eli castigated himself. A call to meet with creditors had not been one of his better ideas. There'd been pushing and shoving over the nasty bit claiming gambling debts, some arguments over place in line, and the predictable demands for immediate payment that had threatened to get out of hand. They were lucky there had not been a riot.

Worst of all, it left Fanny—Miss Hancock—on the brink of collapse. *She doesn't even know the worst of what Edwards threatened.* At least Eli hoped she didn't. The words sickened him. *"I'll take that sister in place of cash if you don't pay me."*

Over my dead body.

Crowd noises had drowned out the threat, but Eli had heard it clearly enough. Unfortunately, the crowd had gotten to the lowlife scum first, shoving him aside before Eli could wipe the pavement with his slime. Eli knew Wil had heard the threat; Eli made a mental note to speak with the boy about not alarming his sister.

For now, they faced financial reconning. Fanny leaned her elbows on the table, her head in her hands, not even looking at their completed lists.

"We can do this tomorrow," he said, sliding a hand across to stroke her arm.

She dropped her hands, ignoring his touch. "Will the size of the debt change?"

He shook his head sadly. "Your idea to return the jeweled stickpins helped. The jeweler took them gladly."

"But we still owe him over a hundred quid. How could Horace buy that many gifts for women in a year? Women!" She shuddered. "At least I assume more than one, or there's a rich courtesan somewhere in Manchester."

Eli's lips twitched. "From what you've said about Rundle, I would guess he had no other way to attract female attention."

"But to leave us with debts for that sort of behavior!"

"Not us, Fanny, me." Wil stood at the top of the stairs. He'd had the job of locking up. "Did you hear Edwards?" The boy came and sat with them.

"I heard him say the debt was yours, yes, but—"

Wil directed his attention to Eli. "He's right, isn't he? I'm my father's heir. Except—" He scratched his head. "Isn't the store Fanny's? It was Mother's, wasn't it?"

Eli pulled his attention from Fanny and his worry that she'd heard all of what Edwards had said. *The law, Benson; think rationally and answer the boy.*

"The store was your mother's, I've gathered. Unfortunately, what was hers became his when she married, and he died intestate—without a will. Unless your grandfather's will specifically left it to your older sister, it is, in fact, yours—or yours and Amy's equally, Miss Fanny not being related to Rundle by blood or law. The ordinary will appoint someone to administer the estate until you are twenty-one and can act for yourself and Amy." He let out a deep breath.

Wil's eyes got larger as Eli rattled that off. "Could Fanny administer?"

Eli searched the face of the woman he admired. Good question. "If I may be so bold, Miss Hancock, how old are you?"

Fanny sat up straight and lifted her chin. "I was twenty last September."

Eli's heart and less respectable body parts took joy in that, relieved he hadn't been lusting after a child, and he suspected he smiled, because Wil and Fanny smiled back. He needed to correct their misunderstanding. "I'm afraid not, Wil. She would need to be twenty-one."

"I will be in three months!" Fanny had her armor on again.

"Even then, a male relative might get preference, depending on the judge." As if that weren't enough to squash their hopes, he went on, feeling like a brute. "Until we sort out Rundle's debts and assets, we won't know if there is anything to inherit, so it may all be a moot point."

Fanny frowned but didn't crumple. She met his gaze head-on. "In that case, Mr. Benson, sooner faced, sooner done. Let's look at what we have." She pulled over the list of debts to study it.

"Is there a way to create an order of importance?" Eli asked.

"Abbot the greengrocer first," she said.

"The mortgage, perhaps? It is pressing and…"

"And impossible," she said.

"We'll set it to the side, remembering that it looms over everything. Home necessities first, then?"

"Yes." She nodded. "The family and the legitimate business expenses first. Horace's personal indulgences move to the bottom."

"Edwards last," Wil reminded them, casting a troubled glance at Eli.

"If ever," Eli agreed.

Wil stiffened, glanced at Fanny, and got up abruptly. "I should seek my bed. Amy has been asleep for an hour." He gave Fanny a one-armed hug and disappeared before anyone could comment.

Wil's instinct to protect Fanny, unusual in one so young, won Eli's admiration.

A WEEK OF emotional upheaval sped by, making Fanny's head spin. It took three of those days to evaluate their assets. They turned Horace's personal goods into cash the first day. Benson insisted on accompanying Fanny to the tailors, who gave them shillings on the pound off their debts, one explaining, "For I fear these will be long out of fashion before I find someone to purchase them." The rest sold for a pittance. Benson insisted they keep Horace's watch for Wil, though the boy would have sold it.

"You may regret it when you're older," Benson told him.

"It will only remind me the sort of man I do not wish to be," Wil answered, breaking Fanny's heart.

None of their suppliers had lined up with the creditors. Fanny dreaded approaching them, even to evaluate their inventory. Local mills provided most of their bolts of cloth. None wished goods returned, and all added sums to their list of debts, though the amounts were modest. Debt continued to rise, with little increase in Fanny's small box of coins.

She and Benson went to the office of the Home and Orient Shipping Company, near their quay along the canal. Their agent took her few bolts of silk, leaving that account even. The woolen agent in Scotland with which Grandfather had established a relationship decades ago, however, had not replied by the end of the week. Fanny had to guess the value of the remaining bolts.

Fanny opened the store for business every afternoon, often leaving Wil behind the counter while she and Benson ran errands. Traffic was thin, and the customers who did come cast such pitying looks at her that she wished they stayed away. After three days, when creditors began stopping by "to see about progress," they simply closed up.

She had no time to write. At the end of the week, she finally found time to tally the finished material stored in the drawers in the store. Benson cautioned her to list it at its lowest likely sale price. Her heart grew heavier with every line she added. She didn't get far before a deepening realization caved her world in.

If we can't pay the mortgage, the lenders will confiscate it all. Those lenders would not give her family credit for as much as these treasures were actually worth. *We could sell it for more ourselves and maybe scrape up enough to pay the mortgage, but then we'd have no money to replenish inventory.* They were trapped in a vicious circle.

Her legs felt like lead weights when she trudged up the stairs. Benson sat at their kitchen table, absently encouraging Amy with her arithmetic while reading some sort of legal tome.

He smiled brightly when Fanny came in. "Finished already?" At her expression, he sobered and stood, pulling out a chair for her. "What is it, Fanny?"

She glowered at him. "Fanny?"

"Miss Hancock."

"I reached a decision," she said.

Benson glanced at Amy, who rolled her eyes.

"I know. Go read in my bedroom. May I go down to Saint Olaf's instead?" Amy asked hopefully. The tiny churchyard was a patch of green in their brick-and-stone neighborhood.

"Go on, then. Take Wil with you. Tell him he's done enough inventory," Fanny told her.

Benson sat across from Fanny, studying her as if worried she might shatter. "What is it you have decided, Miss Hancock?"

"You may as well call me Fanny," she grumbled.

His smile was warm but swiftly gone. "In that case, I better be Eli to you. It may make conversation easier."

Something about using his Christian name made what she had to say more of a confession of sorrow and less like a transaction with her solicitor. She attempted to smile back.

"Eli, then. We aren't going to be able keep the store. You've known it all along."

His expression, equally rueful and open, told her she was correct.

47

He shrugged. "We haven't spoken to the earl yet."

"He might pay the mortgage and some of the more pressing bills— I can't ask him to pay the jeweler. That on Horace, and it wouldn't be right. But we need to sell off inventory to begin to pay some of the rest. Selling quickly means selling below cost, and we'll have no reserves to replace it or keep us in coal. By the time Wil reaches his majority, we'll have had nine years of hand-to-mouth struggle, and he'll have a bankrupt store and two sisters dependent on his earnings. The earl's money might be better spent on Wil's education."

"I confess, Fanny, I couldn't recommend to the earl that the drapery store would be a good investment, not without a large influx of cash immediately and regularly. Frankly, his estate can't manage it."

"How much went to the heirs the old earl bothered to remember?" she asked bitterly.

"Not as much as your situation demands. At least not in most cases. Two sons, including my brother, Rob, got small estates. One was left a store but no cash, and he was cheated out of that. Most got the odd artifact."

"Sons got the land?"

He didn't deny it. "I'm not saying Clarion won't help as much as he can."

"But not enough to enable us to go on as we have."

"Unlikely."

"Will he help me care for the children, Eli?"

"Yes. Or I will.

IF YOU MARRY *her, you can care for all of them.* Alarm shot through Eli at that thought. *Where did that come from? You don't owe the Caulfield family your life for goodness' sake.*

"You mean you'll see that he does," she said, wrinkling up her forehead.

"Yes. That's it. I'll be responsible for administering aid." He stumbled through his words.

"First, we need to sell the inventory. I can slash the prices and still get more than that bank would allow us."

She may be dainty. She may be young. But Fanny Hancock understands business.

"What will you do if you sell the store?" he asked, suddenly curious. "I mean to say, what will you need?"

"A roof over our heads and food on the table, at least until my books are published."

Eli felt as if she had struck him with a brick. "Books?"

Fanny colored brightly and looked away. "A dream." She jerked her head back and raised her chin. "No. A determination. I'm going to publish books. They should bring enough to feed the children eventually."

She had astounded him again. Eli knew next to nothing about the publishing business. Popular novels seemed to sell briskly, but how hard was it to write one? Difficult, he suspected, but even more difficult to get the attention of a publisher. She'd explained her dream, and it turned out to be the one thing he couldn't help her with.

He'd been in Manchester almost ten days, and it was past time he went home. Too many unresolved issues kept him here, however, Edwards chief among them. The weasel lurked about the neighborhood, watching them. Two nights before, Eli had awoken to a sound in the street. The look on Edwards's face through the plate-glass window in the moonlight when Eli had popped up from behind the table, lantern in hand, had been priceless. The miscreant had been holding a brick. He'd run like a coward.

Eli took a deep breath. At least one issue had resolved itself. She had come around to selling without him needing to persuade her to it.

"I'll wish you well in that," he said. "But I have one suggestion."

She waited, one brow raised impatiently.

"The cost of living in Manchester is steep. You cannot remain here. Come back to Ashmead with me." He didn't—he wouldn't—mention Edwards and his threats.

Eli's words hung in the air for a moment while Fanny considered them. She answered at last, "I will come, if just to meet this earl, and only if Wil and Amy may come, too."

CHAPTER EIGHT

IT PAINED FANNY to sell a beautifully embroidered, lace-trimmed table cover for half its worth. She hated even more giving such a bargain to Mrs. Mulligan, a sour-faced woman Fanny had once heard refer to her as "Milly Hancock's little by-blow." Still, it was probably better than having it all pass to new owners, who may or may not use the premises as a drapery.

The estate agent she and Eli had consulted yesterday had laughed when she'd suggested he concentrate on people who might want to continue the business. "Y'want to sell the property as quick as may be afore the bank takes it. We can't be fussy who we show it to. I may start with Thompson's Furniture, the one next to it. They may want to expand."

She hated it, but she hated every part of the whole affair. Presented with their options and the possibility of Ashmead, neither Amy nor Wil had complained. Amy viewed it as an adventure, and Wil clearly viewed it as a relief. An odd, knowing expression had passed between her brother and Eli, some private secret she dreaded to consider. It all left Fanny heartsick.

Fanny removed one more table runner, edged white work and lace all along the hem, and wrapped it in tissue. She ran her hand along the tissue paper, fighting tears. She remembered her mother acquiring this piece from a woman near Eccles, who did particularly fine work. Fanny had already packed some pieces of the woman's to take with her. Wil had the watch. The fine linens would make part of a trousseau for Amy. Fanny had also put aside linen handkerchiefs for their pastor and the parish sexton.

The estate agent seemed certain they would get enough to pay off the mortgage and perhaps a bit more. On that promise, they'd decided to settle a few of the household debts with the coins at hand. Eli had gone to pay off Cramer, and she'd decided to let him handle that brute. She planned to visit Abbot. She had counted out only the amount on his tab into a small purse. The table runner would be a bonus, a gift for Mrs. Abbot.

Wil left to make deliveries for the printer one block down, determined to continue bringing in as many pennies as he could. Fanny decided not to wait for him. She called to Amy to walk with her and locked the door behind her. They could get to Abbot's and back in time to fix supper.

Scurrying down the street, she remembered their once empty pantry. Dinner hadn't been a problem since Eli Benson had come to Manchester. It became another debt pressing down on her. Horace Rundle's were one thing; what she owed the Bensons couldn't be repaid in coin, at least not entirely.

Mr. Abbot motioned her to the side, out of the public eye, before he took the purse and thanked her. When she explained the wrapped parcel, he called Mrs. Abbot from the back, unleashing much acclaiming, much thanking, and yes, a few tears.

"We'll miss you, Miss Hancock, and that's the truth," he told her, shaking his head and pulling away to see to customers.

Fanny wiped her cheeks on her sleeve and turned toward home, steps dragging now, her whole being downcast. Even Amy had gone quiet for once. They had almost reached George Street when Fanny chided herself. "I'll put Mrs. Abbot and her kindness in my book," she told Amy.

"She would like that. When it is published, you can send her a copy."

The narrow alley connecting the main commercial street and a smaller residential lane, the one she forbade Amy to use as a shortcut to the church, opened onto their route just before they reached the corner. Wrapped in thought, Fanny didn't pay attention to it.

Best to face what must be faced. Sooner done, sooner over, she thought just before darkness, in the form of an odoriferous potato sack, fell. She scrambled to pull it off her face, but hands pinned her arms to her side.

Amy shouted, "Leave my sister alone!" The painful screams that immediately followed sent chills through Fanny. Words were said, but Fanny, struggling to breathe, couldn't make them out. Rough hands dragged her along, the sound of Amy's cries faded, and shadows must have fallen, because inside the sack choking her, it became even darker. She kicked and tried to scream until something heavy slammed against her head and she went limp, unable to struggle further.

WALKING BACK TO the drapery gave Eli one benefit. He put his anger into every step. Cramer, the muckworm, had tried to gouge and scrabble for more money, but Eli had held firm. No records, no money.

The blasted man's heart is as black as his coal.

As Eli approached the drapery, his thoughts shifted from the greedy coal monger to Fanny Hancock and the ducklings, much happier images by far. The smile that tickled the edges of his mouth died as quickly as it started when Wil barreled down the street toward Eli, shouting.

"Some man has Amy and Fanny—" Wil skidded to a stop, breath heaving.

Eli felt light-headed, blood draining from his face. "Tell me," he said through clenched teeth.

"A man. Big horse in front of the shop." Wil swallowed, catching his breath. "Amy was shouting, and she screamed when he scooped her up."

Eli, already running, yelled, "What of Fanny?"

"Amy sobbed that a man had Fanny. 'Get Eli,' the man on the horse told me. So I—"

Eli stopped in his tracks. "The man on the horse said what?"

"Get Eli," Wil repeated.

Edwards wouldn't call him Eli. He didn't ride a big horse, either. At least Eli didn't think so. He ran faster.

They found the door to the shop locked. "Fanny planned to go pay Abbot," Wil told him. They set out that way at a run and burst into the greengrocer's premises, demanding information.

"They left here not a half hour ago, Mr. Benson, Miss Fanny and the little one. She said they were going home," Abbot told them. He and his customers demanded that Wil tell him what they knew, but Eli had no time for it.

"She must have walked the way we just came," Eli said, stepping to the street and looking both ways. People flooded out behind him, determined to look for "Rundle's girls."

"Must have gone up the close," Wil murmured.

"Show me!" Eli directed.

They started down the dark alley before reaching the end when their way was blocked by a horseman coming their way. A big horse, both it and its rider familiar and welcome. Eli almost sagged with relief when the rider dismounted, carrying Amy down with him.

"No luck, Eli. Gone without a trace," Sir Robert Benson said, setting Amy on her feet.

Eli pulled his brother into an embrace. "Rob! I don't know what miracle brings you here, but I thank the Almighty for it."

Amy wrapped her little arms around his legs. "I saw it, Mr. Benson. Bad men put something over Fanny's head and dragged her down the close. I tried to stop them. I tried," the little girl sobbed. The bruise blossoming down the side of her tiny face testified to her effort. The injury filled Eli with a mixture of rage and fear.

He knelt to pull her into his arms. "You are very brave. Can you tell me what you saw?"

"What I said. We were walking along, and they jumped out from between the buildings and covered her with an old sack, dragging her." Amy smiled briefly. "I kicked one." Her face fell again. "But they knocked me down and got away. I ran home, but you weren't there. And then the hero came, just like in Fanny's books. On a horse."

Eli glanced up at his brother, who shrugged ruefully.

Amy ignored the byplay and went on, "We rode to the rescue like heroes are supposed to, but they were gone and there's no sign of her." At that she collapsed in tears.

Eli lifted her into his arms and rose, gazing at his brother. "Nothing?"

"By the time the little one showed me where Fanny disappeared, there was no sign of her or of any upheaval," Rob said. He peered over Eli's shoulder. "Are these the neighbors?"

Eli turned to see Wil, Abbot, and several townsfolk staring at the excitement.

Wil never took his eyes from Rob. "He looks like Fanny," he mumbled. "Is he the earl?"

Eli glanced at Rob and back to Wil. "That he does." Damned Caulfield hair and eyes. "But no, not the earl. Wil, Amy, Mr. Abbot, may I introduce my brother, Sir Robert Benson, late of His Majesty's Army, these days posted to security forces in London."

"Perhaps these good people might have some idea who would do such a thing?" Rob suggested.

Several people spoke at once. Rob asked for order, and Eli described Edwards's threats. The neighbors recognized the weasel as a well-known criminal running petty gambling operations in various places but most often in the basement of the Happy Cock.

Rob thanked them. "Our most urgent need is to question people on both streets connected by the alley, while the event is fresh," Rob said. Soon he had Wil and one of his friends canvasing the far street, and Abbot making inquiries down grocery row.

Mrs. Abbot offered to look after Amy.

"I want to ride to the rescue!" the little one protested.

Rob smiled. "Of course you do, but I plan to talk with some boring people. You won't like that."

Eli gave her a fierce hug. "We'll alert you as soon as we know something. And Sir Robert will take you up on his horse when this is over."

She took the woman's hand and walked away, glaring at them over her shoulder every few steps.

Rob spoke quietly to Eli once they all dispersed. "What do you know about this man who held the gambling debts?"

"Edwards. Not much. He had a fistful of her stepfather's vowels." Eli repeated what he'd witnessed, including the lurking about and the specific threat to take Fanny. "You look skeptical. I'm telling you facts."

"I don't question your information. Your description is of a petty criminal. One who would be too busy running his operation to put so much time into stalking one family. A brick through a window is one thing, but he doesn't sound like the sort who could take a woman off the street in daylight or pay two thugs to do it or even know where to sell her."

Sell. Eli's bile rose; he glared at his brother. "He's scum."

"I don't doubt it, but is he powerful enough? Something about this doesn't add up. In any case, we need to act quickly. The longer they have her, the lower our chances of finding her. I have contacts here with the military and local magistrates. I'm going to make inquiries."

"Your boring people? Someone has to go to the Happy Cock," Eli said.

Rob grinned his approval. "Exactly." He clapped Eli on the shoulder. "That's your task. Have faith, little brother. We'll find her."

Eli nodded, tight-lipped. "Just one thing. What the devil are you doing in Manchester?"

"What do you think? You were supposed to be gone three days. It has been two weeks. Da is frantic."

"He must have been, to tear you away from domestic bliss." He liked to tease Rob about his besotted reaction to fatherhood a mere three months before. Rob ignored him. "I'm tempted to complain that none of you seem to believe I can take care of myself, but I'm too glad to see you," Eli grumbled.

Rob had the good grace not to point out the circumstances he'd found when he'd arrived. "Besides, David is cooling his heels in Ashmead after getting your urgent message."

David? "The earl came himself?"

"And isn't happy that his steward has disappeared. Let's find your Miss Hancock, little brother, and get you home." Rob mounted and rode off, leaving Eli stifling his resentment.

Always the little brother. Get over it, Benson; there's no time for pettiness. He set out for the Happy Cock at a dead run.

CHAPTER NINE

ROUGH HANDS SHOVED Fanny to the floor. A door slammed behind her. Free of the brute's iron grip, she crawled to her knees and clawed at the sack over her head, desperate to be free of the torturous thing. It smelled so bad of rotten produce that she gagged and choked. It scratched her skin. It blocked her vision. Several moments of frantic effort later, she yanked it off.

One thing didn't change. She still couldn't see. Total darkness surrounded her. Nothing alleviated the gloom except a tiny sliver of light under the door they had closed behind her. She tried the handle. Three times. With no luck. Locked in.

She clenched her muscles, determined to avoid panic, pushed herself to her feet, and took a step, arms out. Her hands bumped into a shelf of some sort. Running them along it and from side to side, she quickly concluded she had been pushed into a windowless closet a few paces long and the length of both her arms wide.

She sank to the floor and scooted to the back wall. Questions—and fears—flew at her as if a swarm of bees swirled around. *Where is Amy? Did they hurt her? Who would do such a thing and why? Where am I, and how could anyone find me? Does Eli know I'm gone?*

Eli.

She pulled up her knees and hugged them to comfort herself. She clung to one thought: Eli would figure it out. He may not fit what she had looked for in a hero, but he didn't fail people. He would find her.

⟫⟫⟫✳⟪⟪⟪

ELI LEFT THE Happy Cock with a torn coat, black eye, and one solid piece of information. He knew with certainty that people there were afraid of something—or more likely someone.

Rob, damn his hide, is right.

There had been no sign of Fanny. No sign of Edwards, either, but then, it was still midday. Not one person had admitted to seeing either of them. A bruiser had blocked the stairway leading up, and questions about a basement had gotten Eli roughed up for his trouble. Roughed up and tossed out.

The reactions to his questions showed him that some people connected to the Happy Cock had Fanny. Rage urged a frontal attack. Common sense told him stealth would work better and that he ought not attempt it alone. But with time passing and Fanny at risk, every minute counted.

He could go for help, but he needed more information about the layout of the Happy Cock, places they might hold her, entrances and exits, the men who congregated there.

The building next to the Happy Cock stood four floors high, two more than the tavern. A narrow walkway separated the two buildings, more of a close than an alley. The close was no help, but the upper-story windows would give him a clear view of the tavern and more information. He might figure out where they had her.

It took him twenty minutes and a hefty infusion of cash to get past the proprietor of the wine shop on the ground floor and through the door to the apartment overlooking the top floor of the Happy Cock.

There were two windows on that stage. Vague shadows moved behind a shade in the one nearest the street, just clear enough to tell him the Happy Cock indulged in more vices than drink and gambling. Neither of the two figures appeared unwilling. Not Fanny. *Can't be*, he thought, though his heart pounded in his chest. *Think, Eli. Panic won't help her.*

He moved his gaze to the second window, this one with the shade drawn. Two more bruisers sat at a table playing cards, a bottle of gin between them. As he watched, the one from downstairs came into the room. Eli shifted his sore shoulder, eager to give the worm some of the treatment he'd given Eli. It had taken two of them to toss him out. The other must be down in the taproom. That made four thugs. What sort of tavern needed that much muscle? One with the wherewithal to snatch a woman off the street.

From his vantage point, he studied the building. The structure stretched further back than might be obvious from the street, with at least one more room on both floors and yet another on the ground floor, at the back. He pulled out his pocket notebook and sketched out the building. One of the downstairs rooms would be a kitchen.

What is the other? And where is the entrance to the basement gambling den? He had no doubt it existed. A survey of the rear was in order. He clambered down the stairs and asked the wine shop proprietor if there was a rear entrance. The man looked pained but led him out back.

"Mind you, watch out for the bullyboys that come and go back there. Though, think on, you look like you already met them." The proprietor sniffed at him.

"What do you know about what happens at the Happy Cock?" Eli asked.

"As little as possible. Enough to know the neighborhood would be better off without it," the man said.

The shop opened onto a wide alley with a mews behind it. The space narrowed next door where an entire room had been built onto the back of the Happy Cock. Eli quickly added to his notes and sketches, seeing no sign of activity, while the shop owner watched him carefully.

Pulling on his depths of sense, he forced himself to face the fact that he could not invade the den of evil he had sketched. Not now. Not alone. He needed to circle back, check on the children, and find his brother.

"When I come back—and I will—I will not be alone. If you really believe you'd be better off without the vermin next door, look the other way," he told the shop owner.

"What? I hear nothing. I see nothing," the man replied.

Eli grunted and set out the way he'd come.

Lights through the window of the drapery greeted him, reminding him that late-afternoon shadows were forming and Fanny would soon face night. Alone. He fought back sick; it would help no one.

A surprisingly large crowd milled inside.

"Mr. Benson! You look terrible," Wil exclaimed.

"Let me fetch you some tea. Come along, Amy," Mrs. Abbot said.

Amy stood her ground. "Mr. Benson's been in a fight."

The woman shook her head and promised to fetch tea as quick as a bunny. Eli could not care less about the damned tea. He had eyes only for his brother, Rob, who appeared to be enjoying a cup and engulfing a sandwich at the end of the drapery table. Two strangers sat on stools nearby.

"It looks like you may have found our villains, Eli. What do you have to report?" Rob asked.

"Care to introduce your friends?" Eli retorted, wary.

"Hickock and Holliday are inquiry agents on contract to…various government offices," Rob said. He meant, no doubt, Viscount Rockford's shadowing organization. The same one Rob worked for. Contract, though, not employees. *They must be free agents.*

Rob continued, "They have some ideas about crime networks. But first, where did you acquire that delightful bruise? I am assuming at the Happy Cock. What did you find there?"

Wil pushed a stool over to the table for Eli. He looked at the avid faces waiting around him and turned his gaze to his brother. He'd get no more details about Rob's contacts. He described his visit—and treatment—at the Happy Cock. Questions asked; reactions given.

"They wouldn't let me anywhere near the stairs or back rooms. One thing is certain: they're all afraid of something. So are the neighbors."

He pulled out his notes and sketches, describing his survey of the building. "Finally, I took a look out back. This is a sketch of the rear. Odd little extension, that."

"Well done, Eli. Excellent reconnaissance," Rob said, sliding over the sketches. His words soothed Eli's pride, battered by his inability to rush the place.

"They have the means and the muscle to do something like Fanny's abduction," Eli said. "We know Edward's threats are tied to that place. But I saw no way I could get in. Not on my own. If that's where they have her, we don't have much time."

"You did the right thing. You could have been killed, and it might have spooked them into moving her." Rob glanced over at Amy, pulled her close, and spoke softly, "Could you please ask Mrs. Abbot to bring me another of those wonderful sandwiches?"

When the little one ran up the stairs, Rob watched her go before saying, "Holliday here has some experience with white slavery in this part of the country. He thinks they may mean to have her transported."

"Transported? Indentured to the colonies?" Eli couldn't make sense of it.

Rob glanced at the agents. "Holliday thinks the Barbary Coast."

"Young, fresh, and untouched. She fits the pattern," Holliday murmured.

Eli sat as if a boulder had descended onto his head. Slavery. In his worst nightmare, he hadn't considered it. He'd feared rough treatment or forced intercourse at the tavern itself. If they meant to keep her intact to transport her... "Dear God," he breathed.

Wil had moved closer to him.

Eli put an arm around the boy. "I'm sorry you had to hear that." Eli glared at Rob. "But obviously my brother believes you're mature enough to understand what we're up against."

"I want to help." The boy's jaw trembled.

"You already have," Rob said. "Wil found Mr. Reilly there, who saw two men carrying a woman out of the alley, but they disappeared before he could react." He indicated a man dressed as a day laborer, toward the back of the room.

Reilly gave a slight salute. *Former soldier*, Eli thought.

Rob quickly confirmed it. "Reilly served as a sharpshooter in the Peninsular War. He was able to give us a description. Valuable skill, that. I can use a good man like that."

"But now where does that leave us?" Eli asked.

"If the intent is transport, we have a bit of time but not much."

Hancock spoke up, tapping Eli's sketch of the rear of the Happy Cock. "That is an odd extension. There may be a second door on the other side. Flat roof, though. That'll help."

"We'll need people watching the front as well," Holliday murmured.

"That's the plan?" Eli asked, outraged. "We watch?"

Rob nodded ruefully. "I don't like it, either, but taking her when they move her is safer than a frontal assault that would risk injury to Miss Hancock and others."

"But what if Holliday is wrong and they don't plan to move her?" Eli demanded. "Every second counts. They could…" He glanced at Wil. Eli didn't need to put his fears into blunt words.

"The likelihood is they'll move her under cover of darkness. If they haven't brought her out by morning, we'll catch them sleeping." Rob held Eli's eyes. "Eli? Agree?"

Eli nodded. He had little choice. Reilly moved closer to the table, and they began a detailed discussion of tactics and assignments. Tea and a sandwich appeared at Eli's elbow, and he realized he was hungry after all. *You can't go to war starving.*

He listened patiently, adding observations about places the criminals might hide a carriage and four and where they might intercept it. One thought echoed through him. *If the sun comes up, I'm going in there. Even if I have to go alone.*

CHAPTER TEN

FANNY STRETCHED HER aching back. *How many hours have passed?* She thought she had slept a bit, but she'd also used the time to sort through some obvious truths. They hadn't hurt her. They hadn't fed her, either, nor had they allowed her a comfort break, even when she'd called for one. They must plan to move her out of the hole in which they'd stashed her soon.

But for what?

If assault was their goal, they'd have done it. They were saving her for something. She tried not to consider what. Fears for Amy haunted her, and she was less successful in stifling them. She could only pray Amy had made it home and sounded the alarm. Fanny had to believe that.

Someone had flung the door open. "Y'damned fool. Y'din't blindfold her. She can see our faces."

She blinked, blinded and trying to focus. She knew the voice, though. Edwards. Terror warred with rage over Horace's dealings with the toad.

"Don't matter. Who's she gunna tell?" someone else growled. "Help me drag the drab out." That one put action to words, his rough hands squeezing her arms painfully and yanking her to her feet.

"The nob wants her eyes shut, damn it." Edwards crowded into the closet, the smell of unwashed body and garlic sickening her. The nameless brute held her while Edwards blindfolded her painfully; he slapped her when she kicked him. "Let's get moving. They're expecting us in thirty minutes."

Fear accomplishes nothing. She forced herself to think. *If I delay them, maybe...* She tried making herself deadweight and dragging her feet. It did her no good. The ruffian lifted her off the ground, one hammy fist on each arm, and carried her out while she silently cursed her size and kicked in every direction. He tossed her over his shoulder and hauled her downstairs, where they paused. The sound of shuffling told her there were at least three or four of them.

"Put 'er down," a new conspirator said, his voice like sharp gravel. Her tormentors dropped her to her feet. Cool air from an open door struck Fanny's cheek.

A rough hand yanked her chin, foul breath blanketing her face. "Red hair, exactly what the customer ordered. Fresh one, too. Be tempting if she wasn't valuable. Green eyes?" The voice belonged to the new man.

"Aye," Edwards said.

"Perfect. Well done." The man let her go, but she felt him lean in. "You, girl," the gravel voice growled. "Mind your behavior. We're going to walk out. If you do anything to resist—shout, run, kick, drag—we will go back and get that feisty little girl who tried to kick Stink here. There are some that like them young. We can get coin for her, too. We'll take her just before we burn Rundle's precious store down. Edwards warned him not to cross us."

Bile rose. Fanny swallowed it. She wanted to resist in every way the monster listed, but she would go meekly, no matter how it galled, for Amy's sake. She nodded. Silently. They put her between two of them, and she stiffened her back, ready to walk out, head high, to face her fate.

"Eli Benson will protect me," Fanny murmured.

Raucous laughter greeted that. "Benson? The bean counter what's helping ya? Not after the beating Stink and Ralph gave 'im."

⫸⫷

THE CRIMINAL TRANSPORT proved absurdly easy to neutralize. They found it, as Eli suggested, in the mews behind the wine shop, whose owner slipped Eli his spare key and disappeared, preferring to be deaf, blind, and somewhere else when trouble started. The coachman crumpled quickly and lay tied and gagged in the unmarked black carriage.

Eli watched Rob array their troops with silent efficiency before crouching with his brother in the shadow of the wine shop, behind the Happy Cock's foul-smelling rubbish heap. Before long, light from the tavern's rear door, open a crack, spilled into the alley. Eli lunged forward, but Rob grabbed his shoulder, gripping it so hard it hurt. "Signal," Rob growled, reminding him to wait.

Reilly loomed over the alley, from the flat roof on the tavern's extension. Hickock, stationed up there as well, had armed Reilly, the former sharpshooter, with a modified Baker rifle. Holliday lurked in the loft of the mews behind the wine shop; the signal was his to give. Wil, who would not be persuaded to stay away, stood with him.

Eli didn't care for either part of that. He didn't trust Holliday to keep Wil safe, and he suspected Holliday had other things in mind than rescuing Fanny. The inquiry agent had muttered something about catching bigger fish.

Wedged between his brother and the wall, Eli seethed with frustration. They waited for excruciating minutes while the door remained partially open.

When it finally moved, Eli's heart stuttered. The door opened wider, and his beleaguered heart accelerated while every muscle in his body tightened at the sight of Fanny, erect and courageous, between two hulking brutes, who pushed her toward the mews.

Outraged at the sight of her blindfold, he got to his feet, ready to knock Rob over if he had to, to get to her. The kidnappers were almost even with them now.

To hell with the signa—

"Now!" Rob had one of the animals holding Fanny on the ground before Eli reached the other. Holliday ran past them, after a shadowy figure to the rear. Eli plowed into his target, who was twice his size, and knocked him against the wall. The swine bounced off it, flying right back at Eli, fists swinging. Eli ducked, using his smaller size as an advantage, and aimed the crown of his head at the thug's middle. The man went down, and Eli spun around, frantic to get to Fanny.

She turned in confused circles, eyes covered, hands tied together. Eli ripped off her blindfold and wrapped her in a fierce hug before urging her toward the wall and out of the fray.

"Eli!" Fanny screamed, staring over his shoulder, eyes wide in terror. Her shout and the crack of a gunshot were the last things he heard before his world went dark.

CHAPTER ELEVEN

ELI CLIMBED BACK from darkness, terror, and dreams of Fanny being dragged to hell by monstrous half-human creatures, to see Rob's cocky grin.

"Fanny!" Eli flew up—or tried to. Pain shot through his head, almost blinding him.

"Safe. Safe and well," Rob soothed, gently urging him back down to the pillow. "Good to have you back among us."

"What time is it—and where am I?" He lay in a soft bed, in a cheerful room up under eaves. Flower prints livened up walls painted eggshell blue. Sun filtered through lace curtains to the decidedly feminine room, one he had most assuredly never seen before.

"You're in your lady's bower," Rob said, wagging an impertinent eyebrow.

"She isn't my lady," Eli mumbled, absorbing the fact that he lay in Fanny's bed.

"And it's midmorning. Thursday," Rob went on.

Eli started back up again, but his brother stopped him with an arm across his chest. "How can it be Thursday? The Happy Cock. We went there Tuesday night. Have I been sleeping for two days?"

"A day and half, since it is not quite noon. Two nights perhaps. We carried you here shortly after midnight. Do you remember anything? You woke briefly." Rob leaned on his elbows, brow furrowed.

"Nothing. I don't remember anything after…Fanny's look of sheer terror. Where is she?"

"The lady is packing." A shadow passed over Rob's face. "Miss Hancock gave us a detailed description of what happened. It will keep, but you need to know this much. Their 'customer' specified a woman with red hair. I have reason to know that not more than five or six people out of a hundred in this part of the world have hair the color of mine. Even fewer are female, young, and attractive. We need to remove her from Manchester."

Eli digested that, wishing he could spit it out. "What happened to me?"

"The brute you downed didn't stay there. He came at you with a cudgel. He reached for Miss Hancock, but Reilly took him out with a single shot." Rob shook his head. "Brilliant shooting. The man performed every bit as well as he claimed. Some of the miscreants fled. We wrapped the rest up after Reilly's shot, the fight gone out of them. Hickock and Holliday and their men hauled them away in the thieves' own carriage."

"And you brought me here."

"Young Wil ran for the physician, and Miss Hancock insisted on putting you up here. 'Rather than in my disgusting stepfather's bed,' she said. You did wake up briefly, fists flying and frantic. The physician dosed you with laudanum. He said we were to let you sleep."

"That explains the monsters in my nightmares. Keep that stuff away from me please," Eli murmured.

"I'll try to restrain Miss Hancock. Women get carried away when they think something will help a wounded duck," Rob said.

"I'm not a duck! And I don't want laudanum," Eli said more loudly than he intended.

"You're awake." Fanny bustled to the bed, searching his face as if looking for catastrophe.

"I am well, as you can see," Eli said, shoving up onto one elbow. Slowly this time, and very gently. When that worked, he pushed himself all the way up. "My head hurts a bit, but I'll do." He studied Fanny with as much intensity as she examined him.

No sign of injury, thank God. He wished he could see into her heart and soul, for surely there had been injury there. He reached out and took her hand. "Are you truly well? You've recovered from your ordeal?"

"I'm perfectly fine," she said primly, pulling her hand away. "You had a much harder time of it. Should you be sitting up?" She glanced over at the dresser.

Eli saw the laudanum bottle in her line of sight. "Keep that venom away from me."

"The doctor said...," she began.

"That was two days ago," Eli growled.

Rob cleared his throat and rose. "I'll leave you two to argue. But Eli, if you're going to stay upright, you might want to put on a shirt."

Eli glared at his brother's departing back and grabbed for the coverlet.

Fanny turned a remarkable shade of red and gazed at the wall behind the bed. "Rob is right," she said.

My damned brother usually is. Eli stood up on wobbly feet and wrapped himself in the coverlet. "I'll go fetch my clothes. Or I would if I knew where they were."

"You shouldn't be up." Fanny folded her arms across her chest, blocking his way to the door.

"Where have you been sleeping?"

"Across the hall, in Wil's room—and before you ask, he and Rob have been sleeping in Horace's room." Rob, not Sir Robert, he noticed.

"Remind me why I'm not there," he demanded.

"You needed quiet and a room to yourself and... It doesn't matter. Rob said I was right."

Loath though he was to show weakness, Eli sat, suddenly light-headed. "Where are my clothes?"

"Rob brought your valise up here," she said, nodding toward the corner of the room. "The clothes you were wearing when you were injured smelled as if you sat in garbage." She made a sour face as if she could scent it still. "Rob said you hid behind the Happy Cock's rubbish."

Rob again. Eli rolled his eyes. Rob, he'd noticed, wore the same clothing as the other night and was fresh as a daisy. "Couldn't be helped," he muttered.

"They are freshly laundered. I was folding them when I heard you," Fanny said, staring at his chest.

Eli pulled the coverlet tighter. "Do you suppose you could hand me my valise? I have a spare—"

"You should be in bed." Miss Fanny Hancock had a stubborn streak, he noted.

"We're meant to take the remaining inventory to Wagner's Tailoring today." Eli could be stubborn as well, if he needed to.

"Done. Rob and Wil managed the thing earlier this morning, and Rob spun Mrs. Wagner some tale of my sad ordeal until she urged her husband to pay us a bit more," Fanny told him.

Eli stood again, still wrapped in the coverlet. Fanny took a step to urge him to sit but backed off when he glared down at her. His shoulders relaxed. "That's one thing off our list, at least."

"We sold more of the finished goods yesterday, too," Fanny said. "Rob suspects curiosity about the skirmish at the Happy Cock brought the sudden influx of people."

"Ghouls," Eli muttered, making her laugh, a musical sound that gave his tumbling emotions a modest boost.

"Rob said something similar!" she said.

"You and Rob appear to be managing fine." *Without me*, he added silently.

"We are indeed," she said, beaming up at him. "Oh, Eli! He's my brother. I never dreamed such a thing. Amy and Wil can't get over the resemblance. Our births may not have been all that is respectable, but—we're blood. It's a miracle. My brother!"

"He was my brother first," Eli muttered, directing his words to the floor.

Fanny ignored him. "Rob says I am in for more of it when I meet the earl. You didn't tell me the earl is my half-brother as well." Anxiety seeped into her joy. His little warrior let her mask slip, revealing more vulnerability than he had seen before.

"I thought you guessed," he said gently, wanting to sooth the tension from her face.

"No, I never—" Her words caught in her throat even as his eyes captured hers, searching. For what he couldn't say. His gaze slid to her mouth, and a small voice in his head whispered, *She may be Rob's sister, but she isn't yours...*

The moment passed. "If you are going to be stubborn about getting up, your valise is on the chair." She gestured to the corner of the room, then hesitated. "Do you need help? Rob would..."

"I can manage. Tell my brother I'll be down shortly," he said. "And he was my brother first...," he repeated at the door she shut behind her.

FANNY LEANED AGAINST the door, then started down the narrow attic steps. She had to pause halfway down to take a breath, overwhelmed by a maelstrom of emotions. Concern for Eli, and the flow of neighbors and customers gave her no time to deal with her terror and trauma after her ordeal.

When she told Rob Benson and Mr. Holliday about the gravel-voiced man and his words about a customer who wanted a woman with red hair, they'd terrified her with the urgent need to leave

Manchester. She had already agreed to go, but Rob's rush to pack up Grandfather's store and get them all to Ashmead gave her no room to process her grief and disappointment at leaving it all.

She could hear Eli moving around in her little room under the eaves. Seeing him in her bed there had sent shivers of warmth through her for two days—desire to heal, desire to nurture, desire… Desire. She may be an innocent, but she had no doubt about the nature of the emotions and the sensations she felt in her nether regions. They were unexpected, unfamiliar, and unprecedented, and she had no idea what to do with them. Seeing him just now, rumpled and shirtless, sent them spiraling.

Between them, the Benson brothers had her tied in emotional knots.

The sound of Amy's laughter brought her out of her pointless woolgathering. She had packing to oversee. And there was still the estate agent to deal with.

>>><<<

WHEN ELI DROPPED the coverlet and realized he was more than shirtless—he was as naked as his mother had birthed him—he sent a swift prayer that Rob had been the one to put him to bed.

He padded to the corner and picked up his valise. Bending over made him so dizzy he reached out to brace himself on the nearest piece of furniture until the room stopped spinning.

Thankfully it took but a moment. He lifted his hand and looked down at the small writing desk he had been holding on to. Fanny's desk. What had she told him? She planned to publish books. A neat stack of paper sat to one side. A few other papers, whole or in scraps, lay in the center, covered with words, scratches, arrows, and more words.

As they were private, and vitally important to Fanny, Eli had no right to stare at them as he did. Less right to glance at the opening words of the manuscript. "Lady Cassiopeia needed a hero..."

Lady Cassiopeia isn't the only one, he thought.

He shouldn't but he did shift the loose papers in the center to peer at a page of work; an outline; lists of names, buildings, and locations; and a few scraps with descriptions on them. Curiosity was ever Eli's besetting sin. He picked up a piece. Lady Cassiopeia apparently had long chestnut hair and eyes no man could ignore. It made him smile. He picked up another. "Albion" was written on the top. The hero? Eli's conscience pricked him, reminding him it was wrong to look. But he kept reading, suddenly desperate to know what the nascent author envisioned in her hero.

His Fanny apparently liked to examine a man's physique. Tall, sun-bronzed, broad-shouldered, well-muscled all over. But that wasn't all; the man was blond with blue eyes "that sparkled with inner light." At least it wasn't all physical. She went on to describe his character. Commanding, decisive, courageous, and loyal. A rugged out-doorsman. Eli clearly was out of the running for hero, at least fictional hero. Except for loyal. He could manage that. The last line put a period to it. *A man of action, not quiet introspection.*

Eli sighed and tried to put the papers back as he found them, feeling like the sort of idiot who had eavesdropped and heard nothing good about himself.

He put his valise on the bed, picked out a clean shirt, and pulled it over his head. *You are a steward and lucky to be one, not some benighted hero. You came to Manchester to provide Clarion with a clear picture about Miss Frances Hancock's conditions and make a recommendation, not to fret over the blasted woman's ideas about heroism.* Man of action, indeed. *Good luck finding this paragon, Miss Hancock.*

He hoped a good breakfast might cure his foolishness as well as the light-headedness.

CHAPTER TWELVE

T RAVELING HOME TO Ashmead, Eli couldn't shake off the downcast mood that had bedeviled him from the moment he'd woken up to see his brother peering at him. He couldn't think why. He'd always been fond of Rob. He'd been thrilled when Rob had returned to Ashmead as the hero of Waterloo and object of the whole town's pride.

Eli also thought he should find the trip home more enjoyable than the one to Manchester had been. Wil, enchanted as he was by the sights and sounds of the English countryside on his first foray out of the city, made an entertaining traveling companion. Fanny hadn't been as sociable as Wil on the way north; she had traveled in tense silence. The weather blessed them this time as well—which it had not on the way north. His unaccustomed mood made no sense.

There were two problems, Eli finally realized, as they passed through Tideswell. Well, three, actually, if he included Wil's incessant chatter, which had begun to grate on his nerves. First of all, Wil wasn't Fanny. Silent she may have been, but Eli had found her presence at his side comforting. If he were to be perfectly honest, more than comforting.

Damn it, you miss her. Admit it. He'd hardly had a private moment with her since the rescue. He hadn't even had a chance to hear from her own lips what had happened, what she'd heard about their intentions, and how she felt about the increased urgency to depart.

That day had been all planning, provisioning, and packing, directed by Rob while Eli had been pushed to the side, urged to rest by all and sundry. Still, he shouldn't be so downhearted. It wasn't as if he was in love with the girl. Was it?

The other problem, oddly, was the lack of one, at least the lack of a problem to solve, a puzzle to unravel, a situation to analyze—anything to enable him to keep his mind busy and off the rented coach conveying Fanny, Amy, and their luggage, watched over by Rob and, oddly, Reilly, who had become the latest of a long string of unemployed soldiers to find work in Rob's household or his security troops.

Eli still hadn't fully absorbed Rob's belief that the people who'd taken Fanny might try again if she remained in Manchester. There had been little time to discuss it, particularly because they were at pains to keep the conversation away from the children. Holliday believed it and even endorsed the fear that her Caulfield hair made her a particularly valuable target, or so Eli had been told. The horrifying ring that trafficked in the sale of young girls seemed the stuff of someone's fevered imagination, but it explained Rob's urgency to get them packed up and out of the city. And his hiring of an outrider.

Kidnapping wasn't the sort of problem requiring any of Eli's skills; damn it anyway. He could only go along with the plan to get Fanny and the ducklings moved as soon as may be. He couldn't fault the logic, which was why he sped grimly on, determined to simply put miles behind him, Wil at his side, with nothing to do but go over Fanny Hancock's list of qualities she wanted in a hero—none of which Eli possessed.

They pushed on to the little inn on the other side of Matlock, where Eli stabled Cicero, forcing him to stop to exchange horses. He'd pushed the hack past the beast's limit as it was. Eli brought his gig to a stop in the stable yard, eyed the sky, and pulled out his watch. At half past four, they had been on the road since dawn. Now late June, there would be hours of daylight left. With a fresh horse, he might make it to Ashmead, but he wouldn't want to chance it in the dark, not with the boy under his protection. Still, he could bring them within ten miles.

Wil touched his sleeve. "Aren't we meeting the others here? Sir Robert said he would see me at supper." Longing in the boy's eyes was obvious. "He promised to show me how to defend from a knife attack."

"He can do that in Ashmead," Eli snapped. "We're not going to wait around for them to catch up."

Wil's crestfallen expression pricked Eli's conscience but not enough to change his mind. If everyone's hero worship of the great Sir Robert Benson grated on him, he'd get over it. He'd coped with his older brother since Eli could walk. All that adulation certainly wasn't the reason he wanted to push on, he told himself. *You have work to do, Benson. You've been gone long enough. The earlier you arrive tomorrow, the sooner you can get to it.*

⫸⫷

"WHERE CAN THEY be? They were ahead of us, and the gig is speedy." Fanny couldn't stop worrying. She and Amy had been wrapped in the comforts of The Willow and the Rose since shortly after dawn, but now the sun had passed its height above the hills and begun to descend. There was still no sign of Eli and Wil.

"He'll have put up at an inn for the night," old Mr. Benson assured her, not for the first time. "The gig isn't up for overnight travel."

So Eli had told her before. Rob, on the other hand, had assured her they could push on through the night, well-armed as they were, especially with the extra outrider hired for the journey. They'd changed horses twice but hadn't stopped. Considering how loaded down they'd been with luggage, she thought it a miracle.

"He'll be here before long, Miss Hancock. Don't you worry." The innkeeper certainly didn't seem concerned about his younger son. He suggested Amy and Fanny take a walk along the river or make use of the family's shaded bower by the water while they waited for Eli and Wil.

They did both. Now Fanny sat in the quiet spot next to the Afon, reading to Amy, with no sign of the travelers.

When she finally heard steps coming toward them, her heart leapt. Eli had come at last! But he had not.

Rob stood under the shade of the willows, staring at Fanny with a quizzical expression. Except it wasn't Rob. The hair and eyes were identical, but this man's build was slighter, his expression more restrained, for all the resemblance. His tasteful clothing spoke of quality tailoring and fashionable tastes. An air of authority, similar to Rob's but subtly different, radiated from him.

"You're not Rob!" Amy piped up, drawing his attention away from her sister.

The formal manner softened. "No, I am not Rob Benson," he said. "Though you're not the first person to wonder." He gazed back at Fanny and inclined his head. "Clarion, at your service, ladies."

"You're the earl," Amy gasped.

"I am indeed. I understand Miss Hancock came looking for me."

Fanny, bereft of words, dipped a belated curtsey. "My lord," she murmured. "I am Miss Frances Hancock. This is my sister, Amelia Rundle."

When he smiled down at Amy, Fanny saw sadness in the green Caulfield eyes. A habitual, deep-seated sort of sadness, she thought. She felt prepared to like this earl.

"We need to speak about your request for assistance, Miss Hancock, but I'll want to hear what my steward has to say before we see what can be done," he said. "I understand he has been delayed."

Clarion was emphatically not a villain. A new title for her book flitted through her head, *The Elusive Earl*. "Rob—Sir Robert—told us you'd come to the Willow in response to my request. I'm sorry if we pulled you away from weighty matters."

The sad smile came Fanny's way. "Parliament has adjourned for the summer. It's time I came home. My children enjoy the country, and my daughter will be delighted to make Miss Amelia's acquaintance."

"Fanny?" Wil's voice echoed along the river. The boy burst into the clearing. "You got here faster than we did! Eli made us stop for the night, and then there was a problem with one of the hub pins, and—Rob?"

Amy laughed and peered up at Clarion.

"Your Lordship, may I introduce my brother, Mr. Wilber Rundle. Wil, make your bows to the Earl of Clarion," Fanny said.

Wil did as she directed, but his eyes darted from Fanny to the earl and back. He shook his head. "You're my sister, but you look more like him."

"I'm not certain whether it is a blessing or a curse," the earl murmured, offering Fanny his arm. "Shall we go find my tardy steward, Miss Hancock?"

"Eli? You best go swiftly," Wil told them. "He's unloading my bags, but he plans to leave. He has work at Clarion Hall and can't stay. Or so he said."

Clarion sighed. "Ever diligent is Eli Benson. But he can't avoid the inevitable."

"Inevitable?" Fanny asked.

"Family. There will be opinions, Miss Hancock, and Benson can't avoid hearing them. What are we going to do with you?"

CHAPTER THIRTEEN

AFTER A DAY of listening to tenant complaints, paying bills, and reconciling accounts, all of which had accumulated in his absence, Eli sat at his desk in the estate office at Clarion Hall, the center of his domain and his normal place of comfort. Not today. The earl had requested a recommendation. Eli glared down at the estate ledger open in front of him and considered the matter of Fanny Hancock's demands on the estate. He stared at the ledger so long he feared it would burst into flames.

Eli had always prided himself on his cold-blooded reasoning. Allowing emotion to have a role in financial decision-making opened the road to disaster. Even in situations for which he had the utmost compassion, such as Prudence Granger's rightful inheritance or a tenant family's cottage flooded out in heavy rains, the finances had to be analyzed as cold, hard facts. He couldn't create money where there wasn't any, and to give much to one person left less for other equally deserving folks or vitally important needs. Perspective was everything.

He applied his logical mind and legal training to the law even more strictly. The law was the law. One read it, tickled out its subtle nuances, uncovered its hidden exceptions. One did not disregard it.

Why then, he demanded of the universe at large, did he dither over a recommendation regarding Fanny Hancock? Cold, hard fact number one: She had been left out of the old earl's will. Legally the estate had no requirement to help. Cold, hard fact number two: There was no place in the estate's miserably tight budget for the sudden appearance of bastards not covered by the will.

Repairs for a flooded cottage came from a fund set aside for that purpose and were strictly bound by limits and criteria Eli himself had established in order to treat all tenants fairly. Prudence Granger's bequest, like those of others, legally due her under the original terms of the old earl's will, had come from funds retrieved when the countess's fraud had been uncovered. Prudence had gotten what was owed to her, no less, no more. Remaining moneys from the fraud had been used to replenish the estate's operation expenses.

Cold, hard conclusion: The estate need not, could not care for Fanny Hancock.

Meanwhile, his employer, having met Fanny and the ducklings, had taken them to heart. Reserved and formal Clarion might be, but he took the responsibilities of his title seriously. At sixteen the earl had confronted his father about the need to support Alice Wilcox and had done his best for Alice when he'd come into the title. He had also made good on the conditions of the original will with dogged determination. Now he insisted they had an obligation to help Fanny. Moral obligation, yes, Eli agreed, but they would look in vain for an account labeled Long-Lost Sisters. The estate would offer assistance, willy-nilly, and others might assist, but how much and how?

This would be easier, Eli thought morosely, if there was a concrete plan about the sort of help the earl wished to provide. Then Eli could estimate costs. Set her up in business? She might like that, but it would be a risky long-term investment. Marry her off to a professional man, like Alice Wilcox and her curate? The lady should not be forced. She needed time. They may as well take her to London and launch her on the Marriage Mart. She might meet that blond Adonis of a duke, with broad shoulders and sun-bronzed skin, who boxed with Jackson and fenced like a pirate, that she dreamed about. One who didn't expect a dowry. Or they could simply find a cottage for her and the ducklings, as she seemed to want. An empty tenant cottage existed, but Eli didn't deem that appropriate. She wasn't a Clarion tenant and didn't work the land. Besides, her grandfather had left a freehold, and she would insist on ownership. She simply hadn't enough experience to consider other options.

He slammed the ledger shut.

Then there was the matter of Wil and his education. She had already hinted at that, and Wil wasn't even a Caulfield, so hardly a matter for Clarion's steward.

Eli opened his little notebook and surveyed the Hancock-Rundle finances. They'd retrieved a bit from inventory, enough that she did not feel destitute. After they'd paid the more obvious family obligations, there had been little enough in her purse, and Rundle's jewelry and tailoring bills were outstanding. The mortgage hung over them. If the property didn't sell quickly, the bank would simply take it. As luck would have it, they had an offer of sorts.

Eli pulled a folded paper from the notebook. The estate agent had sent round a message just before they'd left. It had come addressed to Eli, which would infuriate Fanny, and he hadn't even had time to discuss it with her. There were no outright buyers, but the agent had found potential renters. He'd offered a sum for the freehold. Less than Fanny hoped but enough to cover the mortgage and Rundle's remaining debts. There might be a few pounds left to put aside for Wil but not enough for university. Then again, the lad may not expect that.

The notebook joined the estate ledger, slammed shut in frustration and tossed across the desk. Wil Rundle's future wasn't Eli's to decide.

Neither was Fanny's safety. If Clarion's sudden enchantment with his new sister centered on assistance, Rob's focused entirely on the white slavers in Manchester. Eli had no role in that, more was the pity. Neither man appeared to have listened to Fanny on either safety or assistance, as near as Eli could tell.

Unable to give his employer the recommendation he wanted, Eli decided to demand clearer instructions. He also needed Fanny and Wil's decision about the estate agent. He rose, stuffed his arms in his coat, and reached for his hat. He would go down to the Willow, where what amounted to a floating welcome party for Fanny had been going on for two days, and try to get someone to give him clarity.

Besides, he thought on his way out the door, *I miss her.*

LATER THAT EVENING, they all sat around the table in the dining room at Willowbrook, the manor house belonging to Rob and his wife, Lucy. Fanny peered around the room at the crowd of Bensons and Caulfields, all of whom seemed to be talking at once, and bit her lower lip to keep from telling her newfound extended family to kindly allow her to make her own decisions.

She had had little enough time to get used to having a brother when she had been confronted with another, the earl, and a sister as well.

The earl's sister—Fanny's newfound half-sister—Madelyn Morgan, had been introduced to her as Lady Madelyn. Emma Corbin had whispered that the earl's sister had been a dowager duchess when she'd married Colonel Morgan but could still claim to be Her Grace, if she chose. She did not. She had asked Fanny to call her Maddy "like our brothers do."

There was a niece—Clarion's daughter, Lady Marj—and nephews. Clarion's son and heir, Viscount Ashmead, tended to be too formal for a boy. Rob's son, on the other hand, was an adorable infant. He'd been introduced as Robert Christopher Benson, but they all called him Kit, there being, as Emma Corbin said, a surfeit of Robs in the Benson family.

Add in the spouses, and it was enough to make Fanny want to hug the ducklings—her beloved, familiar siblings—and scurry back to Manchester.

If she put everyone in her books, they would take her years to write. She wondered if readers would believe it. It was all too much.

She still had no opportunity for a private meeting with Eli, who had appeared at the Willow in the afternoon, interrupting the telling and retelling of Ashmead and family history. She longed for his common sense. Before she could take him aside, he'd asked to speak to the earl privately, and Emma had jumped at the opportunity to whisk Fanny, Amy, and Wil off on a tour of the village, introducing them to all and sundry, with Lady Marj trailing along, hand in hand with Amy.

They returned to find Clarion and Rob arranging a family meeting. "Miss Hancock needs a concrete plan for her future," the earl announced, his sad eyes twinkling for once. "Opinions are welcome." The lot of them had embraced her as Fanny; only the earl held on to the formality of "Miss Hancock." She recalled his earlier comment about family blessings and curses. She tried to catch Eli's eyes, to appeal for his help, but he was deep in conversation with his father.

Opinions, indeed. Now she was getting them in abundance.

The people around the table all acknowledged that "dear Fanny" would make her own decisions, of course, but all were happy to add their advice—their enthusiastic, resolute, determined advice—over filet of sole, herbed chicken, and beans from the kitchen garden.

No one (except Fanny, and she didn't voice it) argued with Rob's adamant—and alarming—insistence that Manchester was not a safe option, but they agreed on little else.

Lucy, Rob's wife—Lady Lucy Benson, to be accurate—saw no reason that Fanny, Amy, and Wil couldn't live at Willowbrook for the immediate future, there being room. After all, she and Rob never lingered in the country, leaving the house often empty. His work called them to London. Eli, apparently, kept an eye on the estate.

Clarion Hall, larger and far more sumptuous, would welcome her, but only if the earl could hire a companion, it being a bachelor residence. Others questioned the added expense. It had become clear to Fanny that the estate and its manor may look opulent, but the estate's finances truly were dismal, and Eli had the job of squeezing funds for expenses out of the shriveled accounts.

Old Mr. Benson reassured Fanny that she and the ducklings were welcome at the Willow as long as they needed to stay. She wouldn't, he told her, be the first more-or-less permanent resident.

Emma Corbin spoke confidentially, "Willowbrook, the Willow, the hall—they're all someone else's homes. You want a place of your own. In town is best, near neighbors, not in some poky cottage miles from everywhere. Eli will work it out."

"What about the dower house?" Brynn Morgan, Maddy's husband, put in. "Now that we have our own country house, it sits empty. I know Eli has recommended that Clarion put it out to rent, but it's an option." He ended on a shrug.

Fanny cleared her throat to remind the earl of her ideas about a quiet life in a place of her own, which she had shared with him at the Willow the first night of this visit. He'd assured her she would have assistance, but his noncommittal responses had not been comforting. He expected Eli to arrange what was "possible."

It certainly appeared all suggestions led back to Eli Benson to sort out, but Fanny hadn't had one private moment with the wretch since he'd arrived two days before. She feared that he avoided her. She glared at him where he sat in the middle of the table, halfway between the earl and Rob, keeping his opinions to himself and studiously attacking his dinner. The man did like to eat, but the uncharacteristic silence irritated her.

"What about London?" Maddy's question brought the table to a silent halt. All eyes shifted to her now. "If we're all intent on giving her choices, she should explore the city. Experience society," Maddy said.

The earl shook his head but said little as the footman entered, carrying a tray of cakes and macaroons.

"London, Maddy, seriously?" the earl asked dubiously, once serving was complete and he'd dismissed the servants.

Rob appeared equally conflicted, but Lucy nodded.

"Why not London? She can always come back to Ashmead," Lucy said. "Three of us have houses there. I don't think Maddy means a Season precisely."

A Season? Presentation at court for an earl's bastard daughter? The very thought threatened to give Fanny palpitations.

Maddy shrugged noncommittally.

"Of course not," Clarion said. "And society is thin in the summer."

"True," Maddy said, "but the shopping is good, and the children would benefit from exploring the capital."

"Marj would be wild to show Amy the Tower," Lucy said, laughing. "Don't you agree, Eli?"

Eli said nothing.

"For a visit, maybe," Rob said, pensive. Fanny suspected he had something on his mind that had little to do with her housing problems.

"Perhaps, but it doesn't solve the larger issues," Clarion argued.

Fanny had had enough. "Please. I know you all mean well, and I appreciate it more than I can say, but I'm—" She faltered on the end.

Eli looked up from the macaroon he had dipped in liqueur, set down the dessert, and cleared his throat as if about to speak.

Fanny spoke first. "Everything you've said seems to come back to Eli Benson. He's also the one who knows the most about our situation in Manchester." She glanced at Rob before peering pointedly at Eli. "Our business and financial situation. I need a private meeting with him. Until I know what is possible, I can't make a decision."

He smiled then, a gentle lift of his lips, one that said he understood. "I would be honored." Their eyes held, and Fanny's heart soared. Eli Benson had never failed her. The more she heard, the more she realized the people around the table all depended on him.

Everything she had learned—and some profound instinct she barely understood—told her to trust him. Eli would know how to create a life for her and the children. Eli would manage it.

CHAPTER FOURTEEN

ELI LED FANNY to the privacy of Lucy's little office. A cacophony of voices (and a few fierce frowns) followed them out of the dining room. He hoped he could finish this interview before the Caulfields, much less the Bensons, agreed on the impropriety of his leading her to a closed room and descended on them.

The office featured little decoration, a simple desk, and a few straight-backed wooden chairs that promised scant comfort. He thought it perfect for what was meant to be, after all, a brief business conversation.

Fanny gazed around, still clinging to his arm, and murmured, "This is different from the one at Clarion Hall."

A laugh bubbled out of Eli. "It is that." He lowered his arm, slipping his hand down hers to grasp her fingers. Their eyes met in a moment of amused accord that sent an electric charge through Eli, one he believed bounced around the tiny room. His gaze dropped to her mouth, and he swayed ever so slightly toward her.

When her lips parted, the temptation to kiss her held him transfixed, but she dipped her head under the force of his gaze and the moment passed.

Keep your senses, Benson. "We best not take long. Either Rob or Clarion will interrupt if we linger," he said.

She nodded, peering at the floor.

Eli put a knuckle under her chin and gently raised her face so she had to look at him. "Do you want to go to London?"

It didn't appear to be the question she expected. Her eyes widened, and flustered words spilled out. "Yes. No... That is, a visit would be lovely, but that's the least of my problems." Her normal energy rushed back through her and, with it, irritation. "Eli, what I want is a little place to raise the ducklings in comfort. It appears you are the only one who can determine if that is possible."

"That's ludicrous. I'm, I'm...," he stuttered at the thought.

"You're the fixer. The one who makes things happen. I haven't been in Ashmead long, but I've already figured that out."

Heat filled him, flushing his face and fleeing as quickly as it came. "I'm a steward. I advise, I don't decide, and I can't tell the earl what is possible unless I know what it is we're funding."

She dropped his hand and scowled. "If it comes back to me, I repeat, all I want is a comfortable place. As lovely as everyone is, I would actually prefer to be above the store in Manchester, business or no business, but Rob forbids it."

Who is the almighty Rob Benson to forbid Fanny anything? Memory of her, blindfolded and confused between two thugs, and of her words about the customer requesting red hair put a swift end to his resentment of his brother. "The store is no longer an option," he said, shards of sorrow pricking his heart.

"It hasn't sold yet," she retorted.

Eli shifted uneasily.

Fanny's eyes narrowed. "What haven't you told me?"

"A message came from the estate agent the morning we left. I haven't had a chance to speak with you with everything else going on," he told her.

"Oh, I have no doubt the Earl of Clarion's business is much more important to you than Miss Frances Hancock's poor problems." Bitterness dripped from her words. "I assume you don't anticipate I will like what I hear."

"Commercial property is valuable, Fanny. Hence the size of the mortgage. It would never do for a home unless you could manage the business, and you agreed in Manchester that you cannot." He held her gaze, willing her agreement.

She hesitated before nodding. "What did the estate agent say?"

He explained the offer. "It has the advantage of speed. It can be done before the bank swoops in." He told her his best estimate.

"There will be little left after we pay Horace's debts," she said.

"And it is Wil's, of course. We can put what is left in a trust for his education." It was the best he could manage with the Rundle inheritance. "That brings us back to your request for assistance from the Clarion estate."

She bit her lip, considering what he said. "You said 'we.' We sell... We pay... Who is this 'we'? Who has the authority to sign the deeds? Didn't you say the courts would appoint someone to act for Wil?"

Damn.

⊱⊰

GONE. *ALREADY GONE.* Fanny thought she had let go of her grandfather's legacy, her childhood home, but grief gripped her at Eli's adamant words, *"The store is no longer an option."* How could Eli make it that cold-blooded? They stood so close in the small office she could feel his breath, and yet he felt miles away.

It isn't his fault. None of it is. He means to help, but there is no "we" in the catastrophe. She pulled herself together. She and the ducklings had to close out their old life and move on. She repeated her question. "Who has the authority to sign the deeds? Who can act for Wil?"

"We will have to petition the ecclesiastical court for you to act on his behalf."

His obvious concern didn't comfort her. "But you aren't certain they will appoint me."

"With Clarion endorsing you, they will." His tone sounded less certain than his words.

She remembered the issue of her age. *They are more likely to seize on the opportunity to appoint an earl Wil's guardian if they get a look at the situation.* She kept that to herself. "Then what? My request for assistance…"

"That rather depends on what you want. An estate like Willowbrook is out of the question," he said.

It hadn't occurred to her, but hearing him say it brought anger to her lips. "Yes. I'm not a son, and I was entirely forgotten. I understand that," she said.

"Fanny—"

She put up a staying hand, one she slowly lowered to his lips. His very warm lips. She could feel his breath on her hand. She could—She pulled it away and called back the thought that had scattered. "I know, Eli. I know. What exactly can a forgotten bastard daughter expect?"

He took a shuddering breath and ran a hand through his hair. "The easiest is a tenant cottage. We have one open. They are clean, dry, and simple."

"How simple?" she asked.

"Two rooms and a loft," he said, grimacing. "The dower house…"

"Brynn Morgan said you had already planned to rent it to someone. Is it excessively grand?" she asked.

"Rather like Willowbrook here but on the Clarion estate and close to the hall. The earl had counted on the rent." He frowned.

"The other extreme, and not available for a freehold," she mused.

"No, definitely not. There's also a steward's house, currently empty because it is rather a wreck and I haven't needed it. That is also unavailable for freehold. Is ownership what you want? Can you be specific?"

Fanny's life had been taken from her; her dreams remained. Ephemeral things, dreams. Space enough for the three of them. A private place to write. Her writing mattered. She would not give that up.

"Fanny," he prodded. "Tell me what you need, and then I'll investigate how to provide it."

"A home of my own, yes. Not one beholden to my brother. One with room for Wil and Amy but with enough space for myself, a private place to write. That's what I want."

"A place for your desk, is that it? A drawing room, a kitchen, and three bedrooms, one of your own with room for the desk?" he asked.

Not space for a piece of furniture. Space for my dreams. Somewhere to be myself. "Or two bedrooms. I can share with Amy if I have an office." She met his eyes. "That's what I need, Mr. Benson. Can the Clarion estate provide it? Because if not, we'll use Wil's education funds and rebuild them with proceeds from my books. There will be proceeds. I will sell them." She held her breath, daring him to mock her dreams.

He winced when she called him Mr. Benson, but he listened, his intense gaze boring into her as if he wanted to reach into her soul. After a long moment, he nodded. "I'll see what I can do."

Fanny, who prided herself on her facility with words, tossed about for the ones to explain, to make him see beyond pence, property, and furnishings. None came. She was spared the struggle by a knock on the door and Lucy's voice.

"Can you finish tomorrow? I came to warn you Rob or David may batter the door down if you stay much longer, and I'm fond of the door to my office."

"We're finished," Eli called back.

Fanny feared they were just that. Finished. He had his hand on the handle before another thought surfaced.

"Wait. What is the next step after petitioning the courts?"

He hung his head without taking his hand off the handle or turning back to her. "Paperwork. I'll have to go to Manchester."

He'll have to? What happened to "we"?

⫸⫷

ELI OPENED THE door. There was no point in provoking two overprotective brothers over a business interview. *That's what this was, isn't it?*

Lucy beamed at them.

"Come in if you wish," he murmured. She did, making it rather crowded.

Fanny wasn't finished with him. "You told me you couldn't be certain I could act on Wil's behalf. We fled Manchester before we could work out the legalities. Now you say we need to go back," she said.

"Not 'we.' I need to go back and handle the legal paperwork," he said. "It isn't safe for you in Manchester."

"I need to be there to defend myself." His little warrior was back, determined and unmovable.

Eli groaned. "We know that is inadvisable."

"But If I'm appointed, I will have to be there to sign over the deeds," she said relentlessly. "Will the court be willing to delay until I'm twenty-one in September?"

"We'll cross that bridge when we come to it. As I said, first I have to petition for a court date and a stay on any actions from the bank." *All of which I could have done before hustling south.* Eli almost wished he had stayed behind to see it through in person, except courts—chancery and ecclesiastical—were notoriously slow. He wanted to kick himself, but that would be undignified. "Depending on how they reply, I'll finalize the paperwork and the sale or I'll appeal. In Manchester."

CHAPTER FIFTEEN

A PLAN, EVEN *a questionable one, is better than no plan*, Eli thought, nursing a pint of ale at the Willow the following afternoon while the ladies took over the Bensons' riverside bower to plan a London visit. Eli's plan didn't include that particular complication, but Lucy, backed by Maddy, had insisted. Fanny and the ducklings were to stay with Rob and Lucy. It was to be Rob's gift.

Eli had spent the morning at the hall, double-checking his numbers and polishing the aforesaid questionable plan so long that the earl had left with Lady Marj and the little viscount to visit with the Rundle children. Eli had followed them to the Willow, where he now waited for his employer, tried not to second-guess his decisions, and pored over a law book.

"Intestate law?" The earl slid into the seat across from Eli in the snug in the corner of the Willow's taproom. He tipped his head to read the title. *"The Disposal of a Person's Estate…"*

"Who Dies without Will and Testament," Eli finished for him. "Two years ago, I would have said wills are simpler."

Clarion laughed and smiled his thanks at Annie, the server who brought him a mug of ale. "I would have thought you were totally weary with inheritance law. Rundle?"

Eli nodded and finished the dregs of his ale, signaling for another.

"How bad is young Wil's situation?"

"Bad enough. If we can sell the store quickly, what he'll have after the mortgage is paid, along with the sale of the assets, should be put aside for his education—if the Clarion estate can provide enough to support his sisters until he reaches his majority."

The earl nodded. "You can see to it?"

"We left Manchester without completing the legalities." Eli shifted uneasily. "I'll need your leave to go back to deal with the ecclesiastical courts and estate agent."

Clarion watched him pointedly. "No wonder it has taken you so long to give me a simple recommendation. You've been dealing with a two-headed monster. The Rundle situation on the one hand and the estate's assistance to our forgotten heir on the other. You care about her."

"Of course I care about them. How can I not? Horace Rundle left them in a dire situation." Eli rushed his words, emphasizing *them*. Clarion's implication made him uneasy.

"I'll hear this plan of yours, and then we'll talk about Manchester." Clarion waited patiently.

Eli handed him the carefully worded report, complete with figures and estimates. "First of all, I'm obliged to make it clear you have no legal obligation to assist Miss Hancock."

"And I'm well aware. My father couldn't bestir himself to remember her existence. Moral obligation is something else."

"I suspect the lady's mother never informed him of her birth, but that's neither here nor there. Last night she made it clear she wants neither ongoing support nor an allowance."

The earl opened his mouth to object, but Eli raised a staying hand. "I factored it in. Are you aware Miss Hancock writes novels? She is convinced they will be able to live on the proceeds, but to my knowledge, she's yet to have one published."

Clarion absorbed that thoughtfully, surprising Eli, who expected vociferous skepticism.

There being no comment, Eli went on, "What she wants is simple.

A small house for the three of them. She has two stipulations, that it be a freehold and that she have enough space for herself to do her work."

"Can we afford it?" the earl asked.

"I think so. Most certainly if we find a tenant for the dower house. With some shifting and economies, even if we don't." Eli laid out the probable range of costs. "It will be easier here than in Manchester. I believe she has become convinced of that. It may take time to find one that fits."

The earl nodded. "One more auburn-haired Caulfield won't shock the neighbors," he said ruefully. "The plan, then, as I understand it, is (1) you will find a suitable property to purchase within the range of costs you quoted and (2) the estate will send you to Manchester to settle Mr. Wil's inheritance as a kindness to my sister."

Annie brought Eli his refreshed ale. He hardly noticed. "In a nut-shell, yes."

"When will you go north?"

"I wrote to the bishop's court, requesting hearing dates, this morn-ing. We'll see." Eli shrugged. "I also sent a formal request to the chancery court to delay repossession of the store pending outright sale. They are notoriously slow, so that is in our favor."

"Good. Then you have time for plan point three," Clarion said.

"There is no three," Eli said, sipping his ale.

Clarion ignored him. "Point three. You will investigate publishers. Rob and Lucy will return to London at the end of the week, bearing Miss Hancock and her siblings with them. You will accompany them. You can stay at Caulfield House."

Eli blinked. London with Fanny? His foolish heart rejoiced. His good sense objected to that nonsense. "You wish me to investigate publishers? She probably knows more about them than I ever will."

"Good. You can ask her assistance and then do what you do," Clarion said with a hand gesture that covered a universe of meaning. "Make lists. Evaluate options. All that."

"Am I not needed here?" Eli asked.

"We'll manage. I will be at the hall, enjoying summer in Ashmead with my children. And Benson, while you are in London, you can post adverts regarding the dower house. You can also pay an unannounced visit to our bank and do a quick audit."

Worded like that, the trip to London sounded like proper use of Clarion's steward. Both Eli and the earl had learned the value of keeping a close eye on the books.

"If we hear from the courts in Manchester, I'll need to know immediately," Eli said.

The earl's lip twitched into a self-deprecating grin. "We'll send word. I think I can manage that."

Eli sat back to finish his ale, his mind already making lists and rearranging tasks.

>>><<<

WHEN ROB AND Lucy invited Fanny and the ducklings to accompany them on their return to London, Fanny accepted, happy for time to get to know her brother better. Besides, London would be an education for Wil. Clarion elected to stay in Ashmead with his children, and Amy begged to stay at the hall with Lady Marj. Fanny agreed with Clarion's encouragement. Brynn Morgan, she'd been told, worked in the capital as well, so he and Maddy would form a sort of caravan with them, enabling a bit less crowding in the Benson carriage. A third carriage would bring maids, nursemaids, and the baby.

On the designated morning, she stood dressed for travel next to Lucy in the stable yard of the Willow while luggage was loaded. There appeared to be some sort of delay, but it didn't last long.

A familiar gig tooled into the stable yard, and Alfred ran over to greet it. The sight of Eli Benson striding across with his ever-present valise bulging with papers came as an unexpected pleasure. She watched him stop to speak with Brynn and Rob while the ostler took his bags, anticipating his company, but her heart sank when he moved toward the other carriage.

Rob came to hand Lucy, Fanny, and Maddy into his carriage. "You ride in Morgan's, young Wil," he said, "but, mind you, my brother plans to work all the way to London. He will not be good company."

Wil grinned. "I know him, Sir Robert."

Rob leaned in. "But you won't have to listen to the ladies, either. Think of that."

Lucy chastised him on behalf of all women, accepted a smacking kiss, and climbed in. Soon they were rolling down the coaching road toward Nottingham, where they would turn south.

Fanny watched out the window as the other carriage moved to follow. "Do you always travel with so many outriders?" she asked. She'd spotted Reilly, now a part of Rob and Lucy's household, and two others who'd served as guards on their trip from Manchester. Rob and Brynn rode beside the carriages as well.

Lucy peered out the window and pursed her lips for a moment before answering, "No, actually. Usually just Rob and one other."

"I confess he asked us to move up our return. He wanted Brynn along as well," Maddy said. "Men worry. I wouldn't fret."

After what happened in Manchester, Fanny decided to take it as a comfort, not a cause for anxiety. Eli had come. All would be well. She didn't pause to question that thought.

She smiled, sat back, and closed her eyes, to entertain herself as she always did. How might she cast Maddy in her story? She was a bit young, but she had the bearing and strength of character to serve as a model for the hero's mother—or his very independent aunt. Fanny could just visualize it. As to Lucy, the heroine's best friend would have just her personality—loyal and smart with a dash of spice.

After Rob rode up alongside and spoke to them through the window to check if all was well, Fanny turned her thoughts to her current hero, *The Elusive Earl*. Elements of Rob and Clarion circled and merged in her mind—physical prowess, protective passion, authoritative air, decisiveness. Of course, she had settled on blond and blue-eyed for her fictional earl.

Satisfied, she let her mind wander. It went where it often did, to Eli. She hoped they might rearrange seats when they stopped overnight. She hoped for a chance to talk to him. *What work is so important he keeps at it in a moving carriage? And what role might he have in my story? The hero's younger brother?* The thought left her dissatisfied. He was that and more.

CHAPTER SIXTEEN

ELI CRAWLED OUT of the carriage and stretched. He needed a walk badly after an entire day traveling. When they stopped at midday, Wil had asked to ride above with the coachman. Before Eli could respond, Rob deemed it safe, and the boy took it as permission. Eli glanced at Fanny to see what she thought, but she and the ladies had scurried off to the privies behind the tavern. Maddy took Wil's spot in the afternoon. He had been relieved it wasn't Fanny, certain her presence would have been too great a distraction from his work.

Who are you deluding, Benson? Just knowing she rode in the other carriage caused her to torment your thoughts and shred your concentration all day.

His attraction to Fanny—and he could no longer pretend it didn't exist—was getting out of hand. He needed to speak to her about his conversation with Clarion. They had settled on a plan, and that should ease her mind. Maybe it would ease his. Even when the stopped for the night, he lost himself in distraction.

"Are you coming?" Maddy stared at Eli quizzically. "I, for one, am looking forward to getting settled in our room." From the way her eyes kept straying to Brynn Morgan, handing over his mount to a young ostler, Eli suspected it was time with her husband she looked forward to, and the thought heated him.

He spied Fanny heading toward the entrance and trotted over.

"Eli! How was your afternoon? Did you get a lot done?" Fanny asked. The conversation around them centered on arrangements for the night.

"I wonder if I might have a private word," he said. *A word. Of business.*

She glanced around at their companions. "Now?"

"I thought perhaps a walk. I certainly need one," he said.

Lucy, preoccupied with a crying baby, waved them on, and Fanny took his arm, walking in silence until they left the vicinity of the inn. Within moments, they strolled onto a country road lined with hedges alive with birds and lined with wild flowers. On the other side, farm fields stretched along undulating hills, where the sun seemed to rest, its lower edge already sinking beneath them. The peace felt too precious to disturb.

Fanny must have agreed, because several moments passed before she spoke. "You wanted a word, Eli?"

"Yes. I thought you would be reassured to know that Clarion agreed to our plan."

"We have a plan?" Fanny asked, turning toward him, brows raised.

He ran his hand along the back of his neck. "I'm getting ahead of myself, aren't I?" Face to face with Fanny anchored at his side, where she held his arm, he found his thoughts scrambled. *Just a word*, Benson he reminded himself, but the urge to kiss her battered his senses.

"Eli? What is this plan?" she asked.

Yes. The plan. He lowered his arm and took hold of her hand instead. That didn't help, but he couldn't make himself let go. "There are two parts. I have Clarion's permission to return to Manchester. I've already petitioned both the ecclesiastical court and the chancery court on your behalf. Clarion believes chancery will hold off on the mortgage until the church court acts on appointing an administrator, giving us time to sell the store."

She nodded. "I will go with you."

He didn't argue; there would be time for that later. Considering how difficult he found it to resist temptation with a herd of family nearby, he could not possibly travel to Manchester alone with her, even if the rest of them permitted it. It would not happen.

A carriage careened down the road, kicking up dust on them, and a farm wagon followed at a distance. He tugged Fanny's hand and led her through a break in the hedge, sheltering her from the road. She didn't object. The trust in her eyes—trust he would probably lose when he went to deal with the courts without her—left him feeling like a knight in armor.

"What is the second part?" Fanny asked.

He dropped her hand. *Words, Benson. Keep it business.* "I described your needs exactly as you gave them to me and put together a budget to make it happen. Clarion agrees. However, it would help if we could find tenants for the dower house. That's one reason he sent me to London."

She gazed up at him expectantly. A man could get lost in that gaze.

"I, uh, I've been deputized to seek tenants and also to find such a haven for you when I get back." His eyes never left hers. "In Ashmead. I—that is, the earl and I—thought that best." He swallowed hard. "Afford..."

She threw her arms around him before he could finish. "Perfect. Just perfect. Thank you."

He had no words. His hands came up to touch her back, but he stifled the urge to pull her tight against him. He didn't have to. The woman had done a thorough job of it herself. His wits went begging. He kissed the top of her head and then the side of her brow.

She tipped her head up, her mouth agape in astonishment.

HE LOOKS AS shocked as I am, Fanny thought. Eli dropped his hands as if he had burned them, and Fanny took a step back. Two steps.

"I—I'm sorry. I didn't mean...," Fanny said.

Eli responded forcefully. "No, I am the one who must apologize. My news made you happy, and you gave in to an impulse. I took advantage as no gentleman should."

"Nonsense! You didn't overstep. You were..." She stumbled over the next word. "Wonderful."

He shook his head. "We were both overcome by the moment. It's best if we forget it."

Fanny glanced toward the opening in the hedge. "We ought to return."

He gestured for her to go ahead of him, but she turned back. She owed him gratitude. "But first I want to repeat my thanks. I am delighted. My brother...the earl... I can't tell you what a relief it is. But you, Eli! I know you'll find me a perfect place."

He gestured to the opening again. "You were correct—we ought to get back." His voice sounded oddly hoarse.

They walked companionably enough, but Eli didn't offer his arm. He loped along with his hands clasped behind his back. After a while, he asked, "So we are agreed that I'm to find a property in Ashmead? Manchester and London being prohibitive."

"Of course."

He nodded solemnly. "I will do my best, Miss Hancock."

The steward had returned. Fanny didn't like it at all.

THE REST OF the way to London, Eli kept to himself and worked on one of his lists, this one entitled "Reasons to Keep My Distance from Frances Hancock." She was his employer's sister. Helping her was his job. His behavior had been inappropriate. She was an innocent with little experience with men. She needed to understand she had choices. She preferred her independence. She was an earl's daughter. She deserved more than a steward could provide.

That last one shocked him. As if he'd even considered marriage. He dismissed it and added, *Lust makes you an idiot.*

When they arrived in London, the Morgan carriage conveyed Eli to Caulfield House, where he let the staff take his luggage to a guest room while he unpacked his valise in the study and set to work. He had announcements for the papers about the dower house complete before supper. Such announcements would, of course, reflect on the earl's social standing, but the entire world already knew what "poor Clarion" had had to endure. Eli decided not to warn the bank of his visit. Unexpected appearances kept them on their toes.

He requested a tray in his room for supper, not wishing to burden the staff more than needed. Clarion traveled with his butler, house-keeper, cook, and most of the maids and footmen, rotating them between houses twice a year rather than employing two full staffs. That reduced whichever house he left behind to a skeleton staff. In London, that meant primarily Mr. and Mrs. Stilson, a taciturn couple that served as maid and groom when the earl was in residence and general caretakers when not. It had been Eli's suggestion and had resulted in satisfying reduction in expenses.

Sitting in morose solitude over cold meats and cheese reminded Eli why he preferred the country. He mulled that thought more than it deserved, using it to keep thoughts of Fanny at bay. It didn't work for long.

He'd never told her part three of the plan. The part in which Eli investigated publishers. It shouldn't be difficult to find them, but how would he tell which were good? The earl had said to ask Fanny. Come to think of it, the entire exercise had been the earl's idea.

For one insane moment, Eli envisioned himself convincing a pub-lisher—a gray-bearded, intellectual sort behind a deep desk piled high with manuscripts—that her words were genius and winning her a contract. A lucrative contract, causing her to gaze at him as her hero.

The daydream dissipated. Even if he managed such an implausible turn of events, she would be more likely to resent the interference than to be grateful.

You need a drink, Benson. Or a woman. Eli wasn't entirely without sexual experience, but he never made use of the women in London's brothels—much less employed women of the street. He shuddered at the thought. That it had even crossed his mind told him how lost he was. He padded back downstairs in stockinged feet. The earl kept his best brandy in a hidden cupboard in his study. He wouldn't begrudge Eli a drink. Or two.

Paying a woman for her favors wouldn't help Eli's obsession with Fanny Hancock, in any case. *Besides*, he thought, sitting behind Clarion's desk, *publishing is a business. How hard can it be to do the research?*

He could do that much. Tomorrow he'd scan the papers for advertisements. Perhaps, like many industries, they clustered in the same area.

Just ask her, a defiant voice told him.

CHAPTER SEVENTEEN

R OB WHISKED WIL off with him after breakfast to Fanny's relief. Apparently, the ladies' first day would be dedicated to shopping and Wil was meant to join the men in avoiding the dreaded experience. Tattersall's and horseflesh were mentioned, but Fanny was left to guess what else they might be up to. When Fanny objected that she had few funds and less interest in feminine whatnots, Lucy grinned.

"What say you to books, art supplies, and sweets?"

"Books?" Fanny sighed.

"Ashmead holds many joys and some treasures. One thing it lacks is a decent bookstore," Lucy declared.

A firm knock on the door interrupted them, and through the drawing room door, Fanny heard the Benson butler hasten to answer.

"Maddy is early," Lucy murmured, but the butler's words of greeting startled Fanny.

"Welcome, Mr. Eli. We weren't expecting you," he intoned.

Even Lucy's eyes widened. She handed the baby she'd been cuddling back to his nurse with a quick kiss and went to the door of the drawing room. "Eli? What brings you so early? I'm afraid Rob has left already, taking Wil with him." Her eyes narrowed. "Did he inform you we needed an escort today? I hope he didn't give you some excuse about being due at Horse Guards because he's meeting Brynn to dither over horses."

Eli peered at Fanny over Lucy's shoulder, warming her to her toes.

"He didn't, but I thought—That is, I'd be happy to serve as escort." He glanced back at Lucy. "Where are we going?"

Lucy laughed and hooked her arm in his. "We're off to show Fanny the true delights of the capital. We are waiting for Maddy, and then we'll be off," she said, leading him into the drawing room.

Eli frowned over at Fanny. "If this means waiting at the modiste while you lot…"

"No, silly, the real treasures. Bookstores and Gunter's," Lucy said, her infectious laugh filling the room. She glanced between Fanny and Eli. "Fanny pronounced no interest whatsoever in fashion." She leaned over and continued in a stage whisper obviously intended for Fanny to hear, "David let Rob contribute to the allowance they plan to set up at Madame Gilberte's establishment. My job is to convince Fanny to make use of it."

Eli smiled, not the least surprised. Of course not. As steward, he was probably the one charged with setting it up. "In that case, I would be honored to escort you ladies while my brother plays least in sight." His eyes never left Fanny, forcing her to drop hers to study her slippers.

Sitting as she was in one of Lucy's borrowed gowns, the hems hastily taken up by Lucy's maid, talk of fashion made Fanny wish she could sink into the floor. She hadn't come to Ashmead to ask for charity but to request her sire take responsibility for her sustenance. Of course, she hadn't expected to be overwhelmed by family, either.

She glanced back up. Admiration in Eli's warm brown eyes—for surely that was what she saw—pushed her embarrassment aside. She sat a bit taller. The frock fit her a treat, and Lucy had insisted it flattered her coloring better than it did Lucy's own.

Maddy arrived, looking a bit paler than normal, and apologized for being tardy. Soon enough, Fanny's newfound sisters were whisking her into Hatchards Bookstore, with Eli trailing behind. Fanny took a deep breath, the smell of leather and ink filling her with serenity.

Maddy laughed when Lucy hurried over to check the newest agricultural journals. "Obsessed!" she said.

"Agriculture?" Fanny wrinkled her nose.

"Has no one told you Lucy is by far the best land steward in all Nottinghamshire?" Eli asked. "She teaches me a great deal."

He must be the humblest. "It isn't what I would have suspected," Fanny said, turning to Maddy for confirmation, but she had disappeared down an aisle of shelves.

Two gentleman and an older lady hovered around a table in front of the window, blocking Fanny's view of the display. A clerk hurried over. "The dark, new work by Mary Wollstonecraft Shelley has caused quite a stir. There are a few copies and other new books back on the fiction shelves. If gothic is your taste, Ann of Swansea's newest is also there. And if I may say so, there is a wonderful four-volume set by the author of *Pride and Prejudice*—two newly published novels in one set."

"Shall we have a look?" Eli asked, offering his arm. Fanny took it, noticing he knew the way.

"Here's the new Ann of Swansea. *Secrets in Every Mansion*. Gothic, he said. Intriguing title." Eli pulled out volume one and studied the title page. "A. K. Newman and Company. Are they important publishers?"

"I've never heard of them," Fanny murmured, running her fingers along the books on the shelf until they came to ones by Selina Davenport. She pulled out *An Angel's Form and a Devil's Heart.*

Eli leaned over her shoulder to peer at it, so close she could feel his breath on her neck and the warmth of him all down her back. Her wits went wandering, and she missed his question. "I beg your pardon?" Her voice sounded breathless, to her irritation.

"Minerva Press," he said, stepping back. "I've heard of them. I think Emma subscribes to their books. Mostly fiction?"

"Yes. And they are one of the few to publish books by women. Notice Miss Davenport has her name on the cover," Fanny said.

"I can see why that might matter. Have you sent them your work?" he asked.

Fanny's heart sank. "Yes," she admitted. *Three times.* "They said my stories lacked danger and suspense."

"Your stories aren't gothic." He made it a statement, not a question.

"I fear I'm not interested in eerie manor houses and insane butlers. Or monks. Nor do I know how to write about them."

"What about this one?" he asked, reaching past her to pull another from the shelf, again enveloping her in his heat, the smell of new leather, and his own hint of cedar scent. He turned it over to reveal volume one of the set the clerk had mentioned by the author of *Pride and Prejudice*.

"*Northanger Abbey* and *Persuasion*. Two full novels. What is the cost?" she asked.

"I can—No, I suppose you wish to make your own purchases," he said before telling her the price. "John Murray on Albemarle Street. Are they also a well-known publisher of fiction?"

"Mmm. They mostly publish poetry, I think. Lord Byron, some Scots fellows. Why are you asking?"

"But this is fiction, so they publish some," he said, removing a notebook from his coat and making a note of it.

Her eyes narrowed when he returned to A. K. Newman and scribbled some notes. Suspicion grew. "Why are you doing that?"

He shrugged. "I know nothing about the business of publishing books, and I'm always eager to learn more. What other publishers have you tried?"

"My books are not your concern, Mr. Benson," she declared.

"Allow me some curiosity, Miss Hancock," he responded, his tone as tart as hers.

"Then exercise it over these shelves, not at my expense. Here." She pulled out one novel after another, holding them out so he could write down the publisher's names and directions.

If he thinks he can treat my writing like a business proposition, he is mistaken. Fanny frowned at her own pettiness. *You want to make money from your books. What is your problem?*

Writing, deeply personal, belonged only to her; she resented anyone's intrusion. And yet she had learned to her regret that publishing was also a business, one she didn't know how to navigate. *What is the point of writing without publishing?* She glanced at Eli from the corner of her eye, and her shoulders relaxed.

PUBLISHERS' NAMES BECAME repetitive, and Eli quickly realized there were a relatively modest number of publishing houses who produced the sort of novels women enjoyed. Not that he knew what Fanny actually wrote. He closed his notebook with a snap.

"Thank you for your assistance." He had upset her. Now awkward and uncertain, he couldn't think what to say next. *Apologies work, you dolt.*

"You are welcome," she murmured, coloring softly.

"And I apologize if I intruded before. Your work is your heart. I know that, and I had no right."

It must have been the right thing to say, because she glowed. He wouldn't forget that again. "Did you plan to buy one?" he asked.

She picked up the first volume of *Northanger Abbey*, and they made their way to the front. Lucy had her journals, and Maddy clutched an illustrated work on exotic flowers for English gardens. The ladies paid for their treasures and handed the parcels to a footman waiting outside. The Benson carriage ferried them to Gunter's Tea Shop.

To his relief, the tension between himself and Fanny eased over ices at Gunter's, during which he and Maddy kept the other two laughing with stories about growing up in Ashmead.

A mellow mood persisted, and when Lucy suggested a stroll through Berkeley Square just across the street, Eli proposed that they walk the few blocks to Hyde Park instead, "since you have such an able escort." He winked at Fanny and was rewarded with a delicate blush.

Lucy agreed that dodging traffic for that distance made walking more attractive. The coachman promised to meet them at the gate of the park in two hours.

Walking next to him on the narrow sidewalk, her small hand in its cotton glove against his arm, Fanny became uncharacteristically quiet. Eli, for his part, feared that the feel of her at his side would torture his nights. It certainly did odd things to his breathing. He almost wished the narrow walk hadn't caused the other two ladies to stroll in front of them. Almost.

The park came as a relief. Lucy directed them down her favorite paths and meandered toward the Serpentine. Eli offered his free arm to the others, and the three women made a game of taking turns. It wasn't quite the fashionable hour, but the occasional carriage passenger nodded greetings at Maddy or Lucy. Curious glances cast at Fanny caused Eli to wonder what the family had decided about introducing her. He soon found out.

A carriage carrying two very young ladies and one old enough to be their mother paused next to them, bringing smiles of greeting from both Maddy and Lucy.

"And who is this young woman?" the older lady asked.

Fanny stiffened at Eli's side, although the woman's gaze appeared kind enough.

Maddy spoke up. "Lady Danbury, may I make known to you my sister, Miss Fanny Hancock? Fanny, the Marchioness of Danbury."

Fanny gave a graceful bow and murmured something unintelligible.

"Welcome, Miss Hancock. I am pleased to make your acquaintance," the marchioness said, studying Fanny closely, with glances back at Maddy. "No one would mistake you for anything other than a Caulfield, and I'll wager there's a story here."

At Fanny's gasp, the marchioness continued, "Never fear, my dear. Your story is your own. Do call on us. We're at home on Tuesdays."

"I don't think that is a good idea," Fanny murmured when the marchioness moved on.

Eli's every instinct was to whisk her back to Ashmead if she was uncomfortable. "You don't have to if you—"

"I disagree," Lucy interrupted. "Lady Danbury is no high stickler."

"Fanny's fears are understandable," Maddy said. "David and I determined long ago to introduce our siblings—our irregular siblings, if you'll excuse the term—as exactly who they are, but there are some who frown on our openness." She shook her head. "Lady Danbury isn't one of those. She and the sort who frequent her at homes are freer thinkers."

"You mean kinder," Lucy said.

Fanny spoke sadly. "The merchant class can be every bit as brutal. There were some in our parish church who cut us because I'm a bastard. That is the word, isn't it? We may as well say it."

Lucy stiffened her back, but Maddy was equally blunt. "I'll be honest—most in the upper classes would ignore illegitimacy in the sibling of an earl. Witness their acceptance of Rob. They are harder on women, however, and your origin in trade is likely to be a bigger barrier to many—not the Danburys, but many."

Fanny met her gaze head-on. "I am unlikely to melt under disapproval, but I don't want my life history pored over. Besides, I didn't come here to be presented to the queen, either."

Fanny's refusal to bend filled Eli with pride on her behalf. They sidestepped two more groups, circled the Serpentine, and were on their way back to the gate before another party approached them. Traffic had picked up; two carriages passed with mere nods and one mildly curious stare. The third stopped, and a rather large woman garbed in yards of purple and an excess of ruffles called out to Maddy, referring to her as "Your Grace."

"Good afternoon, Lady Parmbarton," Maddy sighed. "I trust you are well." Eli thought Maddy would choke on her irritation over the woman's deliberate use of her former title.

Lady Parmbarton ogled Fanny, her calculating eyes missing nothing, least of all the Caulfield hair. "Well enough, well enough, Your— but it is Mrs. Morgan now, is it not?" she said, answering Maddy but studying Fanny.

The old witch undoubtedly knows Maddy eschews the title. Eli fought the urge to push Fanny behind him; it would only make things worse. "This wasn't such a good idea," he muttered.

The witch turned her venom on Lucy. "Lady Benson, is it? Mrs. Morgan hasn't seen fit to introduce us, but then, you wouldn't have been invited to the better parties, would you? And who," she asked without waiting for an answer, "is your escort?" She inspected Eli as if he was a bug.

One cannot throttle a lady, he reminded himself. He bowed politely. "Mr. Eli Benson, Your Ladyship. I am Lady Benson's brother-in-law."

"Brother to a newly minted baronet, are you? Come for some town bronze?" the witch went on, her eyes darting to Fanny.

"I'm here on business for the Earl of Clarion," Eli said.

"Ah yes, Clarion. Interesting family, the Caulfields. I take my leave. We are, I think, unlikely to meet. We aren't the same sort." She waved her carriage on.

"Not her sort? Thank goodness for that," Lucy said, drawing laughs from the others. "What a horror."

"She thinks she's a dragon of society, but the truth is she isn't received many places. Many can't abide her," Maddy said.

"What an unfortunate encounter," a man said, cutting in on their conversation.

Eli turned to see two men on horseback behind them, one fashionably dressed, the other dressed simply. The first man's horse appeared, in Eli's judgment, to be one of those high-strung, overbred creatures that were not to be trusted. Perhaps he'd confused his assessment of the rider with his mount. Both men studied their party with more intensity than was polite. The taller, more plainly attired of the two fixed his gaze on Fanny, or so it seemed to Eli, and hairs on the back of his neck rose.

The fashionable gentleman dismounted and bowed to the ladies. "My apologies. I couldn't help overhearing. That woman is not good *ton*." Tall, blond, and blue-eyed, he was everything Eli was not; he was Fanny's hero come to life. Eli wished him to the devil. "My apologies on behalf of society," the gentleman went on smoothly.

Lucy smiled vaguely at the man, obviously acquainted with him.

Maddy knew him as well. "Miss Frances Hancock, may I present the Earl of Grimsley? My lord, this is my sister, Miss Hancock," she said, her expression challenging.

"Sister!" The earl glanced back at his companion. He rose to the occasion, bowing over Fanny's hand and murmuring, "I'm honored, Miss Hancock. You must be new; I've never seen you in town." He held her hand longer than he needed to, in Eli's opinion, and his gaze swept more than her face.

Fanny made her curtsey and offered brief thanks but said little. Maddy went on to introduce Eli, drawing little more than a nod from the earl.

"Will I see you at Pemberton's musicale on Friday?" he asked, his words for the group but his gaze returning to Fanny.

"My husband is expected at the Austrian ambassador's musical evening that night, I'm afraid," Lucy said.

"The intrepid Sir Robert Benson. Of course," Grimsley said. All of London knew Rob provided discreet security to foreign ambassadors. Most didn't allude to it, working for wages being distasteful at best to much of society. "Perhaps we'll meet another time, dear lady." That time, his gaze never left Fanny.

The earl walked back to his horse, caught his companion's eyes, and turned as if on a sudden thought. "Do you enjoy the theater?" he asked.

"I've never been to the theater," Fanny replied, longing clear in her tone of voice.

"I have a box for the season," he said. "*Rob Roy* continues its run. I invite you to be my guest when it is convenient."

"Isn't that one of Sir Walter Scott's novels?" Fanny asked, her interest obvious.

He smiled. "The play is indeed based on the book." To the group at large, he said, "I invite all of you, of course, even the sober Mr. Benson."

If he expected Eli to produce a smile at that, he was well out of luck. All Eli wanted was to get Fanny, get all of them, out of the park and into the Benson carriage.

The ladies murmured polite gratitude, however, and the earl said, "Shall we say Saturday?"

Lucy agreed on Fanny's behalf, but Maddy demurred, claiming she had seen it already. Grimsley rejoined his companion—Eli judged the other man to be a secretary or assistant of some sort—and rode off while Eli resigned himself to a tedious evening. If Fanny planned to go to the theater with this man, Eli intended to be with her.

CHAPTER EIGHTEEN

L ONDON HAD MANY attractions. Fanny had come to enjoy Eli's company—when he wasn't being overprotective. He had auditing chores to perform for Clarion on some days, however, as he had notified them on the day the ladies went out to Kew Gardens.

When Eli's message had come, Rob Benson had insisted that Reilly, who was now one of his burly footmen, former soldiers all, accompany the ladies. Maddy assured Fanny the company of a footman was the expected thing, but she couldn't shake the feeling that a bodyguard cast a cloud on their day.

By the time they had wandered through beds of glorious flowers and exclaimed over various exotic plants, she had quite forgotten about him. At least, she had until a ruffian bumped into her on one of the upper levels of the Great Pagoda, knocking her to the railing. She might very well have fallen over had the quick-thinking Reilly not grabbed her in the nick of time. Once assured she was well and in the hands of Lucy and Maddy, her savior pelted off after the ruffian but to no avail. The brute disappeared as if into thin air.

Fanny insisted they continue their explorations, but after half an hour, it became clear the joy had gone out of the afternoon. Maddy appeared paler even than Fanny and admitted to feeling ill. They deposited Maddy at her own home before returning to the Benson house, both residences being in Chelsea, near each other.

Later that evening, Rob's merciless interrogation of the footman left Fanny uneasy, and his patently false attempts to reassure her didn't help.

"You don't think it was an accident," Fanny accused. "Tell me why."

"What accident?" Eli, arriving for dinner, peered at Fanny and glared at his brother. He came to Fanny's side and took her hand. "Are you well?" he asked.

"Perfectly fine. Someone bumped into me at Kew. It was an accident," Fanny said.

"A ruffian brushed against her on the eighth level of the pagoda and almost knocked her over the railing. Only Reilly's quick thinking prevented disaster. He pulled her back." Lucy indicated the familiar ex-soldier, standing with slumped shoulders in front of Rob.

"Except I didn't catch the bas—the rotter," Reilly said, eyes downcast.

"Only because you paused to make certain I was well," Fanny said. "Don't berate yourself. Besides, it was an accident."

"Gentlemen—and I use that term in the loosest possible manner—don't run off after an accident. Villains flee," Rob said.

Eli's fierce expression told her his opinion on the matter. He looked prepared to murder, a rather touching turn of events in her mild-mannered solicitor-turned-steward.

"Well, he failed. And Reilly is the hero of the hour," Lucy said.

The butler announced dinner just then. Rob glanced at Reilly. He took a breath and turned to his wife to say, "I'll be with you momentarily." He motioned Reilly to follow and spoke to the butler, who nodded. Eli, Fanny noticed, followed them out.

"Is he going to punish that young man?" Fanny asked.

"Unlikely. More likely they are plotting," Lucy replied.

"Plotting?"

Lucy sighed. "I know the signs. They'll be putting the neighborhood under surveillance. Rob's men—the palace guard—will shadow our every step. I'm guessing Rob—or more likely Eli—will try to curtail our movements."

"That's absurd. Aren't his troops meant to protect ambassadors? One cutpurse—or a clumsy garden visitor—is no cause to declare a national emergency." Fanny frowned.

"Overprotective to a man are the Bensons. Clarion would be as bad were he here," Lucy said. "We ladies have to stand our ground."

Fanny had never had a protective brother before. She wasn't certain how she felt about it. Eli Benson's fierce reaction roiled her emotions even more. She didn't know what to make of it.

>>>—<<<

"HOW LONG DO you plan to push me to the periphery?" Eli demanded as soon as he and Rob were out of earshot of the ladies.

Walking to the servants' hall, Rob answered him over his shoulder, "I don't know what you mean."

Reilly joined the other two footmen across the room while Rob paused in the doorway to speak with Eli.

"Explain," Rob said.

"More than today's incident bothers you, Rob. You've been itchy since Manchester. When we got to Ashmead, you let up, but now I don't know what to think. What do you know that you're not telling me?" Eli said.

"I told you Holliday's belief that someone bigger than that gambler Edwards was involved in Fanny's abduction." Rob paused.

"Yes, the flesh trade. But there's more, isn't there?" Eli held Rob's eyes.

"I brought that to Viscount Rockford when I returned to Horse Guards yesterday." Rob's employer had eyes in every corner of the United Kingdom, and ears as well, trolling for information. "He wasn't surprised."

Eli's eyes widened. "He knew about Edwards?"

"Specifically, no. He has had an investigation occurring in various cities, one I knew nothing about. Involving young girls being abducted off the street. Poor, unprotected ones generally, but lately there have been a series that matched Fanny's situation."

"Her birth?" That puzzled Eli. It wasn't as if illegitimacy could be stamped on her brow.

"No—family member with gambling debts. It appears the criminal, or group of criminals, has been combining their enterprises, using threat of stealing daughters to get fathers, brothers, or stepfathers to pay. There haven't been many, but they've made certain the debtors hear about the other incidents. Five in Manchester. Two in London." Rob let that sink in before going on grimly, "As Holliday suggested, they are being sold along the Barbary Coast."

"Slavery?" Eli swallowed. Hard. He had feared forced brothel labor, but Rob had mentioned the Barbary Coast in Manchester. "You think today is connected? What good would a woman do them if they pushed her to her death?"

Rob shrugged. "More intimidation. Evidence to other victims that they won't give up. Or perhaps today really was an accident. We can't be certain."

Eli glanced at the three former soldiers watching them. "What part do you have for me to play?" He met his brother's eyes. They both knew Eli had none of the skills of Rob's men.

"Stay close to Fanny. I presume that is no hardship?" Rob grinned.

Eli ignored the implication. "I have a few errands to run for Clarion, but I'll manage it. I'll take her to the bank with me if I have to."

"You need to brush up on your courtship skills, little brother, if you think she'll enjoy that," Rob said.

"I'm not courting the woman. I'm doing what I was hired to do—auditing accounts." Eli glared at him.

"If you say so." Rob's cheeky grin disappeared. "Whatever your feelings about Fanny Hancock, it is our responsibility to keep her safe."

Eli nodded and sat to listen to Rob organize his men to protect his house and outline his plans to hire more, there being, Rob said, plenty of their former soldiers who could use the work.

The brothers joined the ladies.

"Our apologies, ladies. Shall we go in to dinner?" Rob offered his arm to Lucy.

"Let's hope the cook hasn't succumbed to apoplexy," Lucy responded tartly, taking his arm and going into the dining room.

Eli hovered near Fanny, her spicy apple scent filling his senses, swelling his heart, and feeding his fears for her. "I'm sorry for the delay," he said.

Her tremulous smile tore at him. "It is a great deal of fuss over nothing."

He forced a smile. "Probably. You will allow us to be protective, however."

"Lucy said you would insist." Fanny did not appear unhappy, and when he offered his arm, she took it.

Eli hated being pushed aside from the action, but hovering close to Fanny would be no hardship. The thought brought a smile to his lips. When she returned it, his world righted and one thing became clear. He would not be relegated to pushing papers, not where Fanny was concerned.

⟫⟫⟫⟩⟨⟨⟨⟪⟪

LUCY ASSURED FANNY she knew nothing. Whatever the Benson brothers spoke about, her husband refused to confide in her. He called it "a project for Rockford."

"Why would Eli be involved in a project for Viscount Rockford?" Fanny asked.

"I can't imagine a reason, but Rob took him to Horse Guards this morning," Lucy said with a shrug.

Maddy sent word she felt queasy that morning and would not join them. When Fanny expressed concern, Lucy smiled slyly and said, "I expect she will be fine in due time."

"Do you think she's—" Fanny stumbled over the word.

"Expecting?" Lucy grinned. "Yes, I do. She'll tell us when she's ready." Basking in the glow of new motherhood, Lucy apparently found the idea wonderful. Fanny had a twinge of envy.

Eli turned up as his usual cheerful self to escort them to the much-avoided visit to the modiste, made no explanation for his time at Horse Guards, and waited patiently while they suffered through measurements and selected patterns and materials, an exercise Fanny found more enjoyable than she cared to admit. New frocks were a joy, but a cottage of her own was a better use of her brothers' money if they wanted to help.

They traveled by carriage, this time with Reilly behind and another of Rob's men up top with the coachman. Fanny pretended not to notice. They took her to Gunter's for ices again, but this time, Eli did not suggest walking.

When he announced they would go directly home, both Lucy and Fanny balked. They would have their walk. He proposed Green Park instead, ordering the coachman to stay nearby. Both footmen—if that was even what they actually were—dismounted the carriage and followed Eli, Lucy, and Fanny at a discreet distance. Fanny again pretended not to notice, but the demand for an explanation lingered on the tip of her tongue. As much as she enjoyed being on Eli's arm, she didn't like being in the dark.

The following day he sent word that he had an early business appointment but that he would arrive to escort them at one o'clock.

Odd, that. He didn't even ask where we planned to go.

Originally, they had considered a visit to the British Museum. Fanny was avid to view the Elgin Marbles. But Maddy begged off, again, and Lucy had another suggestion.

With a sly gleam in her eye, she said, "I think I need new night-clothes and some underlinen."

Fanny raised an eyebrow.

"Something filmy and scandalous," Lucy went on.

Lucy had always seemed practical and down-to-earth to Fanny. "You never struck me as the sort to—" But then, Lucy was a married woman. Who know what sort of gowns she might wear in private? "What are you up to?"

"Think about it." Lucy's eyes brimmed with devilment.

"He will be mortified!" Fanny said when the idea came into focus.

Lucy bit her lip. "Are you up for it?"

By the time Eli arrived, Fanny was bursting with anticipation. Lucy gave the coachman directions to Mrs. Johnson's Stitchery.

"Another modiste?" Eli groaned.

Lucy hugged his arm and let him help her up into the carriage. "You know we ladies need our frippery."

And our privacy, Fanny thought. *He'll be sorry he's sticking to us like a burr.* As much as his hovering protection warmed her heart, she couldn't resist Lucy's plan to tease him.

CHAPTER NINETEEN

E LI'S FAINT HOPE that Rob had invited him to Horse Guards for weapons training or at the very least a strategy session died under a pile of paperwork. Brynn Morgan, who worked as an intelligence analyst in Viscount Rockford's organization, laid out a wide range of facts and figures, some obviously associated with the abductions and human trafficking, more of it related to smuggling in general, broader, and less specific. The viscount himself stopped in briefly, something Morgan described as a sign of how much importance he assigned to the investigation.

"It comes down to ownership. We have an idea about ports, but who owns the ships? What is the money trail?" Morgan said at last. "Some of the answers may be in London, some in Manchester or even York."

It quickly became obvious which of Eli's talents they wanted. He accepted his role with resignation, though how he would pore over account books, port books, and deeds while fulfilling his commitment to Rob to "stay close to Fanny," a job he much preferred, he had no idea.

Now the ladies had him bundled in the carriage heading to yet another clothing shop. They seemed determined to make his life difficult. Maddy had once again sent word she was indisposed. Eli began to expect a happy announcement from the Morgans but knew better than to ask.

Mrs. Johnson's Stitchery looked very little like the Hancock drapery and even less like the modiste they had visited earlier on. The sign above it gave few clues as to its nature. Eli peered at the window decorated with bolts of delicate linens and silks, most sheer, some embroidered, all artfully draped around vases of silk flowers and a few porcelain figurines.

Eli's first hint of trouble came with the sight of a young man—an overdressed elite of the *ton* with a smug smirk on his face—leaving the store with a box wrapped in pink tissue and tied with an elaborate rose-colored bow. The arrogant puppy cast an assessing glance at the ladies until a growl from Eli sent him scurrying away.

What sort of establishment for ladies is frequented by men about town? The answer to that was all too obvious, and Lucy's mischievous grin confirmed it. Fanny refused to meet his eyes.

A tinkling bell announced their arrival when Lucy opened the door. She turned with a dare in her eyes before entering. "Are you certain you wish to join us, Eli? I am positive there is a tavern nearby where you can wait."

When he shot a quick glance at the window, a particularly transparent fall of cloth in an earthy moss green, with heather embroidered on the edge, caught his eye and sent visions of it draped over Fanny—Fanny as the good Lord made her. He groaned and forced the image from his unruly mind.

He knew a ploy when he saw one. They were trying to get rid of him, but he had vowed to stay close to the women—to Fanny—at all costs. It might just come down to that; Mrs. Johnson's might kill him.

"Of course, Lucy," he said sweetly. "I wouldn't think of abandoning you."

The front of the shop, a narrow room, had shelves with bolts of cloth, rather like the Hancock drapery except for the nature of the material. Mrs. Johnson greeted the ladies effusively and cast a gimlet eye on Eli, sizing him up shrewdly. She led them to the spacious interior, where Eli was deposited in a sitting area in a far corner, one with comfortable chairs, newspapers, and the faint odor of tobacco, obviously designed for the use of gentlemen. She took the ladies' cloaks and bonnets and led them to a table where she spread fashion plates.

From where he sat, Eli could see all three women, but not, thank heavens, the pictures in front of them. Fanny had her back to him, a mixed blessing when she leaned over the table to pick up one of the prints. He flicked open a wrinkled newssheet, held it in front of his face, and struggled fruitlessly to read some of the week-old news. Images of the green silk in the window kept intruding. Curiosity about the fashion plates elbowed its way in, and his wretched imagination spun various feminine nightwear made from the green silk. And the pink lace the proprietor pulled out to show the ladies.

When he peeped up from his paper to see Lucy hold out a drawing of a daring negligee to Fanny, he almost bolted. His brother most certainly would not be happy with Eli seeing sketches of intimate garments purchased by his sister-in-law. As to Fanny, he was certain ice baths loomed over his evening and several after. The damned paperwork might help. Sighs, moans, and giggles from across the room didn't.

They held him prisoner there for an hour or more before they gave up and announced they were ready to leave. "Mrs. Johnson has graciously offered to deliver our orders, so you'll be spared another visit," Lucy said with an unrepentant grin.

Eli refused to cower. "Was your time successful as well, Fanny?" he asked.

Pink cheeks rewarded him for his sally, but victory in the exchange went to Fanny. She met his eyes without wavering. "It was certainly enlightening," she said.

Enlightening? How? He dared not think about it. He thrust his hat on his head and followed them out.

CHAPTER TWENTY

F ANNY FROWNED AT the mirror. It wasn't that she disliked how she looked. On the contrary, the new gown that had arrived that afternoon from the dressmaker—due no doubt to Lucy's insistence on a rush order—flattered both her form and her coloring, floating as it did from a high waist to the modest flounces at the hem. The subtle stripes woven into the silk gave her an appearance of added height without shouting to the world their intention. If the neckline revealed rather more of Fanny than she thought proper, Lucy laughingly assured her that was not so. Her frown owed more to her belief that the money might have better served as payment on a home for her siblings, but that thought warred with delight.

Delight won. When she walked into the theater tonight on the arm of a handsome earl, she would feel like a princess. She wondered if the Earl of Grimsley truly was the feast for the eyes that she recalled, all well-muscled form and blond good looks, or had her writer's imagination been at work again? She looked forward to finding out, for he would meet them there.

When they had encountered Grimsley in Green Park one afternoon—quite by accident—he had offered to call to escort Fanny. Eli's insistence that Rob would want to escort the ladies and that he, Eli, would of course accept the earl's gracious invitation had startled her. The Benson brothers' protective instincts crossed the border to possessive. Yet she remembered with a twinge of shame that it had gratified her to be the object of the spark of jealousy she'd seen in Eli's expression. Childish, maybe, but the heat in those brown eyes had given her a lift of feminine awareness.

"Ready?" Lucy asked. "You certainly look it."

Fanny stood tall, nodded, and followed her down the stairs, only to pause partway down at the sight of Eli gazing up at her with naked admiration. The gown, she decided, conveyed some sort of magic. All niggling doubts fled. She would happily enjoy the evening.

Their coachman brought them to the front of the theater, and Rob alighted from the carriage first, turning to help Lucy out. Eli followed and offered his hand to Fanny. The odd tingling she had begun to feel whenever he touched her radiated up her arm, stronger tonight than ever. Sparks she didn't fully understand moved between them when their eyes met as she stepped onto the pavement.

The moment passed quickly. The Earl of Grimsley came forward, meeting them as promised. His gaze seemed to devour her whole, the open attraction causing unease that baffled her. She'd welcomed Eli's; why not this gorgeous man's admiration? His physical attributes proved to be every bit as fine as she remembered. It was as if her sketch of the hero in her current work had come to life. Yet something about him left her uneasy. Perhaps title, wealth, and a pretty face combined into something rather too much for the comfort of an ordinary woman, a mere mortal.

Once in the earl's box, Grimsley helped her to a seat in front, one against the side of the box, where, she realized, no one else could sit on her right side. To her left, Grimsley fussed over her comfort and arranged her shawl just so. When his hand brushed the back of her neck, the hair at her nape stood on end. She heard a faint growl and glanced back to see Eli glowering at her.

How dare he? Who was Eli Benson to judge? Fanny knew her behavior to be perfectly proper. She looked resolutely away and focused on the program for the evening's performance, *Rob Roy MacGregor; or,*

Auld Lang Syne!: A Musical Drama in Three Acts.

Two theater adaptations of Mr. Scott's *Rob Roy* had opened in the spring, one at Covent Garden and the other at Drury Lane. The Earl of Grimsley assured her the musical version presently at Covent Garden was by far the more entertaining of the two.

As she looked about, the Theatre Royal, Covent Garden delighted Fanny. She'd been told that it lacked the modern gas lamps of the new theater at Drury Lane, but she found it marvelous in its own right. She locked all uncomfortable thoughts—worries for her future, Eli's possessiveness, and even the earl's presumption—firmly away in a box, prepared to be enchanted. She wasn't disappointed.

Scottish ballads and stirring action scenes played in Fanny's head when the lights came up for the interval. Ideas for scenes on the written page bounced back and forth in her mind. A sound to her left brought her back to her surroundings to find the earl leaning over her.

Had he said something? He bent a touch too close, and his cloying scent wreaked havoc with her reason.

She sat a bit taller and leaned back. "I'm sorry, my lord. I was lost in the performance and didn't attend your words."

"I suggested we visit the lobby for refreshments," the earl said. He stood and put out a hand to help her rise, assuming agreement.

"I'm sorry, my lord. I need a moment to savor the experience," she said, remaining seated.

Something hard flickered through the earl's eyes, but a slow smile came over this face. "But a visit to the lobby is part of the London theater experience. Let me escort you?"

Fanny hesitated. She truly preferred to stay seated, but did not wish to make a scene. She returned his smile and let him lead her out of the box.

"THEY MAKE A pretty pair," Rob murmured, watching Fanny and the earl leave.

"That gown suits her to a treat," Lucy said. "As for the earl…"

"Pretty is as pretty does," Eli muttered, scrambling to his feet.

"Slowly, Eli," Rob said.

Eli's hackles rose. "What do you mean?"

"The gentleman has escorted her properly. Don't embarrass the lady by rushing after them like the cavalry at full charge," Rob said.

Eli stiffened. *Gentleman?* He had no reason to think otherwise of the man. He took a shuddering breath. "Shouldn't the two of you chaperone? Discreetly," he grumbled.

"Eli is right. Besides, I could use a lemonade," Lucy said.

Rob smiled into his wife's eyes, put out a hand to help her rise, and gestured for Eli precede them.

When they stepped into the hall, Fanny and Grimsley had disappeared. Rob shrugged and led the way to the stairs. They saw no sight of them in the crowd milling around the refreshment tables; alarm flashed through Eli.

"Perhaps Fanny went to the ladies' room," Lucy said. "I'll check." She spun on her heels. "And I don't need a bodyguard for that."

On the first level, a hallway led to offices, storage, what Eli suspected were withdrawing rooms, and ultimately the exit at the rear of the building. Rob and Eli watched Lucy enter a room set aside for ladies' private use before the sound of a disturbance sent them running past it. Another hallway crossed their path just beyond the room Lucy had entered. Two or three people had gathered around the earl, who was pulling on a handle, rattling the door it belonged to.

Fanny's voice, frantic with fear, rent the air, freezing Eli's blood in his heart and speeding his steps. As he ran, he saw the earl glance back at them and put his shoulder to the door, ramming until it gave. A shriek followed the crash.

Eli shouldered past three men, one vaguely familiar, to get to the door, and stopped, one hand on each side of the doorframe, breath heaving while Fanny threw herself into the earl's arms, sobbing. Rob came up behind, putting a staying hand on Eli's shoulder. They peered into a dark, windowless storage closet of some sort.

"Is the lady well?" Rob demanded, his commanding officer voice on full display.

Grimsley straightened and removed his arms from the utterly inappropriate—and in Eli's opinion, unnecessary—embrace, only to put one around her waist to support her. "Shaken up, I think," Grimsley responded. "Let me find you a place to recover, Miss Hancock."

"Come this way, my lord. The business office is a few steps away," a portly little man, one of the men that had apparently come in response to her screams, said.

The earl led a trembling Fanny from the closet and down the hall. She glanced at Eli briefly and opened her mouth, but the earl moved her on before she could speak. Rob and Eli could only trail behind them to the office. When they reached the main hall, Lucy hurried up to them, shouldering her way through a crowd that began to gather. The three of them slipped into the office, and Eli closed the door behind them.

Soon the theater manager had Fanny in a chair with a glass of lemonade. "I can't imagine what happened," he fussed.

"Yes," Rob said. "Do explain it to us, Grimsley."

"It was entirely my fault. I thought I knew the way to the ladies' retiring room. We took an incorrect turn and opened the wrong door," the earl said. "Miss Hancock tripped somehow, and the door shut behind her and jammed. I couldn't get it open. The darkness frightened her." He knelt and took Fanny's free hand. "I'm so sorry. Are you well?"

Fanny gazed at the earl with a wan smile. "It is a good thing you were able to break down the door quickly," she said.

The lady and the hero of her dreams. Eli had never felt more useless in his life.

Fanny shook herself, put down her glass, and looked about the room. "I should be the one to apologize for making such a scene. It was nothing, really. I overreacted."

"After what happened to you in Manchester, it's understandable," Lucy said, laying a hand on Fanny's shoulder.

Fanny retrieved her fingers from the earl's grasp and covered Lucy's. "Thank you," she whispered.

"We should get you home," Eli said.

"The crowd will dissipate when the program resumes," the fussy little manager said, his expression dubious as if he didn't quite believe his own words. He turned to Rob, deciding he was the one in charge. "I, ah, my lo—" he began.

"Sir Robert Benson. Miss Hancock's brother." Rob's clipped, no-nonsense words added to the man's nervousness.

"I am so sorry for Miss Hancock's unfortunate accident. We will see to that door. I guarantee it." The theater official wrung his hands.

"See that you do!" Rob turned to Fanny, his voice softening. "I'll have the carriage brought round to the rear."

Eli thought for a moment she would argue with them and demand to finish the play she so clearly enjoyed, but she did not.

While they waited, Lucy urged sips of lemonade on Fanny. Fanny, for her part, expressed embarrassment until Eli thought his heart would break.

"It wasn't your fault," he told her. "The door was faulty." How that could be he couldn't quite imagine. It didn't make sense.

"Mr. Benson is correct. Blame me, dear Miss Hancock," the earl said, hand to heart, thoroughly irritating Eli.

Rob appeared sooner than they might have expected, to Eli's intense relief. "The crowd is gone, Fanny. You'll be fine."

Fanny groaned. "There will be gossip. I can only pray the victim will be described as 'unknown woman from the country'... At least it is unlikely to follow me to Ashmead."

"Ashmead? A village? Is it as quaint as it sounds?" the earl asked.

"It is home," Eli muttered, wishing he could wipe the earl's self-satisfied smile right off his face.

Eli offered Fanny his arm before Grimsley could, but she turned to the earl when they exited to the hall. "Thank you for your rescue, my lord. I'm sorry I ruined the evening."

"Not at all, dear lady. I will beg the privilege of calling on you tomorrow, to make certain you are well," the earl responded.

"That won't be necessary," Fanny told him. "I am well."

Something flitted through the earl's expression, as if he wanted to argue with her, something that sat poorly with Eli.

"The lady will wish to recuperate in peace," Eli said, glaring at the man.

A condescending smile quickly replaced the ugly expression that had flickered in the earl's countenance. It happened so fast Eli wondered if he had been mistaken.

"Of course," Grimsley said with a bow. He hesitated a moment longer as if to follow them, before he surrendered and took his leave.

"About time," Eli muttered, walking toward the exit with Fanny on his arm.

"Don't be rude, Eli Benson. Grimsley was a perfect gentleman. I don't know what I would have done without him," she said.

You might have stayed in the box. With me. Eli clamped his jaw shut lest he give vent to his opinion about her hero's perfection.

CHAPTER TWENTY-ONE

SUN SEEPED THROUGH narrow windows in the records room of the new custom house. Eli pinched his nose and leaned back in the wooden chair only to stretch upward to relieve his back. Six hours poring over port books left him as ignorant as he had been at dawn. He would much rather have escorted Fanny and Wil to the bloody Tower as promised, but Fanny truly did need to stay home and rest after her ordeal. With them all safe at Rob's house in Chelsea, he'd decided to begin the investigation into shipping that Morgan and Rockford had suggested.

He rose on a yawn, paced to the window, and gazed down at the river traffic. So many ships and boats of all sizes. So much going and coming. But none of them gave him a glimmer of light on the issue of abducted women and girls.

Neither did the port books. Obviously, no captain would list human cargo in customs declarations, but he had yet to find any record that customs agents had uncovered such an atrocity, either. Records from the cruisers and revenue cutters patrolling the coast had nothing specific to offer. The list he assembled of ships involved in the illegal trades, laid side by side with the list of known abductions provided by Rockford's men, revealed no patterns, no direction for further research. The abductions had clustered in the northwest in the past five years. Even if he focused his attention on that area, there were too many ports. Too many ships. Too many ways to evade detection.

None of it added up.

He strolled back to the table, twisting his neck from side to side to relieve stiffness. A charred port book from 1812 caught his eye. Records for London were spotty due to the fire that destroyed the custom house in 1814. This had been a fool's errand. He returned the record books to the clerk on duty and packed up his notes. He had to think. To do that, he needed lunch.

Descending the stairs to Lower Thames Street, he considered the next steps. What had Rockford told him to do? *Follow the money. What money?* He paused in the lobby and sank to a marble bench.

The mews behind the Happy Cock shimmered into focus in his mind. The smell of rotting trash. Fanny blindfolded and bullied. The street toughs who'd held her. His stomach clenched, and rage momentarily blinded him.

What are you doing shuffling papers, Benson? Illicit trade means ill-gotten money. You won't find it in port books. If you want to nail these bastards, you have to get your hands dirty.

He was approaching the problem from the wrong end. He had to begin at the point of abduction. Money moved among the gamblers and cheats. Money passed hands on the docks. He had to trace it to the mastermind, from the street up.

Standing on Lower Thames Street, searching for a hackney, he realized he had two problems. For one, he needed to learn more about the language of the docks, how money changed hands legally and illegally—how ships were bought, sold, disguised, and hidden. He needed to spend time in the docklands, in the taverns, and among the workers. He lacked the sort of vocabulary needed to ask the right questions.

He could go immediately, but a quick glance at his suit and valise stuffed with notes put a period to that notion. He couldn't just pop into a tavern in the Isle of Dogs, looking like the solicitor he was, and expect to learn something useful. It would have to keep for tomorrow.

When he finally flagged a hackney to take him to Caulfield House, he sat back to contemplate his larger problem. He would have to return to Manchester and run the trade to ground, starting with whoever paid the bullyboys and working his way up the chain to the ultimate villains. He couldn't do that as long as Fanny remained in London. He wasn't certain about Rob's suspicion that the same people that abducted her meant to do her harm here, but the incidents at Kew and the theater had made it obvious she wasn't safe. Certain devious earls sniffing at her skirts posed another threat. Grimsley could not be trusted to treat Eli's Fanny with honor.

Eli breathed a sigh of relief that the ladies had agreed to stay home that day. That thought led to another. He called to the driver and changed directions. *I need to make sure my Fanny has recovered.*

My Fanny. He could no longer pretend his interest in her was business. Perhaps it never had been. He had fallen in love and had no idea what to do about it, at least not while Fanny tried to make a life for herself. What did Eli have to offer her? She had an earl dancing attendance. Grimsley may be insincere, but he matched her description of her hero perfectly. Eli devoutly hoped Fanny would see through him before she had to disabuse any dishonorable intentions.

That thought didn't help. Even if Grimsley faded away tomorrow, there would be others, more honorable men who would see her worth. The upper levels of society might cut up rough over her mother's family being shopkeepers, but others would happily accept the daughter of an earl, even one born on the wrong side of the blanket. Eli could do nothing to compete; he could only hover nearby to make sure she got the life she wanted.

Morose thoughts engulfed him until he arrived at Rob's house in Chelsea, paid the driver, and climbed the steps to be greeted by Mullins, Rob and Lucy's butler.

"Greetings, Mullins. How did Wil survive his 'boring' day? Is Miss Hancock in the drawing room?" he asked, handing over his hat and valise.

"Mr. Wil found solace in the mews among the horses and is there still. I'm sorry, Mr. Benson, but the ladies left two hours ago. The Earl of Grimsley invited them for a drive out in his carriage." Mullins betrayed his disapproval with the slightest pinch of his lips. Eli felt sick.

ACCEPTING THE EARL'S invitation had been a mistake.

Grimsley's sympathy fell flat on Fanny's ears, and yet she had no reason to doubt him. Perhaps her general misery dampened her response to his words. Lucy, for her part, bit her lip and clasped her hands tightly in her lap, no doubt also regretting their impulsive decision to accept his invitation.

If Fanny had realized he meant to parade them through Hyde Park at the fashionable hour, she would have refused. She had been told London society thinned in the summer. If so, she never wanted to visit during the Season. Summer crowds were certainly no kinder, and the crush of vehicles had been maddening. Once trapped in the line of carriages, there had been no way to demand that they return home immediately. She could only endure.

"You mustn't take it to heart, truly," the earl droned on. "Lady Parmbarton and her cronies are not as influential as they pretend."

Fanny cared nothing for the old crones' influence, but they were even more cruel this time. She smarted from their venomous barbs. It quickly became obvious that the story of her incident at Covent Garden had been served up for entertainment across London.

She breathed in sharply when they pulled up in front of the little house in Chelsea that had become a refuge to her. Grimsley leapt down as a gentleman ought and extended a hand to Fanny. She took it, eager to get inside, and allowed him to help her down. The gesture, perfectly proper, felt uncomfortable when he retained her hand longer than he needed to, rubbing her palm with his thumb until she turned pointedly to Lucy. Forced to recall his other guest, he let go of her hand.

"Lady Benson."

Fanny heard Grimsley say the words, but she was already at the door.

"Thank you for bringing us directly home," Lucy murmured, drawing Fanny's attention back, embarrassed she had failed to thank him. Grimsley, his smile firmly in place, stepped toward her.

Surely he doesn't expect to come in!

The earl's expression wavered when the door opened behind her. Something unpleasant shone in the narrowing of his eyes, though the smile stayed.

"Yes. Thank you for seeing the ladies home." Eli, speaking behind her, didn't sound grateful. He stood so close his voice vibrated down her back. Fanny had to stop herself from leaning against him.

They stood frozen in place for a moment until Lucy walked around the earl, who had all but turned his back on her. She bobbed a curtsey when she passed. "Good day, my lord," she said firmly.

After a moment of hesitation, the earl inclined his head and departed. What else could he do?

Eli closed the door and turned his penetrating gaze on Fanny. "You're trembling! Have you had a fright?"

"No, no," Fanny said. "Nothing so dramatic."

The butler gathered the ladies' wraps. "Tea may be the thing," he suggested.

"Good man, Mullins," Eli agreed, wrapping an arm around Fanny's shoulders and pulling her toward the drawing room. She leaned into his warmth, though all the while, he cast accusatory glances at Lucy, who followed Mullins a few paces and spoke to him quietly.

Eli led Fanny to a plush wingback chair near the hearth. "Is it cool in here? Shall I make up the fire?"

It had been hot all day, but now? Fanny nodded. She craved comfort.

Lucy joined them and pulled up a small chair next to Fanny. "I asked for tea sandwiches. I also sent a note to Maddy. If she had been here, she would never have let me talk you into going. Oh, Fanny, I am so sorry." Unfortunately, Maddy had sent round notice that she felt poorly.

"What exactly happened to upset Fanny—and what were you thinking driving out without me or Rob's men? I thought we had all agreed." Eli glowered at Lucy.

"We agreed? We? You and Rob decided!" Fanny frowned back at him. Her burst of spirit spent, she sank back against the chair. "In this case, I wish we hadn't gone at all. The palace guard, as Lucy calls it, wouldn't have made any difference."

"She's right on both counts. What happened today didn't require male oversight. Our problem was cats," Lucy said.

Eli pulled up another small chair, closer than was strictly proper. She didn't care. When he reached for Fanny's hand, she gave it gladly, desiring his warmth.

"I thought you planned to stay in. You told Grimsley you weren't receiving today," Eli said.

"Actually, *you* all but told him to stay away," Lucy said. She sighed deeply. "And of course, you were right. Fanny needed today to recuperate and to let the blasted cats move on to some other prey."

"I take it the cats in question are of the human variety?" Eli raised one eyebrow.

Fanny nodded. "On full parade in Hyde Park."

"You did the fashionable see-and-be-seen march through the park?" Eli gasped.

"If I realized what he intended, I wouldn't have gone," Fanny said. "He's always seemed a perfect gentleman. And he did rescue me last night. He was very kind."

"A gentleman wouldn't have invited you in a closed carriage," Eli murmured. His opinion had come to matter, and his criticism stung.

"Maddy would have known better. I'm so sorry, Fanny. I'm still new to this world," Lucy said.

"Maddy certainly would have refused the closed carriage," Eli said, peering from one to the other sternly.

Fanny groaned, feeling like the ignorant provincial Lady Parmbarton had dubbed her. She had been not so subtly enlightened by the old witch on the matter of riding out in a closed carriage with a single man. Even now, the memory made her heart sink.

Lucy dropped her gaze to stare at her toes. "I almost turned back when I saw it, but it was a glorious afternoon."

"And we were cooped up in the house," Fanny added.

"I didn't want to make a scene, so I went along," Lucy said. "He offered to show Fanny some of the prominent buildings."

"And he did. Whitehall, Horse Guards...," Fanny murmured, damning her curiosity for leading her into his carriage.

"Mostly he seemed eager to point out the homes of what he called 'those who matter.' He drove us through Mayfair, turned around Bedford Square, and of course pointed out his own townhouse, one certainly larger and more fashionable than we're sitting in." Lucy sounded bitter.

Fanny leaned toward her. "Are you implying he meant to puff up his consequence at your expense, Lucy?"

"Perhaps he merely meant to puff up his consequence for your benefit, Fanny, rather as a peacock displays his tail."

Fanny felt her face flame. *I hope I'm no peahen to be impressed with foolish display.*

ELI HAD TO like Lucy's peacock analogy, even if it did make him wish for an excuse to pluck the earl's blasted tail feathers.

"First, he preens. Then he drags you to Hyde Park to display you to the cats, as you call them, knowing full well they would be happy to sink their claws into Fanny while the story of her accident last night was fresh in their minds. Your hero is less than he seems, Fanny."

She paled, and he wanted to kick himself.

"He isn't my hero," she muttered.

The tea cart, that blessed English bastion against an excess of emotion, arrived, to Eli's intense relief. He sat back and let Lucy manage the time-honored ritual of pouring and serving.

He watched Fanny sip her tea, watched the color gradually return to her face, and watched her sit straighter, a true lady, her back never touching the chair. His dainty warrior had returned, and his heart began to beat normally.

"We'll deny Grimsley the door," Eli said, determined on the matter.

"Isn't that a bit extreme?" Lucy suggested.

"He intruded after we asked him to stay away. He's a strutting peacock. He—" Eli sputtered.

"He rescued me last night," Fanny pointed out softly. "I cannot treat him so shabbily."

"Ah yes. He's your hero." Eli sounded like a jackass to his own ears—or at least a rude bully. He wanted to bite his tongue.

"He isn't my hero," Fanny said. She clipped her words with insistence.

"He looks like your description of one," Eli snapped without thinking. Now he knew for certain that his wits had gone begging, for Fanny narrowed her eyes and glared at him.

"How—" Fanny waved a hand as if to brush the thought away. Now she knew he had looked at her writing. Eli suspected she would berate him when Lucy couldn't overhear.

"We can't deny Grimsley the door without London knowing. The man gossips skillfully. I learned that much watching him today," Lucy mused. "Besides, Fanny, didn't you promise him a dance at Danbury's soiree?"

"What soiree?" Eli asked.

"The invitation arrived yesterday, and we accepted. The marchioness is kind, and Maddy believes it is a comfortable venue for Fanny to experience society," Lucy explained.

"Grimsley is invited?" Eli demanded.

"Why wouldn't he be?" Lucy asked. "I know you don't like him—and I don't find him charming, either, truth be told—but he's perfectly respectable."

Eli held on to doubts about that. His face pinched, and he kept back comment. He would have to attend this soiree; he suspected an invitation lurked in the pile of mail he had neglected. "When is this event?"

"Tuesday," Lucy said, sipping her tea.

It was Thursday. The soiree would be the following Tuesday. Five more days. He needed to convince Fanny to return to Ashmead, where family would keep her safe. Could he show Wil the Tower of London, visit publishers, and do a foray or two to the docklands in five days? He would have to. "Will we return to Ashmead after the Danbury soiree?"

Lucy opened her mouth, but no words came out. Fanny merely blinked.

"What I mean is, how long do we plan to remain in London?" *And can I keep Fanny away from Grimsley until then?* Eli wondered.

"Yes, we need to return to Ashmead." Fanny's words flowed like balm over Eli.

"So soon?" Lucy's distress showed on her face.

"I can't be at peace until I know I have a home for Amy and Wil," Fanny said. She reached for Eli's hand, and his heart sped up. "Find me that cottage we discussed and you'll be my hero." The edges of her mouth—her most attractive lips—tipped up, and Eli was lost in the sight. "And Clarion will, too, of course," she added, bringing Eli down with a thump.

Of course. Her hero. The earl. What had she called Eli? The fixer.

Chapter Twenty-Two

ONE WAY TO avoid unwanted callers was to be out. Eli made it his priority to keep Fanny busy and at his side. He wouldn't make Thursday's mistake again. With the weekend looming, he decided visits to publishing houses would be their first task Friday morning.

"I'm not certain what you expect to accomplish," Fanny repeated for the third time after he handed her into the Benson carriage. Susan, the maid Lucy had sent along for propriety's sake, sat in the rear-facing seat. Eli climbed in beside Fanny.

"Clarion asked me to investigate publishing houses and report back. It is, in fact, the final task on the list he gave me, and I'm determined to do it."

"Why is my presence required?" she asked tartly.

"Required? No. He suggested you knew much more about the business of books and publishing than I, which would not be difficult considering I know nothing at all," Eli said.

"Now tell me the truth. Why is Clarion suddenly interested in publishing? Does he plan to invest?" she asked.

"Alas, he is forced by circumstance to invest carefully and that particular industry seems risky to us. They will not know that, however," he said.

"Truth, Eli," she demanded, tapping one finger on her knee. "Did you tell him about my ambitions?"

"I may have mentioned it in my report. He asked for all matters pertaining to your needs and plans. Do you mind, truly?"

"I'm gratified that he took my ambitions seriously enough to send his steward to learn more about the business. Pleased, really, but promise me you don't plan to introduce me to these men as a writer," Fanny said.

He studied her slowly, unable to ignore her palpable tension. "How have you communicated with them in the past?"

"I wrote to them. I sent manuscripts—no easy task. I sign my name as F. Hancock," she explained.

"Masking your gender? Wise, perhaps, but unfortunate," he said.

"It was that or 'The Rose of Lincolnshire,' and that made me sound foolish," she replied.

That bit of nonsense made him grin, which bought him an answering smile.

She fumbled in her reticule. "I made a list for you because I knew you would ask."

"List?"

"Of the three who have seen—and rejected—my work in the past," she explained, handing it over.

"You came prepared!" He scanned it quickly. "Minerva, T. Hookham, and R and W Dean. That's it? Not A. K. Newman? I thought they—But we'll get a feel for all of them."

By the second office, they had a successful process. Eli introduced himself as an agent of the Earl of Clarion, leaving Fanny's role vague, although her incessant note-taking could be interpreted as the publishers chose. He would allude to a general interest in the industry without ever explicitly stating an interest in investment. He would ask three questions: What are your sales figures? What sorts of books do you publish (looking, of course, for romantic fiction, which Fanny had suggested defined her work)? How do you judge a new author?

By lunchtime, when they found a lovely little tea shop just off Regent Street, Eli had information about six different publishers, two of which he could eliminate out of hand, and an animated companion. Her enthusiasm for the project overflowed.

"Shall we continue? We can visit a half dozen more this afternoon," he suggested. Her passionate yes gratified him more than he could put into words.

The little maid, who had loyally followed them, waiting patiently in the carriage at each stop, had blushed when Eli had brought her in to sit at a small table at the rear of the shop. She smiled as they climbed back into the carriage.

"Thank goodness for Rob's carriage, if you plan to seek out six more. I'm afraid walking would leave me too weary to speak," Fanny said, her face a mask of joy.

"I think you would walk the length of England to publish," Eli retorted. He directed the coachman to T. Hookham on Bond Street.

Hookham's premises were fine, and the owner's sons struck Eli as professional. He would rate them as "possible," though they had rejected Fanny's work once. Markington-Hughes was easily dismissed after twenty minutes with the smug and ingratiating owner, whose interest appeared to be political. He continued to think A. K. Newman was a possibility.

John Murray proved to be less somber than he feared, yet fiction amounted to a minor part of their business. The publisher made certain they understood the success of *Northanger Abbey*, reminding Fanny she still needed the final two volumes.

They concluded their day at Hatchards so Fanny could do that. She also bought one of the Minerva novels for Susan, in thanks.

Eli took the proprietor aside and soon had a pile of books, one from each of the publishers he deemed "likely," ones the bookstore workers assured him were typical of the publishers' offerings. When Fanny tried to protest, he insisted he would need them for his report for Clarion. If he also planned to suggest that she evaluate them and analyze her own work for type and appropriateness for each publisher, well, he would save that for later.

It took the clerk two trips to carry their purchases to the carriage, where the coachman stowed them in the boot. Fanny bounced on her heels with happiness, and Eli's heart soared.

Fanny sank back into the seat of the carriage with a heart full of hope and a mind full of ideas. "Sometimes, I think heaven is a library."

Eli, who had always envisioned green meadows and flowers, closed his eyes and pretended to consider the matter. The only thing that danced through his mind was Fanny. Fanny walking at his side. Fanny filled with happiness. Fanny in his arms. Fanny… He cut the thought off there.

He might not be her idea of a hero, but he had found a way to give her joy. It was enough for now.

"A LIBRARY. LIKE Clarion's. I hope the earl will let me use it. Will the books be stored at the hall?" Fanny mused.

"Perhaps. After you've read them and made notes on the publishers," Eli said with a wry grin. "We need a plan."

"Plan for what?" Her brows pulled together. Fanny's writing, too precious, too personal, did not need meddling. "You will kindly tell your employer he is not to interfere. I appreciated the opportunity to learn more, but—"

"Duly noted, madam author. As your business adviser, however, I would suggest you need a plan. We will review our notes, examine their offerings, and settle on a short list of target publishers." Eli, who was across from her in the back-facing seat, leaned his elbows on his knees. "Then we will decide which of your works most suits each one and write a targeted proposal to—"

"Are you?" Fanny asked, suddenly sober.

"Am I what?"

"My business adviser." She sorted the words in her mind. Adviser. Not dictator.

"I think I have been since the day we met." Eli looked into her eyes, searching and probing, but she couldn't think what he sought.

Business adviser. She liked the sound of it, as if she managed her own business. As if he worked for her. That part didn't sit perfectly well, however. *Partners* sounded better, but still, her heart sank. *Is that all we are to each other?*

〉〉〉✕〈〈〈

FRIDAY HAVING BEEN a long day, they made a late start Saturday. Rob was needed at work, leaving Eli to escort Fanny, Lucy, and young Wil to the Tower of London. Reilly trailed after them. Maddy again pled indisposition. Mornings laid her low.

"I'm sorry Viscount Ashmead isn't here. He promised me history," Wil said.

"Lady Marj said he would give you the gory bits," Fanny commented. She couldn't quite imagine Clarion's sober little son getting up to mischief.

Wil grinned. "That, too."

"I'm sorry Amy is missing this," Fanny said.

"She's more interested in running in the woods with Lady Marj," Eli pointed out to Fanny's agreement.

The visit didn't disappoint. Wil pronounced the lions and other beasts "rather sad, really," and Eli couldn't disagree. The boy found the various armories, especially the Spanish Armoury, with its trophies from the defeat of the armada, much more to his taste.

"Shall we have a look at the Jewel House?" Eli raised his brows and peered at Fanny. "Unless, of course, you're done in." Her quick grin pleased him. "Lucy? Are you up for more?" he went on. Lucy had almost begged off because the baby had the sniffles, until the nursery maid had assured her the boy was better and would be fine.

"For the jewels? Always!" Lucy said.

Fanny linked arms with her brother. "I wouldn't miss it. And stop rolling your eyes, Wilbur Rundle. They are the gems of your sovereign."

Their laughter cut off abruptly when two men coming toward them blocked their way to the jewel display. Eli recognized Grimsley's stern-faced companion from previous encounters. As before, the man hung back and Grimsley didn't introduce him. Eli glanced back at Reilly. Grimsley's companion was rather better dressed than a footman, but perhaps he was a bodyguard of some sort as well.

"Well met, ladies," the earl oozed, inclining his head. "Enjoying the delights of the Tower?" His gaze trailed to Fanny rather more often than Eli liked.

"We are, indeed, my lord. We're on our way to the Jewel House," Lucy said, glancing pointedly past the two men.

Eli kept silent, wishing they would get out of the way.

"Not the lions?" Humor lurked in Grimsley's expression. No one shared it. He flicked a glance at Wil.

"We visited the menagerie earlier," Fanny said.

Grimsley rearranged his expression to convey disappointment, but his sharp eyes glittered. "I'm downcast. I had hoped to show you the exotic beasts myself. Did you see the baboon?" A growl started in Eli's throat when the dandified earl glanced over at him. He controlled it. Grimsley seemed to have less command over his tongue this afternoon than in the past.

The earl went on as if he noticed nothing. "Of course, I would be delighted to escort you to the Jewel House. I should have known the ladies would fancy that exhibit." He offered his arm to Fanny, managing to nudge Wil away. Unable to politely decline, she placed the tips of her fingers on his arm after a moment of hesitation.

When they turned on the narrow path, Grimsley's companion

stood between the earl, Fanny on his arm, and Eli, who escorted Lucy. When Eli leaned to the left to peer around the man, Lucy tugged him back and glared, wordlessly telling him not to make a scene.

Arriving in front of the cage surrounding the royal regalia, Fanny retrieved her hand, turned to Wil, pulled him forward—putting an arm around his shoulder—and began describing knowledgeably what they saw. Grimsley stood close to her other side.

"Saint Edward's Crown?" Wil asked. "Who was he?"

"The king who died in 1066," Grimsley interjected before Fanny could answer. "He's a cautionary tale about leaving no heir." He gestured about the building they stood in. "His conquering successor built this fortress and took the crown, which was made for Edward."

"Actually, Edward's crown was destroyed under Cromwell," Fanny said, contradicting the earl. "They melted down all the royal jewels. The crown had to be recreated for Charles II."

Her knowledge impressed Eli. Forced to stand behind them, he kept one eye on the companion, who hung back to the earl's right. Eli was gratified to see Reilly hovering nearby, his posture alert.

Grimsley growled. "It shows what happens when rabble goes unchecked."

Something in the earl's manner and in the presence of his servant—if that was what he was—made Eli uneasy. He felt a fool, standing tense and vigilant as if he was back in the alley in Manchester, facing street toughs, yet the hairs on the back of his head stood on end and he couldn't shake his sense of menace. Perhaps it was the open way Grimsley ogled Fanny. Even the companion cast intent glances her way, but why would he? Eli wondered if he was letting jealousy infest his judgment.

Perhaps not. The earl's remark about the lower classes brought a fierce frown to Wil's face and caused Fanny to stiffen.

Grimsley took no notice. "This display must be impressive for someone from—Ashmead, is it? Isn't that in Nottinghamshire?"

For one so high in the instep, the earl took an inordinate amount of interest in Fanny. He likely believed the saying "blood will out," or some such nonsense, allowing an earl's bastard in his charmed circle but patently excluding her brother. And Eli. Eli contemplated the consequences of bloodying the man's nose. They would be unpleasant.

Wil spoke up, "I would think it would impress any Englishman. And I am a Manchester man," he said proudly, blushed, and glanced apologetically at Lucy and Eli. "But I'm coming to enjoy Ashmead."

"Manchester? You, too, Miss Hancock?" the earl asked.

Fanny nodded, but before she could speak, Lucy, who had been studying the jewels quietly at Wil's side, turned to her companions. "This has been lovely, but I fear I grow weary," she murmured, to Eli's relief. Fanny turned toward Lucy, giving Grimsley her back. Lucy reached for Wil's arm, and Eli offered his to Fanny, earning a wary smile. He patted her hand to reassure her.

Once a few steps away, Lucy peered back at Grimsley. "Do enjoy your visit to the Tower, my lord. I was surprised to find you here. Do you come here often?"

The earl stiffened. "Of course. It is our heritage, and the day is lovely."

"We'll leave you to your tour, then. Good day, my lord," Eli said.

Grimsley's eyes narrowed. "I'll see you again on Tuesday, Miss Hancock. You promised to reserve a dance. Perhaps you can tell me more about your life in Manchester then."

Fanny blinked. She had obviously forgotten about the soiree. Eli led her to the door, half expecting Grimsley or his companion to intervene or attempt to separate them. Reilly may have thought the same, because he moved to their back.

Out in the sunshine, they saw other people enjoying outings at the Tower, and Eli relaxed a bit. He didn't stop their march to their carriage, however. None of them spoke until they were in it and on their way, Eli and Wil facing back, the ladies facing forward, and Reilly up top.

Eli groped for something wise to say to explain what had just happened or to turn the subject, but Fanny couldn't keep anxiety from her expression, and words wouldn't come to him.

"That was strange." Trust Lucy to put it into words. "Why would Grimsley be strolling around the Tower grounds? Do you think he came specifically to meet us?"

"How would he know we were there?" Fanny asked.

How, indeed. Eli wondered the same thing. "An odd coincidence," he said.

"Is he the one you said rescued you at the theater?" Wil asked. "He didn't seem particularly pleasant to me."

"Understatement, young Wil. He neglected to bring his charm today," Eli said.

"That's exactly it. He has always been at pains to exhibit his charm. Not today," Lucy said. She pulled her brows together in thought. "Not that he has ever been particularly amiable in the past, before he met Fanny at Hyde Park." She glanced up at Fanny. "Rob and I skirt the edges of high society, as part of an earl's family, though the highest sticklers ignore us and others keep our connections to Clarion vague. I'd have put Grimsley in that first group before."

"Perhaps he regrets taking an interest in an earl's by-blow," Fanny murmured.

"That doesn't explain his turning up during our tour," Eli said. Privately, he believed himself to be the primary target of the earl's hostility. He resolved to speak to Mullins about the staff at Rob's house and to question servants at Caulfield House. He couldn't shake the belief someone had told the vile earl where to find them. He had no idea why the man cared.

He resolved to speak to Rob. Since they'd gotten to London, his dratted brother had spent entirely too much time providing security for—and likely spying on—diplomats from much of the civilized world and too little paying attention to his household. For which, of course, he was well compensated.

CHAPTER TWENTY-THREE

THE BENSON HOUSE in Chelsea fell quiet the following Sunday. Fanny ought to have used the silence to write, but she couldn't muster the energy. She spent the afternoon finishing *Northanger Abbey* and beginning the second novel in the four-volume set she'd bought, finding as always that a good book soothed her nerves.

Wil spent his time in the mews, in the company of their coachman and horses. Fanny suspected he'd seen enough of London and would be perfectly happy to return to The Willow and the Rose in Ashmead. On the whole, she believed she would, too.

Fanny hoped to avoid the Marchioness of Danbury's soiree on Tuesday. She wanted to speak to Lucy about the protocol of dropping an invitation one had already accepted, but she hadn't the heart to interfere with Lucy's peaceful afternoon with her husband, who was home for once. Fanny had to smile at the two of them enchanted with the miracle of their little son, thriving now at just past four months of age.

When Eli arrived, his gaze went to Fanny as soon as he entered the house. Her heart leapt. He would listen. He always did. She'd come to rely on his steady presence. If she was honest, she'd begun to crave it. She wondered if he might take a turn in the garden with her.

He went immediately to Fanny's side. "I see you're making progress," he grinned, nodding at the book. "How is it?"

"I think I like *Persuasion* better than *Northanger Abbey*," she replied, eager to revisit their discussion about publishers.

Before she could formulate an excuse to take a walk, Eli knelt on the carpet where his nephew lay, having his tummy tickled by a cloth bunny in his father's hand. Eli joined in the play for a moment. When the little one's face puckered up as if he might cry, it was Eli who picked him up.

"Did that clumsy father of yours get too rough, Kit?" he asked soothingly as he snuggled the boy against his shoulder. His ease with the baby filled Fanny with admiration. It occurred to her that Eli had experienced the infancy of Emma's children from the time he'd been Wil's age, while Rob had been off at war. The boy quieted and pulled his head back to stare at Eli before grabbing him by the nose.

Rob burst out laughing. "You show him, Kit!"

A nursemaid appeared at the door. "It is the lad's nap time, Sir Robert, Lady Benson," she said.

"Well, nephew, we dare not break routine," Eli said, giving the boy a smacking kiss and handing him over before addressing his brother. "Actually Rob, I'd like a private word, if I may."

Fanny wondered what he didn't say, but Rob didn't look surprised by the request. Very quickly he and Rob disappeared into the study, leaving Fanny bereft. She thought perhaps she might at least have that talk with Lucy, but as her friend watched her son disappear to the nursery, she claimed fatigue and went off for a nap.

Fanny sunk back on a sigh, left with only her novel for company. Her question about invitations went unasked.

ROB OPENED A cabinet beneath the window and retrieved a bottle and two glasses.

"Whiskey?" Eli wrinkled his nose.

"An acquired taste, I agree. Mine comes from a glen in the Highlands, via a friend." Rob poured two glasses and urged one on his brother.

"Da wouldn't approve," Eli murmured, taking a sip. He dipped his head to one side, considering the matter, took another sip, and murmured his approval. They both took chairs in front of Rob's desk, setting their glasses on it.

"Begin. What's at the top of your mind?" Rob asked.

"Yesterday."

Rob's brows shot up. "The Tower? I expected word about your visit to the custom house."

"Customs records were no use. We knew there would be no blatant evidence, but there were no patterns, either. Nothing. I can spend a week at the chancery looking at deeds and sales of ships, but I would be spinning my wheels." Eli told his brother his conclusion: dirty business leaves a dirty money trail, not tidy record books. "I need to go back to the beginning. We know of several abductions from Manchester. I need to interview witnesses and families and trace the cash transactions from the street toughs up."

"Holliday should handle that. He may have already done some of it. Do you plan to go back north?"

Eli gazed up at the ceiling. "Good question. I want Fanny and Wil safely in Ashmead first."

Rob sputtered a laugh. "You think I can't protect her here?"

"As long as you keep her at home. Good luck trying. I don't think your work will allow you to escort the ladies around the city. Even your evenings end up at diplomatic dinners and balls. Do you plan to bring Lucy and Fanny with you? In Ashmead there will be family around her and strangers stand out."

"Point taken. What really bothers you, though? Grimsley? A woman with experience as narrow as Fanny's is bound to be flattered by attention from an earl."

Eli nodded. "What did Lucy tell you about yesterday?"

"That he behaved like an ass. She said, 'He left his charm at home.'"

"There's something not right about that man," Eli said.

"Other than the stiff-rumped arrogance of his class—some elements of his class?" Rob asked.

"What do you know about his shadow?" Eli asked.

"You mean Bateson? Peculiar, for certain. I've only seen him a few times, always out in public. He doesn't attend *ton* events. He wasn't at the theater."

"Yes. He was. I saw him in the crowd when I shut the door to the office," Eli responded. "I've seen him on the streets with Grimsley three times including yesterday. How do you know his name?"

"Grimsley generally doesn't acknowledge me, but I overheard him at Tattersall's once. The Marquess of Danbury all but demanded an introduction. Grimsley referred to him as his associate."

"Associate. Business partner? He doesn't have the deferential manner of a secretary or steward, neither of which would trail after an earl around London. I suspected bodyguard, but why would an earl require one?"

"There are endless reasons he would have one, but a bodyguard is more likely to look like Reilly or my security squads—watchful but compliant—than Bateson." Rob bit his lip in thought. "What concerns you?"

"Fanny, of course. You're the one who feared for her after Manchester. You're the one who insisted on security. Your home is guarded. You told me whoever is selling those women doesn't like escapes. That they would kill her rather than let her go free. That they use murder to terrorize others who owe them money and reinforce their threats."

"I did, indeed. The word from Manchester and other cities in the northwest is that the abductions and gambling operations are linked."

"Someone tried to push her off the Great Pagoda." Eli held his brother's eyes.

"And we stepped up vigilance," Rob said.

"And then there's the theater. Something about that just doesn't make sense," Eli said. "I don't trust Grimsley."

"It wasn't an attack. She was locked in a closet. What possible motive would there be for that?" Rob appeared to be searching his thoughts for an answer to his own question.

"Perhaps Grimsley hoped to gain her trust by first frightening her and then rescuing her, putting himself in the role of hero. Perhaps he knew being in a locked room would terrify her," Eli suggested.

"Eli, are you implying Grimsley is somehow involved in the nasty business in Manchester?" Rob gasped. "You may not like him, but that's a stretch. Are you sure it isn't jealousy talking?"

Eli drained the remains of his whiskey. "No. That is, no, I'm not certain it isn't jealousy," he said, meeting his brother's laughing eyes.

"Should I be asking your intentions or is that Clarion's role?" Rob teased.

"Don't jump to conclusions. What do I have to offer Fanny Hancock? She's lovely and the daughter of an earl."

"Do not hand me some taradiddle about her being above your touch, Eli. You are a land steward—a highly respected professional position, more than physician or solicitor in most people's minds. Well able to support a wife. To have done it by your age is remarkable."

Eli shifted, uncomfortable. "Luck. Events at the hall simply needed my skills," he murmured.

Rob rolled his eyes. "I hope you have no illusions that Fanny could look for a title or some such nonsense. The titled classes might accept an earl's bastard as long as that goes unmentioned—I should know—but Fanny is a shopkeeper's daughter and a shop clerk herself. No blue-blooded fribble will ever accept her, Clarion's acknowledgment notwithstanding. Besides, you're worth two of them."

The words gave Eli hope, more than he would admit to his brother. "Enough, Rob. If I decide to court Fanny, it is she who should be asked, not you or my prim and proper employer."

Rob bit back a knowing grin. "Don't let your feelings cloud your judgment where Grimsley is concerned."

"You may be right. I don't trust him, though, and I trust that 'associate' even less," Eli said. "Can you ask Viscount Rockford what he thinks of the two of them?" Rob's chief had his thumb in many pies. If anyone knew about Bateson, it would be Rockford.

"I'll see him at the Spanish ambassador's reception on Monday. I'll drop the name. Either he'll know something or he won't. Either way, it will put the name in his mind. He forgets nothing," Rob said. His next words made Eli sit a little taller. "What are your plans, then?"

Rob was asking, not telling. That had to be a first. "I've finished the things Clarion sent me to do. I have duties in Ashmead, and I should have word about Fanny's case in the church and chancery courts soon. That will necessitate a trip to Manchester. I can confer with Holliday then. In any case, I plan to take Fanny and Wil, if she agrees. To Ashmead, I mean. We need to keep her out of Manchester."

"Lucy believes the Marquess of Danbury's soiree on Tuesday is important. She and Maddy want Fanny to experience the better side of society after the nasty experiences she's had in the park." Rob raised a brow and waited.

"I'll talk to Fanny. We can depart the day after."

"And then what? Will you leave the investigation to us— Rockford's people and Holliday?" Rob asked.

Eli blinked. *Will I?* "Maybe."

AN HOUR OR more passed before the two men emerged, sober but silent, and Lucy returned to the drawing room. A tea tray followed. Conversation seemed stiff to Fanny, but she put that off onto her own somber mood.

"Do you suppose a stroll would be acceptable on a Sunday afternoon? We've been cooped up all day," Lucy asked.

Rob brushed crumbs from his hands and gazed at his wife. The naked longing sent heat up Fanny's neck. The warmth traveled lower, if she was completely honest.

"The physic garden will be closed," Fanny sighed.

"All gardens are," Rob said. He turned to Eli with a wink. "It is the law, isn't it, my solicitor brother?"

Eli cleared his throat. *"An Act for Preventing Certain Abuses and Profanations on the Lord's Day Called Sunday,* alas, does indeed cover Sunday strolls through public gardens, even ones with medicinal purposes. And it is enforced."

"I, for one, will never understand the logic behind denying people simple pleasures on the Sabbath," Lucy said.

"They hope the lack of choices will drive the heathens into the churches," Rob said.

"Not that it works with all heathens," Lucy said tartly. She had accompanied Fanny and Wil to church without her husband that morning. He'd claimed he had work.

"An Act for Preventing, etc., etc. wouldn't stop us from having a dignified and somber stroll along the river," Eli said, lips twitching. He cast a glance Fanny's way that raised her spirits.

"Unfortunately, I have a little person to feed," Lucy said.

Rob grinned wickedly. "Even better. That is one of my favorite activities to observe. I'll join you," he said, causing his wife's face to flame red. "But the two of you should enjoy what is left of this fine day. You have plenty of time to get to the river and back." He glanced pointedly at Eli. "Take Reilly."

Fanny's heart sank. She did not want a chaperone; she wanted Eli.

CHAPTER TWENTY-FOUR

TWO MORE DAYS. It had been agreed he would escort Fanny and Wil to Ashmead on Wednesday. Two more days.

Eli lay in bed Monday morning, contemplating the ceiling in the silent house. No servants disturbed his rest. Caulfield House's skeleton staff gladly left him to care for himself. He had wondered for the past week if he shouldn't have stayed at Rob's instead of the earl's townhouse.

His stroll with Fanny Sunday night had put that thought to rest. A walk at sunset, merely a walk, Fanny at his side, her dainty body pressing close when she had stepped on uneven ground, her spicy apple scent filling his senses, had paralyzed him with yearning, heated his dreams, and confused him about his future. Staying under the same roof would make it all worse.

Rob could handle her security. Eli would sort her legal problems in Manchester, find her that dratted cottage, and—What had he called himself? Her business adviser? He must have been mad. Someone had to take a closer look at the money trail from gambling hell to ships, however. Someone.

After that, I'll put my suit to the test. The thought, unexpected and unbidden, hung in the air. He sat up and held his head, his elbows on his knees. It felt right, but it terrified him. *What is the worst thing that could happen?* he asked the universe. A mocking voice in his head responded, *She could say no.*

He flung his legs to the side of the bed, dressed quietly, and went down to the kitchen, where Mrs. Stilson already had coffee brewing and breakfast breads purchased from a shop she preferred. Blessedly the staff left him to his thoughts.

After his second coffee, Eli reached a decision. He would ramble about the docks and see what he could learn. Fanny, energized after their walk to the river, declared her desire to stay in and write, leaving him free.

He cleared his throat and broke the silence. "Stilson, do you suppose the grooms left spare clothes a man might borrow if he wished to look a bit less like a solicitor?"

The older man eyed him carefully. "Are ye wishing something from the rag box or decent working man clothes?"

Shrewd question. "Something a man seeking work on the docks might wear."

Stilson thought a moment. "Per'aps a bit of both?"

Two hours later, a hackney let him off along the Ratcliffe Highway, dressed in a mix of borrowed clothing and discards, with no firm plan other than to observe and listen. He meandered about the London docks. When he paused to watch one crew unloading cargo, their chief offered him two hours' work. He took it.

He said little lest his speech betray him, but the dockworkers' cant clarified in his ears quickly. They all understood customs law and process well enough. None seemed averse to petty theft. When, job done, they all pocketed their coins and wandered toward a tavern where both ale and other work could be found, Eli asked them if they'd ever witnessed abducted women. He'd have sworn to his own mother they were horrified. "None. Never. Not even Africans. Not in this port." He believed them.

He wandered past the docks to Wapping. Once there, he found the Thames River Police easily, but he stood outside, looked askance at his appearance, and wondered if they'd toss him out.

A man about to enter glowered at him. "You, there, what are you doing? You need the police?"

"Yes, I rather think you might help," Eli said, his cultured accents at war with his appearance.

The man's eyes went wide, and he motioned Eli inside. "Oy, Danny, I think we have a story here," he said.

The man named Danny studied Eli grimly. "Lost your sister, have you?"

It cut close enough to startle Eli. "Not exactly. But what do you know about abducting girls for sale?"

"Sale? To the brothels in the stews? That's not our patch. And you're no dockworker."

Eli grinned. "I was for a few hours today." They directed him to a rickety chair next to a desk that belonged to Danny, who appeared to be some sort of leader.

Eli wiggled to get comfortable, and leaned an elbow on Danny's desk. "Not that kind of sale. I mean transporting. Overseas. To the Barbary Coast."

The river police didn't shock easily. Two more came closer to listen.

Danny leaned forward. "You mean selling English women? I've heard of it, but..."

"I know such a trade is probably customs cutters' 'patch,' as you call it, or maybe the Royal Navy even, once at sea. But you see the coming and going. You know trade. How would a person—or likely a gang of people—go about it? In your opinion."

Three of them began to talk at once, first to express their disgust and then to speculate. It would, Eli was told, depend. The ones responsible would need to hide cargo like that. They wouldn't use customs docks.

"Inlets like coastal smugglers?" Eli requested paper to take notes.

"Aye, but some o'them are bold as brass," one policeman said.

"Might use private anchorage," another suggested.

"What sort of ship would I be looking for?" Eli asked. "Where would it be registered?"

"It wouldn't," one officer laughed. "No name, no flag, sail on moonless nights."

"Or the opposite," Danny said. "Rich man's yacht on a private dock. Who would search it?"

"Why wud a nob do that?" a rugged-looking officer asked.

"Same as a street thief: greed. Maybe less need but no less greed," Danny said.

"Where can I find out about traffic from that sort of dock?" Eli asked.

"If you got lucky—really lucky—th'harbor master might know. Some of 'em travel in and out like that. It would be worth some questions, wouldn't it?" Danny looked from face to face. His men nodded. "Not the London or East India docks so much. Out toward the sea, on past Greenwich, maybe. Where are these girls being grabbed?"

"A few in London. That's one reason I'm here. You might keep your eyes and ears open. More up north. Lincolnshire. Manchester. No docks there."

"No," one of the men, a rail-thin fellow a good head taller than Eli, said. "You might try Liverpool. Or even Beaumaris."

An hour later, the rail-thin policemen, who called himself Benny, led Eli on a tour of some of the seedier riverside taverns along the Isle of Dogs and across to Greenwich and the Surry docks. Nothing of specific use came up, but Eli counted himself well educated.

Long past dark, he returned to Caulfield House and asked for bathwater. The Stilsons brought him warm stew and tea while the water heated. If he didn't know better, he might have thought they had worried.

He soaked in the bath and thought of Fanny. She'd promised him she would remain home that day. He had given her every incentive to do that. "You must miss writing," he had said. "Lucy has been distracting you."

That should have done the trick! He sank deeper into the warm water, grinning widely.

FANNY SET HER pen on the blotter and reread the last words she'd written.

"The sound of footsteps blundering through the woods alerted Cassiopeia to hide. She sank behind the briars, breathing heavily."

Her heroine, having survived an attempted abduction and learned to repent her vanity, hid in a croft in the Highlands, living on what she could find in the forest.

How on earth is my hero going to find her? Rob might have a suggestion.

Fanny quickly dismissed that notion. She could never bring herself to lay out the plot of her current novel about the enigmatic earl and the granddaughter of a brilliant but impractical scholar. Too many family details had crept into it since she'd first traveled to confront the earl.

What would a hero do? Charge off after her, tracking her movements? *Perhaps that is him blundering through the forest now.* Not in this case. He didn't know she ran to evade the clutches of his evil cousin. Said cousin has poured poison in the earl's ears about her disreputable behavior, claiming she ran off with another. She bit her lip. *Have I boxed myself in? What would Eli think?*

She had even less inclination to find that out. The wretch had already snooped on her desk in the old house. Still, he hadn't run away in horror. His survey of publishers amused her, and she believed none of that would hurt. Research might help her sell her work. All that business wouldn't get the books written, however. Only she could do that.

She tapped one finger on the table, lost in thought. What had he called himself? Her business adviser. She wasn't certain she wanted one. She wasn't clear on how one would help. She was sure about one thing, however. Eli Benson's presence—and his touch—complicated her work.

Every time she tried to write about the hero as she had described him—tall, blond, granite-jawed, and masterful—she kept seeing brown hair, kind eyes with laughter lurking in them, and quiet competence. She kept seeing Eli. He made her heart race.

She sighed, picked up the pen, and wrote, *Chapter Fourteen. A man came into view...*

Light filtering into her bedroom window began to fail before a gentle knock at her door and Lucy's voice brought her back to reality. She called to her to enter and set her pen down. Lucy carried a tray with a plate covered by linen. Susan followed with a pot of tea, and a footman brought up the rear. He set up a folding table and took his leave.

"When you didn't come to tea, we thought tea should come to you lest you wilt away," Lucy said with a teasing grin. She sobered too quickly for Fanny's taste and softened her voice. "Are you well, truly? Are you still brooding over Grimsley's behavior on Friday? Or did Eli say something to upset you?"

"No, not at all," Fanny said. *Drat the man, anyway.* His gaze had been so heated when they'd paused at the river, sheltered among the viburnum, Reilly a discreet distance away. She'd thought he would kiss her. He had not.

"I can see I disturbed you by bringing it up." Lucy arranged the tea things on the little table, her face darkened with concern, while Susan lit candles. Lucy dismissed the maid and sat on one side. "Tell me how my brother-in-law has distressed you."

Fanny shook her head and joined her at the table. "Eli Benson is a perfect gentleman."

A gleam lit in Lucy's eyes. "Is that what you're unhappy about? You hoped he'd let his gentlemanly instincts slip a bit as the moon rose?"

Fanny's heated blush said more than words.

"Aha!" Lucy gloated.

"There is nothing between Eli Benson and me, at least nothing personal. I'm a task assigned to him by the Earl of Clarion. The closest he has come to speaking personally is to call himself my 'business adviser.'" The words tasted bitter on her tongue.

Lucy's hilarity over that took a few moments to subside. "Business adviser? No man of business would look at you the way Eli looks at you. At least no respectable one. Perhaps we should rejoice that he's a gentleman."

"I don't know what to make of it," Fanny admitted. "Sometimes I think he's interested. And then he's all business." She grimaced. "There's that word again."

"Rob thinks he's uncomfortable. David—Clarion—is his employer," Lucy said.

Fanny wanted to voice her horror that Lucy and Rob would discuss such a thing, but something else burst out first. "What does that have to do with anything?"

"You're David's sister. Eli would never trespass on David's goodwill. Besides, you're an earl's daughter—"

"That is ludicrous. I'm a shop owner's granddaughter. A store clerk, and illegitimate besides," Fanny said.

Lucy indicated the pile of papers on the desk with a nod. "Judging from that, you're a prodigious writer. You haven't shared it with me, but I'm guessing that is a novel, and knowing you, whatever you set your mind to is brilliant. Eli dragged you to publishers Friday. He must know. Perhaps that puts him in awe of you."

"More likely it gives him a disgust—a woman who wishes to earn coin by writing," Fanny retorted.

Lucy snorted. "Eli is not so big a fool as that. Have you asked him? What happened with the publishers?"

"He called it research. Clarion suggested it," Fanny said.

Lucy bit the inside of her lip. "Interesting. I wonder if he meant to throw you together."

Fanny didn't respond to that nonsense. "They think I need a business plan—I'm a writer, Lucy, not a wool manufacturer. How does that require a business plan? Perhaps they hope it will make me financially independent." She sighed. That certainly aligned with her own hopes. "In any case, Clarion has agreed to purchase a cottage for me and the ducklings. A place where I can write in peace."

"That's what you want? Wil and Amy won't be with you forever. Then what?" Lucy asked.

"Then I'll have my house and my writing," Fanny said firmly. "I can now say I've visited London. Once will be enough. I'm already looking forward to Ashmead. Don't you miss it?"

Lucy took the hint and the change of subject. "Every day. But my home is with Rob, wherever that takes me. We'll be back at Willowbrook by Michaelmas for my quarterly visit to oversee the estate. I check on the fields, the tenants, and my bees. Rob makes himself comfortable at the Willow and visits with old Robert, who delights in Kit. Then it will be back to London until Christmas. It works."

"I'm glad to know I'll see you regularly," Fanny murmured. She polished off a sandwich. She'd been hungrier than she'd realized. For a moment, she thought she was safe from Lucy's speculation.

"You need to ask him," Lucy said, cutting up the peace.

"What do you mean?"

"Eli. Ask him what he thinks about your writing." Lucy leaned forward. "Better yet, tell him you'll entertain his attentions. With only Wil and Susan for chaperones on the way, you'll have ample opportunity."

"Lucy!" Fanny's horror wasn't feigned. A lady didn't say such a thing to a gentleman.

Did she?

CHAPTER TWENTY-FIVE

I N SPITE OF Fanny's reluctance, Tuesday evening began with promise. Maddy arrived to go with them, looking pale but determined, her attentive husband, Brynn Morgan, at her side. A new evening gown gave Fanny confidence, and the Marchioness of Danbury proved to be as gracious a hostess as described. Most of the guests addressed Maddy as Lady Madelyn or even Mrs. Morgan, respecting her wish to avoid her former title. None drew back in horror when Maddy introduced Fanny as "my sister, Miss Frances Hancock."

All of London knew the story of the Earl of Clarion's bastards. One simply ignored the unfortunate fact and accepted them as they were. As predicted, some guests squirmed awkwardly at the hint of commercial enterprise in Fanny's background, but for the most part, the evening went smoothly with few questions asked. Meanwhile her friends and family took turns making sure they never left her on her own. Eli gave Fanny over to Maddy, who made introductions and put her on the arm of Rob, who in turn subtly handed her off to Lucy.

The soiree, an evening party, had been described to Fanny as "small," but at eighty attendees, it had thirty or forty more people, casually gathered in a series of rooms, than Fanny had ever seen at one party before. They clustered for conversation on couches, around refreshment tables, or over cards. There being no sight of the Earl of Grimsley, Fanny gradually relaxed. She floated from group to group, smiling, nodding, and often genuinely interested in the cultured and knowledgeable conversations. She discovered she quite liked the Danburys' friends.

When the marquess announced that Lady Isabelle, the Danburys' youngest, would accompany those who wished to dance, Eli appeared at Fanny's side, offering his arm for the first dance, and Fanny's evening reached perfection. She glided out onto the dance floor.

"I longed for this all evening," he whispered close to her ear when the figures of the dance brought them close. His nearness left her breathless, unable to formulate an answer. She let the rhythm of the dance carry her away only to have her heart soar when it brought them close again. His eyes never left her. She knew because hers never left him. Something had shifted between them. Something Fanny didn't fully understand but was happy to explore.

When the music ended on a glorious chord, breaking the spell, Eli bowed gracefully, and she dipped into a curtsey. As he walked her toward Maddy, who now sat near some tall, potted ferns, he murmured, "I'd ask you for a second dance, but it would cause talk. Besides, it appears other gentlemen wish an opportunity."

Fanny danced with a man introduced as a viscount, who carefully confessed he was the son of a duke—a fourth son—and an "honorable" clad in uniform. Her last partner led her to a chair near the French doors rather than back to Maddy. The doors were open against the heat of the evening and the crush in the informal ballroom. The air felt lovely, and giving in to an impulse, she stood, stepped nearer the door, and tipped her head up to the draft, half turned away from the dancing.

"There you are, waiting so patiently for me. I haven't forgotten our dance." Her breath caught at the sound of the Earl of Grimsley's voice behind her. Before she could formulate a reply, or even be certain who he addressed, she was on his arm and out the door.

Though torches lit the terrace, clouds skittered across a crescent moon, casting shadows across the far recesses of the Danburys' garden.

"Kind of Lieutenant Probst to deliver you to me. Your family's tenacity has made getting you alone a tedious exercise." Grimsley pulled her to the edge of the terrace, where a path led out into the darkness.

Fanny, every sense on alert, dug in her heels.

Grimsley's smug laughter grated on her. "Oh, come, Miss Hancock. You aren't going to turn missish on me now, are you? You were happy enough in my company earlier this week."

To Fanny's horror, she realized he had pitched his voice so anyone on the terrace or near the door might hear him.

ELI BACKED AWAY from the refreshment table with a lemonade in one hand. Brynn and Rob found conversation with the marquess and his cronies and subjects of economic and political interest irresistible, leaving Eli to see to the ladies. Maddy had been drawn to the dancing earlier yet had tired quickly. Eli left her looking weary to fetch a cold drink for her. He nodded to a friend, sidestepped a couple in rather closer conversation than was seemly, in the hallway, and came back into the ballroom via a side door, making his way toward Maddy. He wondered absently at what point a woman in expectation of a blessed event might best avoid social activity. He certainly had no idea about the answer, but he stood ready to fetch Brynn if she asked.

She glanced up wanly and accepted the glass he offered. "When did he arrive?"

Something in her emphasis on "he" had Eli following her line of sight, peering through pulsing lines of dancers. His eyes narrowed on a gentleman making his way toward the open terrace doors with determined tread. Grimsley. Eli sucked air and frowned.

Seconds later he turned his back on Maddy and weaved his way toward the door through which Grimsley had disappeared, taking Fanny, who in Eli's opinion, didn't look willing. He stepped outside and blinked to adjust to the torchlight and darkness beyond. Fanny stood several feet away, her back to him, her feet planted a foot apart and firmly on the terrace.

Striding across the flagstones, Eli didn't make out every word Grimsley said, but his tone sounded clear enough, one meant to belittle and intimidate. He came around Fanny's side, and when she turned and the torchlight illuminated her face, her obvious relief grabbed him by the throat, forcing him to swallow.

"Kindly unhand Miss Hancock, my lord," he said in measured tones, clenching his fists at his side. He longed to use them, but good sense and upbringing urged caution. Making a scene helped no one. "The lady has promised to dance the next one with me."

Grimsley's eyes glittered with malice. "And how does a jumped-up clerk think to interfere with an earl, the guest of a marquess?"

"Miss Hancock is a guest in this house, my lord." Eli glanced at Fanny, whose gaze begged for his help. "I suggest you let go of the lady's arm if you wish to be invited here again."

"Whose audacity would deny me the marquess's invitation? The nouveau baronet, your bastard brother? Or that half-pay colonel with coal dust under his fingernails? You, clerk?"

"Mine would, Grimsley. I suggest you take your leave quietly." The Marchioness of Danbury came up behind Eli, speaking in tones no less crisp and clear for being quietly said. "Perhaps if you leave London itself quietly, some of the less discerning hostesses might have you back in the spring."

Vile emotions twisted Grimsley's face, but he dropped Fanny's arm and backed up a step. He cast a baleful glance at Eli before inclining his head to the marchioness. "My lady. This is a misunderstanding. I don't know what lies this man has—"

"I have eyes and ears, Grimsley. Kindly leave my garden now." She indicated the back gate with a subtle movement of her head.

Grimsley looked briefly as if he might object, but he thought better of it and faded into the shadows.

"Thank you, my lady," Eli breathed, earning a faint smile from their hostess.

"Fanny, dear, I'm so glad you were able to join us this evening," the marchioness said, pitching her voice to be heard and hugging the girl. "I must show you the new painting by William Turner, in the green drawing room. I know some people find his style outlandish, but I'm intrigued. I would love your opinion. Yours as well, Mr. Benson, if you care to join us."

Lady Danbury drew back toward the ballroom, Fanny in tow. Eli didn't move.

The marchioness sighed wearily and murmured, "If you wish a word with the earl, perhaps you might do so outside my garden?"

Eli heard her meaning. *Don't be overheard or cause a scandal.*

Trailing after the earl through the dark garden, Eli weighed the satisfaction of knocking the earl down with a simple warning to stay away. The warning had fewer complications but would be significantly less satisfying. Still, attacking a peer could have ugly results. The decision made itself; he did neither. The sounds of voices distracted him.

"What were you doing in the garden?" Grimsley's words vibrated with anger.

"Seeing whether you ignored my orders." *Bateson?* Eli rather thought it was, but how was it the associate would be giving orders to the earl? Eli inched forward to the gate, standing in the shadow of the garden wall to the right of it. From that angle, he could see them. A street lamp illuminated Grimsley and his companion, a taller man. Bateson for certain. A carriage waited to the rear of both men.

"I don't take orders," Grimsley snarled.

"Oh, I rather think you do. The consequences to you of doing otherwise would be dire. She eluded me in Manchester, and it was only by the greatest stroke of luck she turned up in London. You have no idea how valuable she is."

"Because of her bedamned hair? Red signals an ill-tempered, soulless—"

Bateson's vile laugh churned Eli's stomach. "Don't tell my customer that. Did I tell you the potentate met the Duchess of Glenmoor? Met and wanted? When the dog found out I had the duchess's sister, my price spiked. He wants her untouched, you fool. My orders were for you to get me a close look at the chit and perhaps frighten her a bit to keep her uneasy but leave her unmolested." Bateson's cold voice, clear in the night, horrified Eli.

"She'll flee back to Ashly or Ashmore or whatever godforsaken backwater she wants soon enough," Grimsley whined. "I just wanted a bit before she did. Now the Danbury witch ordered me to rusticate. Can you believe that?"

"The marchioness is smarter than you are, Grimsley. Do it," Bateson said.

"I damn well—" Grimsley's words stopped on a gurgle. From his vantage point, Eli leaned forward, trying to make out what happened in the shadows. Bateson's silhouette merged briefly with Grimsley's shape. Grimsley staggered back, gagging and choking.

"You know what I'm capable of, Grimsley. If you value your inheritance, your sister, and your manhood, I suggest you do as you're told." Bateson turned on his heels and strode away.

Grimsley lurched to the carriage and clambered in. Eli sank back against the wall, breath heaving.

What the hell was that about? He needed to talk to his brother— almost as much as he needed to see Fanny.

DAZED AND DISTRACTED, Fanny smiled on cue as the Marchioness of Danbury swept her through the sea of guests, referred to her as "our Miss Hancock," and led her into the nearly deserted green drawing room, where two ladies' chatted on a settee and another couple spoke softly by the far wall. The lady drew her up in front of a painting.

Fanny stared at a sweeping panoramic view of a valley, an ancient manor house in the far distance, the sky a roiling mass of dark clouds. She saw little else in the work, absorbing instead its air of doom, a mood too close to her own at that moment for comfort.

"A grim view of the family pile, I know," the marchioness said. "But I rather like the drama. Our Mister Turner is never one for the sweet and pretty." She tilted her head to Fanny and whispered, "Simply look thoughtful. You'll feel better momentarily."

Fanny swallowed convulsively and did as the lady suggested, forcing her gaze to the painting while her thoughts ran to Eli. She might have thrown herself into his arms when he'd appeared at her side, staring down Grimsley, if the vile earl hadn't held her arm is such a tight grip. She'd longed to when the villain had walked away, but the marchioness had more concern for Fanny's reputation and her own. Fanny owed her a debt of gratitude—one she might give words to if only she could speak.

"Breathe," the marchioness murmured.

She did. It helped. *Where is Eli? Has he gone to confront Grimsley? He's not a man prepared for violence.* Her heart stuttered at the thought of what might happen to him. She choked back tears. The shock of that brought her to her senses.

You are made of sterner stuff, Fanny Hancock, and Eli Benson is no fool. She inhaled deeply.

"Good girl," the marchioness murmured. "Better? Shall I take you to Lady Benson?"

Fanny nodded. "Thank you, my lady. I can't begin to express my gratitude."

"Nonsense. I enjoy showing off my paintings." The lady patted her hand and winked. "Ah, here is our Sir Robert, come to find his sister."

Rob's piercing inspection of her person told Fanny he'd heard what had happened. She hoped it was Eli who'd spoken with him, not one of the other guests. He pulled his expression under control and smiled at the marchioness. He took Fanny's hand and placed it on his arm.

"Your soiree has been a joy as always, Lady Danbury. My family appreciates your hospitality more than I can say," he said.

"You enrich the assemblage every time you gift us with your presence," the marchioness replied. "Are you leaving us? The hour is not yet so terribly late."

"Alas, Lady Madelyn has grown weary and needs to go home. I think it best we accompany her," Rob replied.

Eli strode to the door and stood watching, his eyes boring into Fanny. He appeared sound. Fanny saw no blood, no bruises, only grim determination. Though relieved, she pursed her lips. His expression would draw attention.

Their hostess glanced toward the door. "I see your handsome brother has come to join you. I'll have my staff order your carriage brought round." She left them there.

"Eli, would you kindly escort Fanny to the carriage while I see to my wife?" Rob said, giving him a pointed look.

Her smile trembled when she took Eli's arm, but her mind was clear enough. He looked ready to murder. She had to put a stop to that. She peered back at the painting. "Really, Mr. Benson, the painting does have a grim air about it, but I think you exaggerate."

Startled, he glanced up at Mr. Turner's work.

Fanny whispered, "Your fierce expression is drawing stares. People will think I've offended you."

Eli's eyes, the color of warm chocolate, melted into tender appreciation when he met hers. "Never." A sad sort of smile accompanied his words. "Never."

They took their time walking to the entrance, glancing at each other often. "Wasn't this a lovely evening?" Fanny asked, her gaze challenging him.

"It was indeed," he replied. Dropping his voice, he added, "We'll talk on the way home."

⟫⟪

"ONCE MORE, ELI. Don't leave out a detail," Rob demanded in the dark carriage rolling toward Chelsea and home.

The six of them huddled in the Benson carriage, Rob and Lucy side by side, with Fanny next to Lucy on the back-facing bench. Eli sat next to the Morgans, across from Fanny. They faced forward as a courtesy to Maddy's delicate stomach. Eli endured his brother's questioning, but his eyes—and his heart—were fixed on the woman across from him.

Eli described what he had witnessed on the street outside the Danburys' garden in Mayfair one more time.

"Bateson threatened Grimsley, you're absolutely certain?" Brynn Morgan asked.

"As certain as can be. At first, I couldn't be positive it was him; I was that startled. But he stood in the light, I'm certain. The associate ordering the earl to do his bidding. It makes no sense." Eli had gone over it in his mind several times. There could be only one conclusion.

"Grimsley wouldn't put up with that unless Bateson has some sort of information or leverage to do great harm," Rob murmured, voicing Eli's conclusion. "What we thought was a bodyguard may be a shadow."

"That Grimsley has no honor where women are concerned is not a shock. The rest of it, though..." Maddy shook her head and let her words trail off.

"It is lucky Eli followed the worm and overheard it," Rob said.

"The information matters."

"Not luck that I followed. I intended to rearrange his filthy mouth when I caught up with him," Eli muttered.

"Then it is our good fortune we didn't have to help you avoid transportation for assaulting a peer of the realm," Rob said with a sly smile. "You have to do that sort of thing more discreetly. Dark alcove. Unknown assailant. No witnesses."

"Are you offering to teach me?" Eli asked hopefully.

"Stop it, you two. Violence won't help!" Lucy exclaimed, the words bursting out. "Grimsley's obsession with Fanny appears to be for the crudest of predictable reasons. Some people believe an elevated title gives them privilege to act in the lowest possible manner."

"At least we're free of the slimy earl and know him for what he is." Maddy didn't sound confident.

"I'm not such an innocent as to be stupefied by how horrid he turned out to be. Looks deceive as well," Fanny replied. "I've come to the conclusion our nasty earl pushed me into that closet at the theater. He did it so he could rescue me, as a ploy to earn my trust. He underestimated me. Men often do because of my size."

That's my little warrior, Eli thought. Fanny's pluck and backbone were what had attracted him to her that first day.

"Do you think Grimsley will heed the marchioness and leave London?" Fanny asked.

"People like Grimsley value their social status. She could ruin him, and he knows it. He'll retreat for a while," Maddy said.

"But where does that put us?" Lucy asked.

"With Bateson to deal with," Rob murmured, peering at Eli.

Eli's met his brother's eyes. He had one thought, one he suspected Rob shared. *We need to get her to the security of Clarion Hall.*

Silence permeated the carriage until they reached Caulfield House.

"Does all this mean you'll stay longer?" Lucy asked hopefully as they came to a stop.

"No," Eli and Fanny spoke over each other.

"I have to get home to Ashmead; I have work to do," Eli explained.

"Since some of that work is on Wil's behalf, I need to go with him," Fanny said.

"I—" Eli started to declare that he could take care of the business in Manchester on his own but thought better of it. He would save that fight for Ashmead. He said something else entirely.

⟫⟫⟫✕⟪⟪⟪

ELI'S HESITANCE WHEN the carriage pulled up at Caulfield House surprised Fanny. Dropping him first was logical, but his reluctance to leave them was not.

He leaned across to her and took one hand. "Fanny..." He glanced at his brother. "With Rob's permission, may I have a private word?"

Rob seemed as startled as Fanny. "Of course. A *brief* word."

Eli handed her from the carriage and a step or three to the right of the door, putting his back to the window. His hands held hers, still encased in gloves. His thumbs rubbed circles in the palms of her hands.

"Fanny, I... Uh." He stuttered to halt. "Are you well? I need to know if what happened tonight caused you distress. That is, I know it did, but I—That is..." He sighed. "I just—You must know that you— that is, your safety—is vital to me."

"What are you trying to say?" Fanny's heartbeat sped up. She swayed toward him.

He mirrored the movement until their foreheads almost touched. For a long while, they stayed in place, her eyes searching his in the lamplight, his studying her face until they focused on her lips. For one heart-stopping moment, she thought he would finally kiss her, but then he spoke softly.

"I will come at first light tomorrow to escort you safely to Ashmead. We will find that cottage you want. You will have your heart's desire soon."

"Thank you," she breathed. *Is that all? That can't be all.*

He gave his head a shake and turned so he could hand her back into the carriage, firming his grip on her left hand to do so.

"Thank you," she repeated. "For everything." She would have her heart's desire. Once, she'd thought she knew what that was. Now? She wondered.

CHAPTER TWENTY-SIX

"I DON'T SEE why Mr. Benson can ride outside and I can't. He isn't one of the guards," Wil grumbled.

Since they traveled at a moderate pace, there were two overnight stops between London and Ashmead, and they were three-fourths of the way to the second.

Wil had been enthralled at first by the outriders, not only Reilly, who'd become their loyal protector, but Corporal Goodfellow, a member of Rob's troop, one of the men Lucy called the palace guard. Fanny was less comfortable, worried what it meant. There had been discussion of hiring two more, but in the end, four men, including Williams the coachman, had been deemed sufficient. Eli had muttered that he hoped they wouldn't regret that decision. He'd been tense throughout the trip; he had in fact seemed so since the encounter with Grimsley in the garden.

Wil was considerably less pleased when it became clear he was to ride inside with Fanny, though Goodfellow hinted they might loosen that restriction the next day.

Truth be told, Fanny felt as frantic for a change as Wil did after two days on the road. Neither her brother nor Susan had much by way of stimulating conversation. She tried writing in fits and starts, but it didn't go well.

If she was honest with herself, she longed for Eli's company. She couldn't fault him for attempting to maintain propriety, but she thought his efforts excessive. After all, Susan rode with her, and he'd shared a carriage with Fanny before.

What had changed between them? Her hopeful heart whispered that he wanted her, wanted her in all possible ways, but he hadn't spoken. She chastised herself for her unruly thoughts, yet she saw it in his eyes. *Can a woman ever be certain? Why does he hesitate?*

"Tell him you'll entertain his attentions." Lucy's words haunted her, but they implied a forwardness Fanny wasn't prepared to demonstrate.

She picked up the page on her lap desk, reading through it, searching the next fragment of dialogue she meant to write. Soon enough she let herself get lost in the story. So absorbed was she that she had no warning before the carriage lurched to a stop, horses screamed, and a shot rang out. After she was brought to alertness, the second shot galvanized her thoughts.

"Get down, both of you!" She went to her knees on the floor and tore at the box affixed to the vehicle's door while Susan and Wil complied.

At least Wil got to the floor; he didn't stay there. "Reilly is down," he called from his knees, at the window. "Goodfellow is firing from horseback. I think the bandits are—"

"Bandits?" Fanny cried. "Get down." She yanked open the box as Rob had demonstrated and pulled out the pistol stored there.

"What else? Bandits. One is on the ground, and one—no, two others—are trying to go around."

Fanny turned to pull Wil back from the window. The door behind her rattled. She spun back and landed on her fundament just as the door was pulled open. The man who stared at her wore a mask. His brows rose at the sight of the gun she aimed at the center of his chest.

"You're supposed to come with me, not fool with that barking iron," the bandit growled.

Fanny eased back the hammer on the pistol as Rob had taught her. The man hesitated for a moment, let lose a string of curses, and reached for her. The recoil when she fired knocked her back into Susan. Blood spurted out of the bandit's shoulder. She'd hit him off-center and slowed him but not stopped him. When he grabbed one ankle and leaned forward to pull her closer, she reared up her other leg and kicked right where she had shot him. Hard. He howled and went to his knees, hitting his chin on the bottom of the carriage door on the way down.

"Well done, Fanny," Wil crowed while Susan sobbed.

She scrambled to grab the door, relieved when it pulled shut. The man she'd shot must have fallen clear of it. "Find something to use as a cudgel," she ordered Wil. She turned the now useless pistol in her hand to use it as a club, burned her fingers on the hot barrel, and dropped it.

She pulled out a handkerchief and wrapped the handle just in time. The door opened again. She raised her improvised weapon to defend herself and almost whacked Eli on the head. She threw the pistol to the floor and herself into his arms, lucky she didn't topple him.

Panic set in. "We have to get down!" She pulled away; he tugged her back, holding her tenderly. He kissed her hair, and his hands gently caressed her back. "They're gone, Fanny. We wounded one, and Goodfellow killed another and chased two away. Reilly is down, but—"

Fanny froze at the sight of movement on the ground next to the coach. The man she'd shot attempted to stand, failed, and crawled toward his pistol.

"Gun!" she shouted.

Eli leapt on the man, spurring Fanny into action. She stepped on the bandit's hand so he'd release the gun and kicked the weapon out of reach.

Eli knelt on the man's back and had him by the scruff of the neck quickly enough, but the ruffian bucked and fought while Eli tried to get an arm around his throat. Fanny looked around frantically, picked up a rock, and bashed the man on his head, stunning him long enough for Eli to get a good grip, bending one arm behind the brute's back and tightening the choke hold. The man moaned in agony.

"I shot him," Fanny said.

Eli's wide grin delighted her. "Did you really? That explains why this hurts so effectively." He pulled on the bent arm harder to demonstrate what he meant by "this," and the would-be bandit fainted. "Well done, my love, well done."

Danger and mayhem faded away. *My love... Did he mean it?*

ELI WANTED FANNY safely in his arms more than anything, but there was no time. He lowered the attacker to the ground, keeping a firm grip on his arm. "Do you have a scarf or rope or anything we can use to tie this animal up?" Eli asked.

Fanny considered it for a moment before she pulled up her skirts to tear a flounce from her petticoat. He took full advantage of the glance of shapely ankle she provided. When she looked up to hand him the frilly binding, she caught him looking, and a peculiar expression crossed her face. He didn't stop to consider its meaning.

Goodfellow galloped up. "The rotters got away. I daren't leave you all to pursue," he said, sliding off his horse. "It looks like you got another, though, Benson. Maybe we can get information out of this one. The one you shot may not be long for this world."

"Not I. Miss Hancock shot this one and, if I'm not mistaken, is responsible for that nasty whack on the chin. I merely leveraged her work to subdue him the rest of the way."

"Well done, Miss Hancock!" Goodfellow grinned at her. "Young Wil is seeing to the wounded. I best help him," he went on.

"I'm sorry. I ought to be doing that. You make sure those horrid men don't come back!" Fanny lifted her skirts and ran around the coach.

Goodfellow helped Eli drag the wounded man to the other side of the carriage, where they took stock.

Fanny and Wil hovered over Reilly, who lay unconscious on the ground. The boy held a pad, which looked suspiciously like cloth from a petticoat, tight against a seeping wound in Reilly's side. His shirt had been torn off and used to bind another in one of his legs. Fanny secured the dressing on his side with another strip of ruffle from her clothing. She ordered Wil to keep pressure on the wound and rose. To Eli's horror, she wiped her bloody hands on her dress.

She caught his look and smiled sadly. "It is ruined in any case. We did what we could for Reilly. Wil had the sense to bear down on the bleeding quickly. If we can get him to help, he should recover." She put the back of her hand to her forehead, brushing hair back, and left a smear of blood. "We need to see to those men."

She gestured toward the three bandits lying in the dirt. One had died from Goodfellow's shot that went neatly through his forehead. Eli had shot the other in the belly with the blunderbuss. He still breathed but wouldn't live long.

"There's nothing you can do for that one. Leave him," Goodfellow said. "Unless you keep laudanum at hand."

Susan called from the box in front of the carriage, where she tended to the coachman, that she had some in her reticule in the coach.

The man Fanny had shot lay on his side, his arms tied behind his back, the wound in his shoulder seeping. Eli bent to look at it while Goodfellow went to round up Reilly's horse. Eli wanted to throttle him for daring to touch Fanny, but basic humanity won out.

Fanny stooped down as well. She stopped the rogue's bleeding readily enough using a piece of the man's own shirt. "It's dirty but will have to do," she said.

The wounded man groaned and glared at her. "You din't have to shoot me."

"You didn't have to attack us or attempt to grab me," she retorted.

"Got paid to take you, din't we? If they'd have handed you over, no one needed to get hurt."

"Interesting. Perhaps if you tell us more, we'll get a physician to see to that wound before we give you to the magistrate." Eli shoved the man's shoulder to emphasize the point.

A gunshot brought Eli to his feet. He shoved Fanny toward the coach, pulling Wil along, before searching the road.

Goodfellow returned a moment later, leading two horses. "Reilly's had to be put down. The vermin wounded it. They left us these two in exchange," he muttered. He glanced up at the carriage's box. "How are you doing, Williams?"

Their coachman's wounds were slight. "I'll do. Concentrating on getting you lot and the folks inside, they were. You kept 'em busy, but Mr. Benson there made good use of the blunderbuss under the seat," the loyal servant said while Susan cleaned the graze on the side of his head. A bit closer and it wouldn't have been minor in the least. One hand, which had become tangled in the reins in the confusion, lay limp in his lap.

Goodfellow surveyed the situation. "We'll leave those two here," he said, indicating the dead and dying criminals. "Can you ride, Williams?"

"Easier than driving, I think, sir." The coachman lifted his battered hand.

"We aren't far from the Rooster's Haven. Benson, can you drive the coach? We'll lay Reilly on the floor. Unfortunately, we'll have to put this piece of garbage"—Goodfellow prodded the man Fanny had shot, with the toe of his boot—"next to him."

"Susan and I will ride inside with Williams and see to them," Fanny said.

"Reload that pistol first," Eli muttered, bringing a wry grin from Goodfellow.

"Young Wil, can you ride?" Goodfellow asked.

"Yes, sir," the boy said eagerly. "At least some. A few times. In the city."

Goodfellow laughed. "Perhaps best if you ride up next to Benson. Can you shoot?"

"Show me how, and I will," Wil answered.

Fanny did not look pleased at the thought, but Eli saw the sense.

"Take a minute to reload the blunderbuss and show him the basics. Emphasize safety," Eli said, giving Wil a penetrating gaze he hoped got the point across. "I'll supervise. He won't touch it except in dire necessity."

They made quick work of lifting Reilly into the carriage as gently as they could. They retied the wounded bandit so he could lie on his back, retrieved Susan's laudanum, and gave him some before laying him next to Reilly, grateful when he lost consciousness.

Eli dosed the dying man with the rest, stared down at the mess his shot had made of the man's stomach, and grimaced.

Goodfellow put a hand on his shoulder. "Is this the first time you've killed a man, Benson?" the corporal asked.

Eli nodded. He'd had no choice and wouldn't second-guess himself, but the horror of it would haunt him.

"It needed doing," Goodfellow said, clapping him on the shoulder. "Think on the things you protected."

When Fanny slid up next to Eli and put an arm around his waist, he turned her away from the sight of the brigand's wounds and pulled her into an embrace. Eli soaked in the comfort she offered, thanking God she had not been injured.

Fanny went up on her toes and kissed the side of his chin. "We best get Reilly to a doctor," she said, her voice thick and wet.

He kissed her fiercely then, pouring all the wanting, all the passion, all his need for comfort into that kiss. When he raised his head, still holding her, Goodfellow studiously saw to the tack on his horse, but Wil stared openmouthed.

Eli almost asked Fanny to trade places with Wil, needing her by his side, but she'd be safer inside the carriage. One thing he knew for certain. Once they got to the inn, he wouldn't let her out of his sight.

CHAPTER TWENTY-SEVEN

GOODFELLOW, AWKWARD AND ill at ease, stood next to Reilly's sickbed at the Rooster's Haven. He cleared his throat, peered down at the man on the bed, and eyed Fanny nervously. Eli knew the man—though a year or two younger than Eli himself—to be skilled at all manner of security concerns, loyal as they come, and brave. He was one of Rob Benson's finest. He was, however, no diplomat.

"If we could speak privately, Benson...," Goodfellow rasped.

Eli prepared to argue, but Fanny got there first. "This concerns me, Corporal Goodfellow. I will not be excluded from this discussion."

The Rooster's Haven, which they had reached within two hours with no further trouble, had turned out to be somewhat isolated. It was only the greatest of good fortune that a physician had been among the guests. The man pronounced Williams—the coachman—fit and Reilly "likely to survive barring infection." The bullet that had struck Reilly's side, he'd said, appeared to have missed major organs and, "God be praised," his intestines. "We'll know in due time," he'd murmured.

The physician had pronounced their prisoner well enough to question, appeared indifferent to the highwayman's survival after that, and suggested they leave him locked in the inn's stable until the magistrate sent someone. "He may live long enough to be transported. Or may not," the doctor had said.

Fanny had remained in the sickroom with Wil and Susan during the interrogation to protect them from hearing the worst and to care for the injured, but she'd chaffed under the necessity of it. As soon as Eli had returned, she'd demanded to know what they'd learned and the plan going forward.

Eli was torn between the desire to shelter her from fear and the need to keep her close. Now that he'd returned to her side, however, he didn't plan to leave it no matter what Goodfellow proposed.

She's mine to protect, he thought fiercely, even more determined to keep her where he could see her after what he had just heard.

"Wil, we've spoken for another room across the hall. I've ordered tea for the ladies. Would you kindly escort Susan there?" Eli asked. The boy glanced at Fanny. Seeing no reprieve there, he did as Eli asked.

Fanny's hand brushed Eli's where it hung at his side, sending a frisson of awareness through him. He liked her where he could touch her even better. He took it, their hands half-hidden in her skirt as she glanced down at the wounded man on the bed. "If Reilly here can bear what must be said, so can I, Corporal Goodfellow," she murmured. "What did you discover?"

"Precious little, Miss Hancock. The weasel we captured knows only the name of the man leading the attack, and he's dead. They were paid by someone—our prisoner claims not to know who—and threatened with retribution if they failed." Goodfellow frowned. "It fits with what we know about the criminal enterprise."

Eli agreed. "Low-level criminals report to local miscreants, but a more powerful figure is driving the entire filthy operation."

"Bateson's enterprise?" Fanny demanded.

Eli touched her cheek gently, searching her face for distress. "Likely. The prisoner was clear about one thing. They were to abduct you or die trying. Rob was right. Bateson, or whoever is behind what happened in Manchester, has not given up and will not give up."

"That is ludicrous! Die trying? How can I matter so much?" Fanny retorted.

Eli reminded her of Bateson's description of his buyer. "A great deal of money must be at stake," he said.

"We may be dealing with a madman, ma'am," Goodfellow said. "We do know he uses threats and intimidation to control his minions as well as those who owe him money. They've used abduction and threats to support their gambling businesses many times."

"What are we going to do?" she asked.

She said "we." Eli took strength from her trust even as her determination worried him. His little warrior would not be sidelined no matter how hard the men around her tried to protect her.

"We have few choices, Miss Hancock," Goodfellow said.

"We know those men weren't robbers. They were sent to abduct me. Given what he said and past incidents, we can assume they will try again. The question, then, is, How do we keep me safe without endangering the rest of you? Do I have that right?"

"Yes. We beat them back once. If our prisoner told the truth, they'll likely try again between here and Ashmead. *Very* likely if they're under threat," Goodfellow said.

"How safe are we here?" Fanny asked.

"I'd feel better if we could get you to Clarion Hall and the earl's people," Eli told her, squeezing her hand.

"So would I. This spot is isolated," Goodfellow said. "I wouldn't expect another frontal attack like on the road, but the inn is vulnerable. We'd have to secure every door and window in this place to guard against a determined kidnapper, and there are few enough of us."

"I'm fit. I will help," Reilly put in, rising on one elbow. His pallor argued otherwise.

"Would they give up if I'm not here?" Fanny asked. Eli frowned down at her, but she went on, "Reilly, Williams, Susan, and Wil are all at risk near me. Could the three of us go on to Ashmead and send back assistance?"

"We beat them back when there were four men defending. I'm not sure we can risk doing it with two," Goodfellow said.

"Four men and a woman," Fanny corrected tartly.

"I have another suggestion." Eli lifted her hand to his lips. "How well can you ride?"

"Are you going to suggest we leave the carriage behind?" Goodfellow demanded.

Fanny met Eli's eyes, and he watched her sort it out. "I suspect he means something else entirely. Are you suggesting a decoy, Eli?"

The corporal's face lit up. "We could divide our party and use the carriage as a decoy. Is that what you mean?"

Eli nodded. "I will take Miss Hancock across country by horseback. You make a great show of staying here. I suggest we leave the carriage in a prominent spot for the world and whoever watches to think we never left."

"It would be safer if I came with you," Goodfellow said, rubbing his chin.

"That would put everyone else at risk when they try to get in to get to me. We already said the inn isn't secure. We need a diversion," Fanny insisted.

"She's right. Fanny and I will be safe that way, but the rest of you have to leave here. You could take the carriage on to Ashmead in the morning with Reilly and Williams. Leave Susan and Wil," Eli said.

Goodfellow sorted it through. "You two would be long gone before that carriage moves in the morning." Still, he looked unhappy, but he made no alternative suggestion.

"Yes, overland on horseback. Eli and I," Fanny agreed.

Goodfellow sighed deeply. "It would work but not if they are watching us leave and see the empty carriage. We'll need a volunteer to dress as you, ma'am. Dare we risk the boy or your maid? One of them could wear the disguise."

Her stricken expression tore at Eli. "Fanny, these men want you. If they stop the carriage, they'll leave everyone alone once they figure out you aren't with them. Susan can dress as you when she boards the carriage and discard the costume on the road."

"Wil would be better." Fanny spoke through tight lips. "He looks more like me. But I don't like it."

"What alternative do we have?" Eli asked.

"None," she replied.

Goodfellow nodded. "Can you do it?"

Eli peered at Fanny.

She tightened her grip on his hand, lifted her chin, and met his eyes. "Yes, we can."

It was decided. There was some squabbling over details, and multiple opinions about how to manage Wil and Susan.

Eli and Fanny crossed the hall to consult the two of them.

So much for keeping them protected, Eli thought ruefully.

The maid proved to be remarkably brave. "I'm sure I don't want to sit here like a sitting duck. I'll be safer with Corporal Goodfellow," she insisted. Wil reacted with characteristic enthusiasm, glad to have a role. An argument broke out between the two of them, both of whom wanted to be the one who dressed as Fanny to board the coach. Wil won.

AFTER A HURRIED supper, Fanny made Eli leave her so she could change clothes. She suspected he paced the hallway outside the door. Wil went to sit with Reilly.

Fanny left her discarded clothing, quickly adjusted, in a neat pile for Wil. She planned to borrow Susan's spare gown, but the maid made a startling suggestion. "You'll be safer as a boy, ma'am. You ought best to wear Mr. Wil's spare clothes."

The idea shocked Fanny, but it made sense. "It will be easier to ride one of those great, hulking beasts if I'm not in skirts," she murmured.

"You need a dark shirt, though," Susan said. "So you won't be seen so easy in the night."

"Williams always wears black and gray. Go ask him." Fanny sent the maid across the hall and dug through Wil's bag. Now that she was alone and faced with the reality of what she'd agreed to do, fear settled in her belly. She'd told the men she could ride. It wasn't a lie. She had ridden Horace's mount from the drapery to the port many times. On city streets. Sidesaddle. In the daylight. This would be very different. She shook off her anxiety. Any other choice exposed Wil and the others to even greater danger. She feared for Eli as it was.

Susan returned waving the shirt in triumph. It proved to be much too large, but the two women belted it in.

"I'll have to wear my own half-boots," Fanny murmured.

The maid nodded. "Can't be hobbling along." She studied their handiwork. "This won't work close up, but you'll do," she pronounced.

A knock interrupted them. "Night is upon us, Fanny. We need to be off," Eli called through the door.

Fanny stepped out, and Eli's jaw dropped. He stared but said nothing, as if he'd swallowed his tongue at the sight of her in her brother's spare trousers.

"Susan's suggestion and a practical one," she told him briskly. We were going to cut my hair, but there wasn't time."

"Thank God for that much!" he said.

Her auburn tresses had been pulled back in a tether. She lifted her hair to stuff it under Wil's hat while Eli's warm gaze raked her from her black half-boots to the place where the shirt stretched across her chest, tightened by her uplifted arms. "No one will believe you're a boy. Trust me on that, Fanny."

She almost got lost in his heated gaze before he tore his eyes away.

"Goodfellow is waiting in the stable."

She reached for his hand and took a firm hold on it and her courage. The corporal met them with two horses, one of them his own. His eyes widened at Fanny in boys' clothing before he quickly looked away.

Two pistols and a pouch of shot lay on a bench next to Goodfellow. "Miss Hancock, this is the carriage pistol, the one you made good use of before. It is loaded. I found a shoulder holster for it. Are you comfortable carrying it?"

When Fanny hesitated, Eli said, "I can carry both. If we happen to need it, I'll hand it to her."

The corporal nodded his approval. "Benson, I have given you Reilly's pistol and kept his musket. Agree?"

Eli nodded grimly. "Sensible," he muttered.

"With luck, you won't need them," Goodfellow said.

The two horses, saddled and ready, fitted with saddlebags, drew the party's attention next.

Goodfellow patted his horse—his personal mount—with pride. "I suggest we put Miss Hancock on this fellow. He's steady and has had a bit of rest. He can get you safely to Ashmead." Goodfellow shrugged. "This other is one of the bandits' horses. He appears to be a sturdy fellow if a bit skittery. You can manage him, Benson." Eli helped Fanny up and mounted the other horse, bringing it under control when it sidled nervously.

With that, Eli and Fanny—dressed in dark clothes and armed as heavily as their little party could spare—walked two horses from the innyard and disappeared into the night, heading roughly northwest.

CHAPTER TWENTY-EIGHT

E LI, INNKEEPER'S SON, had grown up around horses and knew enough to be painfully aware of the dangers in riding cross-country at night. He set an easy pace across the meadow that fronted the road behind the inn, but feared the terrain would be hillier and less easy as they went. As to the night, the quarter moon helped, but clouds glided over it periodically.

Fanny lagged behind.

"Are you managing?" he called to her.

"Well enough," she replied. He didn't like the sound of her voice.

He slowed his mount and came up alongside. "Tell me the truth. Have you ridden before?"

"Yes," she said, a tremor in her voice. "Just not like this. Not in the dark."

He cursed under his breath.

"I'm sorry, Eli. It is our only choice. I'll manage."

"You're a brave one, Fanny, but we can't take unnecessary chances. I would hold your reins, but it is safer if you keep them and stay beside me. You hang on. We won't be galloping neck or nothing. At least we won't unless we have to."

They passed a sheepfold and skirted a fenced field, keeping to slim lanes where they could. When they came to a dense wood, Eli paused. His sense of direction told him the surest line to Ashmead lay directly through, but hazards to horses and riders would abound in the wood, where moonlight would be of no help. A narrow track followed the edge of the tree line. He turned them left, which he presumed to be due west, and they rode for another hour along the dirt trail following the edge of the wood.

Sometime after midnight, still following the tree line, Fanny swayed slightly in the saddle.

"Fanny!" Eli hissed, coming to a stop. When he reached out an arm to steady her, both horses sidled uneasily.

She grabbed the pommel in a fierce grip and pulled herself up. "I can manage! I—"

Eli dismounted, went around to her side, and held up his arms. "Come down, Fanny. That's enough."

"No, we need to go on. We have to get to Clarion Hall. We—" Her voice cracked.

Eli took her by the waist and pulled her down into his arms. Her trembling vibrated through him, and for a moment, he thought she might fall to pieces, but this was his brave Fanny. She took a shaky breath and lifted her head. It was almost more than he could bear.

Before he could lean down for the all-consuming kiss his whole being yearned for, she pulled away. "I can stand. I'll man—"

Eli caught her as her legs went out from under her, and she sank toward the ground. "Managing, are we?" He cradled her close, and she snuggled her face against the folds of his cravat.

"I'm sorry Eli," she whispered.

He kissed the words away then, a gentle and respectful salute meant to reassure. "No need for that. You've been brilliant," he murmured against her lips.

They'd been riding for hours, and Eli's legs ached from controlling the bandit's skittery horse. He shuddered to think how she felt. He let her slide down to her feet, but they stood like that, Fanny wrapped in Eli's arms, her head nestled against him, for several long moments while their mounts stood patiently by, cropping the grass in the dark.

Her hand came up against his chest, and she pushed back. "I can stand. I need..." She glanced toward the woods.

Eli took her hands. *She needs to relieve herself.* He cleared his throat. "Don't go too far, and step carefully." He waited while she walked into the woods, listened to her rustling the underbrush, and cringed when he heard a loud squeal. Alarm shot through him.

"Fanny!" he shouted.

A creature of the night, disturbed by her movement or his shout, shot from the woods, spooking the horse Eli had been riding; it recoiled, spun, and ran off into the night. Goodfellow's better-trained mount shied briefly but held his ground, ears alert, and pawed nervously. Eli grabbed the reins of Goodfellow's horse, running his hand down its neck and speaking soothingly.

Fanny ran up, breathless. "What was that?"

"A roe deer, I suspect. I didn't get a good look. What happened?" Eli asked.

"The brush is thick. I scratched my...self. Where's the other horse?" she asked.

"Terrified. He bolted, probably running home. Thank God one of them has a valiant heart," Eli said, still soothing their remaining horse. He looped the reins loosely over a low branch.

Fanny moved up against him. "Dear God! What are we going to do?" He could feel her body quivering.

"We'll ride together," he said. *We'll have to.* "You're shivering." He pulled her closer.

"I'm freezing.," she admitted.

Of course she was. Cold. Hungry. Frightened. Alone with a man miles from anyone. Worried how they would manage, since one of their horses had disappeared. Utterly vulnerable. And it was entirely Eli's fault. What had seemed like a brilliant idea in the middle of the afternoon now struck him as the most dunderheaded decision he had ever made. He had placed her in this position.

He opened his coat and wrapped it around her, holding her to his body for warmth.

"We should push on," she murmured against his chest but made no effort to move. "Perhaps we'll find the beast."

"No, I think not. We've taken a great risk riding in the dark, we've seen no sign of the kidnappers, and we're both exhausted." He inhaled deeply and rested his chin on the top of her head. "I believe what's in front of us is Spencer's Wood. It is miles wide, and we'd have to go around all night. The other side of it is twelve miles southeast of Ashmead. If we wait until morning. we can go through." At least he hoped so. He wished he felt as confident as he tried to sound.

"Sleep on the ground? I think right now I could sleep on rocks. Is there a blanket?" Her trust in his judgment humbled him.

He removed Reilly's gun from his belt and unbuckled the shoulder holster with the carriage pistol; he set them against the broad trunk of the largest tree near them. He then stripped the saddle and saddlebag from their horse and located two skins of water. He saw to the horse first, removing his hat to water the beast. Their safety would depend on him.

"There's only one blanket," he murmured.

"But there is cheese in here. A bit of bread and apples," Fanny told him while she rooted through one of the saddlebags. Goodfellow seemed to have thought of everything. She removed half. They would need the rest tomorrow.

Eli pulled a knife from his boot and cut one of the apples into slices, feeding it to the horse while Fanny stretched the blanket out in front of the tree where he had placed the pistols. "Wait," he said. "I have a better idea." He pulled the blanket up against the trunk of the tree to protect her back and put the saddlebag on it to hold it in place. "Sit and I'll wrap it around you."

She didn't move. "Where will you sleep?"

"Nearby."

"That you will not. The blanket is wide enough to wrap both of us. We'll be warmer together," she insisted, stooping to push the saddlebag off the blanket and pick up the food.

He couldn't argue with her logic, but neither could he spend a night with Fanny in his arms and hold on to any fiber of the claim he was a gentleman. He had battled his growing arousal all evening, made worse by the liberties he'd already taken.

"Sit and eat. I need to do as you did. In the woods." He stumbled over his words, causing her to laugh.

"Hurry and come back because I am getting colder. I need you."

"I need you." Is she trying to kill me? He moved far enough down the road that she might not hear him and stepped behind the nearest tree, devoutly wishing cold air and discomfort would cool his lust.

Dark though it was, he returned to her effortlessly as if drawn by invisible threads. She had wrapped the blanket around her, but she flipped it open. "Come and sit by me. Keep me warm."

Eli tried his best not to think how he would like to keep her warm, but he suspected he would fight that fight all night. He sat, keeping the weapons at a short distance, still within reach. When she snuggled close, draped the blanket around them both, and handed him some bread and cheese, he realized he was ravenous for food almost as much as for Fanny.

They ate in silence until they had finished their supplies. When Fanny laid her head on his chest, he wrapped an arm around her to support her. She sighed sweetly as if he had put her on silken sheets. He thought she drifted off to sleep, but several minutes later, she spoke.

"Eli?"

"Yes?"

"Thank you."

"What for?" All he'd done was bring her misery.

"For taking such good care of me," she said, her voice trailing off at the end.

That time, he knew she actually had fallen asleep, leaving him to consider his failures as a protector, not least the acute desire for the warm little body pressed next to his. His painful arousal, a penance for sure, would plague him all night.

Be careful what you wish for, Benson, because you may find what you desire most dangled just out of reach. It would be a long night.

⟫⟫⟫✕⟪⟪⟪

COLD AIR DISTURBED Fanny's sleep. She tried to snuggle deeper into the blankets, reaching for her pillow. There was none. She blinked awake, and reality returned. Eli had left her.

She sat up, groaning over sore muscles, and peered around. The sky had lightened, but she thought it wasn't quite full dawn; trees along a bend in the road blocked the view to the east, so she could not be sure. She had slept through the night thanks to Eli's warmth and the protective blanket of his care.

Where is he?

Without Eli, she felt lost, alone, and vulnerable. She scrambled to her feet but saw no sign of him.

He can't have gone too long ago. Her instinct told her she would have known, that she must have awakened right after he had.

The crumbs of their makeshift supper still lay on the ground next to the skin of water, open saddlebag, and one of the pistols. The missing horse, however, had not magically returned overnight. Their other mount, noble steed, calmy nibbled grass nearby.

Fanny picked up the pistol and stood in the narrow lane, peering as far as she could, first one way and then the other. With no more warning than a rustle in the underbrush, Eli exited the wood, and the urge to run to him overtook her. She had gone several strides when she realized how foolishly she behaved, skidded to a stop, and set the pistol down carefully.

Memory of her clinging to him the previous night churned up embarrassment. *What must he think of you?* She drew a calming breath and let him approach.

"What is it, Fanny? Are you upset?" He reached up and tucked a lock of hair over her ear. Wil's hat had come off in the night and lay on the ground. The touch of Eli's hand set her heart racing, and with difficulty, she restrained herself from trying to impose her body on his.

"You were gone. I knew you couldn't be far, but I almost panicked," she said.

"I was exploring. Look what I found. The treasure of late summer!" He reached in his shirt pocket and handed her two blackberries. "They are abundant. I would have picked more for our breakfast, but I heard you moving around. Let's pack up and I'll show you."

With little enough to sort, he soon led her into the woods a short way. As promised a massive bank of blackberry brambles, heavy with fruit, greeted them. He handed her their tin cup. "You harvest. I'll see to our equine friend and saddle up."

She grabbed on to his coat. "Don't leave me. Please. I feel safe when you're near me."

Eli's arrested expression puzzled her. His eyes bored into her, and she waited for him to kiss her, longed for it. He blinked and broke the tension, plucking a blackberry and popping it in her mouth before making a mock bow.

"Eli Benson, white knight at large, at your service, madam," he teased.

She gave him a poke. "I'll alert you if I see any dragons," she laughed.

They stuffed themselves with berries, returned to the clearing next to the road, and packed. "I wish we could find water," she said.

"Me, too. There's little here, and I think our friend Galant here needs it more than we do," he replied, nodding at Goodfellow's horse. He took a sip and handed the waterskin to her.

"Is that his name?" she asked.

"It is now. I didn't think to ask when we left." He saddled with the same efficiency Eli Benson brought to every task, humming to himself. Fanny found the sound comforting. She took a sip of water from the skin and poured the rest into Eli's hat to water the horse as they had the previous night.

Eli set the folded blanket over the pommel. All in readiness, he held his hands together to give her a lift onto the horse before climbing into the saddle behind her.

"Are we going to go through the woods?" she asked over her shoulder. She sat, back straight, rigid in front of him.

"The undergrowth here is thick—as we discovered. I suggest we follow this track a way until we find an opening."

"Perhaps we'll find our other horse. He can't have run too far," she said.

"Or he may be in Cornwall by now," Eli muttered. "Are you comfortable? You look a bit stiff." He put an arm around her waist and pulled her against his chest. "That's better."

It was. His arm felt secure, and she relaxed against him. She wanted to sink into his warmth.

Eli had been correct in his confidence that they would locate an opening, but it was another hour before the woods thinned. They saw no sign of their errant horse. Eli turned them into the canopy of trees, at a moderate trot, on what appeared to be a path.

Thank goodness Eli Benson came into my life. I wish— Fanny wished many things. Some of them centered on the sturdy body behind her. Those thoughts brought a blush to her face. Some of them were contradictory. For now, she simply wished they would reach Clarion Hall safely. She couldn't shake the fears that haunted her after the attack and a night traveling. Perversely, she wished they could stay out on the road, a world outside normal life, where she could nestle in Eli's arms without censure.

CHAPTER TWENTY-NINE

ELI BROUGHT HIS gig to a halt in front of Clarion Hall at dusk, rousing Fanny from her sleep where she leaned against him. They had stumbled into the stable yard of the Willow less than an hour before, staying only long enough to hand Galant, limping yet steadfast, into the hands of Alfred the ostler and hitch Cicero to Eli's gig.

Eli had known Alfred since boyhood and trusted him to care for Goodfellow's loyal horse. Eli explained that he had removed a stone from Galant's hoof but there was a crack in the frog, the soft sole in the center.

"Probably stepped on a piece o'flint. Sharp edges on flint," Alfred murmured, soothing the animal. "Needs poultices and care, but he'll heal. Be right as rain in time." He lifted his eyes and nodded at Eli. "You did well to dismount and walk, Mr. Eli."

Eli had no energy for relief. After Galant had begun to limp, they had walked all day, leading him. Three wrong turns and a swollen creek hadn't helped. Now they arrived at last, filthy, scratched by brambles, aching from their misadventures, and utterly exhausted.

Eli climbed down from the gig, the muscles in his back protesting, and went around to help Fanny. She put her hands on his shoulders. He took her by the waist, but when she sagged against him, he swept her into his arms and carried her up the steps to the hall.

Harris opened the door. His eyes flew open wide, and he hissed a command at a waiting footman.

Eli reached the top, paused to lean against the frame momentarily. He took two steps into the hall's massive entranceway before the sound of running footsteps came from the hallway leading into the lower rooms. Goodfellow dashed forward first, but the Earl of Clarion hurried behind him, came to a halt, and with what looked like deliberate effort, wrapped his customary dignity around him.

Other voices sounded above, and the nursery denizens scrambled down the massive, curving stairs. Several people spoke at once.

"What has happened to Miss Hancock?" the earl demanded.

"What took you so long?" Goodfellow asked.

"Is Fanny dead?" Marj asked with a tremor.

"Is she sick?" Amy demanded with no less horror.

Clarion took command, directing Eli to carry her to the nearest parlor. He spewed a spate of orders that Harris most likely would have known to do without being told. "Send to the kitchen for food—and tea. Bring Miss Hancock's maid to assist her, and have bathwater sent up to the room we prepared for her."

"Water," Eli interjected. "Quickly." He knelt at her side.

"Send for Dr. Farley," Clarion continued, smoothly.

"No need." Fanny's voice sounded weak and thready as Eli laid her on a sofa. Wil's hat came off in the process, and her hair tumbled around her shoulders.

"Every need," Clarion said.

Eli took her hands in his. "We're home," he said rather pointlessly.

Fanny smiled wearily, her eyes fixed on his. "Thanks to you." Her eyes flickered over his shoulder at Clarion. "I'm sorry to be such a weakling. It has been a trying day."

Amy pressed close to Eli's shoulder. "Are you truly well, Fan? You frightened me."

Fanny pushed herself upright with a groan. "Merely tired."

"Exhausted. And scratched to bits and..." Eli's voice trailed off when she raised her hand.

"But not shot. Not kidnapped. Not abducted to some horrid place." She glanced up at Goodfellow. "Thanks to my heroic protectors."

Eli's heart twisted. *Of course. Goodfellow is the heroic one. And Reilly. Reilly!* He looked up at Goodfellow. "How are Reilly and Williams? Was there a second attack?"

"Both are healing nicely." Before Goodfellow could continue, the pot boy bustled in with a jug of water and two mugs, awed to be in such an august assembly.

Fanny's hands, Eli saw, trembled while she downed first one mug of water and then another. He did the same.

She dropped her head back against the sofa. "Heaven. The most glorious drink I've ever had," she said.

"It was only water, silly," Amy told her. The little girl hopped up next to her big sister, and Fanny gave her a one-armed hug.

"I pulled Eli's gig around to the stables. Harris sent his gear to his rooms and Fanny's to hers." Wil came directly to the group huddled around his sister. "Are you well, Fanny? You look a mess."

"Do not insult your sister, young man," Clarion said sternly. "She has had an ordeal."

Wil ignored him. "We did well. Reilly said I looked just like you. I practiced walking like you do, so I just sauntered up to the carriage and Corporal Goodfellow handed me up like a real lady."

Fanny spoke simultaneously, "I must look a fright. We slept on the ground last night."

"May I suggest we allow Miss Hancock to bathe and rest? We will send supper up on a tray, and Farley should be here within an hour," Clarion said. His word was *suggest*, but Eli knew a command when he heard one. The children were sent to the nursery with a promise of a visit from Fanny in the morning.

Eli struggled to his feet, prepared to assist Fanny to rise, but Clarion got there first, offering her a hand and then his arm. "Feel free to eat, Benson, but I'll have your report after I escort her to her room."

Eli trailed after them as far as the drawing room door. Fanny glanced back at Eli once, but she leaned on her brother's arm as he led her up the stairs and appeared to reassure him as they walked.

It was over. They were back in the real world, and Fanny, his Fanny, was back in the care of her brother. The earl. Eli's employer.

⤜⤛

FANNY SANK DOWN into the warm water scented with lavender and emptied her mind for a moment. It didn't last. What crowded back was Eli. Eli holding her through the night. Eli feeding her blackberries. Eli leading her by the hand, cajoling, bullying, and teasing so she could walk one more step and then another. Eli carrying her up the stairs, bringing her home. Peace settled over her. Her future may still be murky, but she knew the bone-deep peace that comes when someone cares for you.

"Shall I wash your hair?" Susan, safe, well, and cheerful, offered.

"Yes, please."

Soon enough the maid had her scrubbed, dressed in a soft nightgown and buddled into a thick robe. Susan arranged the contents of the supper tray on the table while Fanny dried her hair by the fire and Susan chattered about her own adventure.

"Only two of 'em came, because our men had already taken three of theirs the first time. 'She ain't here,' Goodfellow told them. 'Leave afore we do you like we did your fellows.'"

"They simply left?"

"No, ma'am. They demanded to see. The boss one, he sent the other over, and Goodfellow set a gun up alongside his head, but he looked in anyway, knocking on the seat like you were hidden in the hallow. But you weren't, of course, and they left. Wil asked Goodfellow why we didn't shoot 'em, and Goodfellow said as how it was safer not to start shooting with us in the carriage. I think your brother was cast down that there was no fight."

"Where?" Fanny asked.

"We were past Nottingham. Right on the road to Ashmead. Took nerve, that. After noon it was."

Eli and I were just coming free of the woods. Miles from the devilish louts. She cast another prayer of thanksgiving heavenward.

Fanny dragged herself to the table, believing herself too tired to eat. Two bites reminded her how long she'd gone without food, and she tucked into a savory beef stew with vigor.

I wish Eli had come up so we could eat together. She knew the thought for ridiculous as soon as it passed through her mind. *In your bedroom? You dressed in nightclothes, Fanny?* She missed him.

A knock interrupted her train of thought. Susan opened the door to Clarion and a gentleman Fanny recognized from the Willow, Dr. Farley.

The physician beamed at her. "It seems nature, a bath, and a good meal have done my work for me," he said.

Susan tucked Fanny in bed at the physician's bidding and hovered nearby. In short order he had checked her pulse, dismissed any thought of fever, and pronounced her fit and healthy. "A good night's sleep should finish the job," he said.

"Is Eli—"

"He is my next concern, Miss Hancock. You're not to worry." His avuncular smile might have comforted her on a different night. She found the maelstrom of her emotions too difficult to sort and had no energy for the man.

Clarion gestured toward the door. "Sleep well. We can talk tomorrow."

They were gone before she could say more. She stared at the ceiling a moment in frustration, sighed, and reminded herself she could talk it all over with Eli in the morning. Her lids drifted shut, and she slept.

⇥⇥⇥⇤⇤⇤

ELI WAS URGED to the kitchen, where Goodfellow and the staff hovered around, plying him with warm bread, savory stew, and an apple tart delightful enough to bring joy to the most hardened heart. Wil followed, making short work of more tart. All the while, the threads of stories twisted and folded around one another—the carriage ride, the pretense, the robbers in one thread; the horses, the woods, the sleeping hard, walking miles in another—until they both came to a neat conclusion, everyone safe and at Clarion Hall.

Paul Farley popped in, reassured Eli repeatedly that Fanny was fit and well, pronounced him equally so, and happily accepted an apple tart.

Clarion joined them just then, and all rose to bow. He waved them down and sat across from Eli. "I won't keep you long. You'll want a warm bath and a good sleep, I warrant. I've already heard Corporal Goodfellow's account. I must say I had my doubts about the decision to send Miss Hancock cross-country with only one man for her protection and would not have countenanced it if I'd been there."

"We had few good choices, my lord," Eli said.

The earl nodded. "I can see that, and it ended well enough but at some cost to my sister. How is it you came to be on foot?"

Eli explained about bolting horses and rocks under shoes, flooded streams, and brambles.

"Am I to understand she slept on the ground?" The earl appeared horrified.

"She did, indeed. I sat with a weapon nearby." Eli didn't mention she'd slept in his arms.

"You were alone with her all night," the earl said, brows raised.

"Yes, my lord. Her safety demanded it." Eli didn't like Clarion's troubled expression, but the earl gave a firm nod at his words.

"Well done, Benson. Thank you for your vigilance. She's safe here." The earl rose. "You'll want to bathe and change."

"That won't be necessary. I'm fit—as the good doctor here can vouch." He nodded toward Farley, who had risen as well. "I'll be at my desk tomorrow. Perhaps I can begin looking for that property we discussed."

"For my sister and her siblings? Not as long as there is any sort of threat. They are safer here. Goodfellow has the security well in hand. You rest tomorrow."

"I'm sure work has accumulated on my desk."

Clarion smiled one of his sad smiles. "I'm certain it has. In addition, word has come about your inquiries in the Manchester courts. I'll have it put on your desk in the morning as well." He turned at the door. "How did your tasks in London go?"

"Without problems. Bank audited. Dower house rental posted to the papers. I'll give you my report on publishing houses tomorrow."

"Well done, Benson, efficient as always." The earl left him, and the cook pushed another slice of tart his way.

That will be my epitaph. Eli Benson—he was an efficient soul. His appetite gone, he gave the extra slice to Wil.

CHAPTER THIRTY

E LI ROSE AT dawn as was his custom, went to the kitchen for coffee as he always did, and took a brisk walk to shake off sleep as was his habit. He ate his breakfast in the servants' hall like he normally did and checked with the stable master, the butler, and the housekeeper, while they were all together, for any burning issues. There were none.

He missed Fanny, the feel of her, the smell—the taste. He hesitated in the hallway only briefly, staring in the direction of the breakfast room, the other public rooms, and the family quarters to which Clarion had swept her up the previous evening. It wasn't a place Eli felt comfortable.

He pulled his spine straight and turned on his heel, to his own domain, feeling awkward and unsure, all his confidence and determination to press his suit—as soon as he completed the business in Manchester—dripping away.

The office greeted him as expected. The desk neatly organized. The chair comfortable and adjusted exactly as he liked it. His favorite watercolor paintings of the valley of the Afon River on the wall. Incoming complaints, invoices, and reports stacked in the proper basket. Work awaiting his attention. All familiar, all exactly as Eli liked them. None of it gave him joy.

Why can't you get to work, Benson?

He tapped his pencil on the edge of the desk, unable to decide where to begin. He knew the answer. He wanted to run up to the family wing to check on Fanny. He reminded himself that he had brought her safely to the hall, where she could be guarded closely and cosseted as befit the daughter of an earl. In this world, she wasn't his to care for, at least no more than any of the people of Clarion Hall.

Rob seemed to believe Eli had a chance with her, and he clung to that thought, but for now, the work the earl had assigned in her regard wasn't finished. He still had to deal with the paperwork in Manchester. He wouldn't have her company when he did. His heart ached.

The only cure is work. Get to it, Benson. He pulled the basket forward and began to sort the mail, the bills, and the other items that required attention, into piles.

"You have visitors, Mr. Benson." John, the most diligent of Clarion's footmen, held out two thick packets of paper, the responses from the chancery and episcopal courts in Manchester, no doubt. Their seals, Eli saw, had been broken.

"Visitors?" He accepted the papers, his mind on the contents. *Who on earth would be here for him at this hour?*

"I don't need to be announced, young man. I know my way!" His father's confident voice brought him to his feet.

"Da! I didn't expect you." He leaned both hands on the desk and grinned at the old man and Emma, right behind him.

"Did you think to slip in after all we heard and not let your family see you? Alfred said you came in looking like something that had been dragged through the sheep meadow by his feet tied to a bolting horse, took your gig, and left without a word to me." Da's stern expression shamed Eli as effectively as it had done when he'd been ten.

"I'm sorry, Da. I had Fanny to care for. I needed to get her under this roof as quickly as I could." To Eli's irritation, his face felt hot. He probably looked red as a beet.

Emma made free with one of his side chairs, seating herself, brows raised. "Tell us about how the two of you came to be wandering in on your own."

Eli breathed in sharply and glanced at John, watching avidly from the door. "That will be all, John. Do stop and tell cook to send tea." He gestured to the second side chair, and his father sat. Feeling a fool to be sitting behind the steward's desk, talking to family, he pulled his around, and they formed a circle.

"What do you know about what occurred?" he asked them.

They knew a bit, as it happened. The decoy caravan had passed the Willow early in the day, and Da had sent Alfred up to the hall to ask about it.

"You were missing at that point, and we kept a sharp eye out all day. If it hadn't been the evening rush, I would have spied you in the stable yard," Da said. "Word in the kitchen is Miss Hancock—our Fanny—is safe and well. Alfred had her at death's door."

Emma glanced at Da. "It was all I could do to keep him from tearing up here in the dark to check on you," she said.

"Thank you for that! Miss Hancock is fit and well," Eli said. At least he hoped so. He forced himself to rely on Farley's word. "We had a time of it, so Alfred's alarm is understandable. She was so exhausted; she was ready to drop. She slept all the way up from the Willow."

"When did you separate from Goodfellow and the others? Alfred reported it was two days ago." Da leaned forward, and Eli retold the story for what felt like the dozenth time, emphasizing Fanny's strength and courage, leaving out the way she'd collapsed in his arms. Or slept in them.

When he finished, his father gazed at him intently, probing the hollow places in his soul with a father's unerring concern. The old man spoke softly. "You cared for her well, son. You can feel good about that." His eyes searched Eli's for a response.

Eli glanced at a painting of the Willow and blinked twice. "Certainly. The plan worked as we designed, hard though it was on her. We fooled them."

"How is she this morning?" Emma asked, curiosity vivid on her face.

"I don't know. I don't pay attention to what happens in the family wing, and it isn't my place to query the staff about them." He glared pointedly at his sister, daring her to ask impertinent questions about Fanny or his dealings with her. Da's knowing eyes were bad enough.

Tea arrived, and they chatted briefly, Emma exclaiming over his overnight adventure, her hints about his relationship with Fanny becoming more obvious. Da deflected her efforts with local gossip until Eli pointedly picked up the papers from Manchester. "This, I fear, is urgent. I may be returning to Manchester again on the Rundles' behalf, at the earl's direction."

They rose and Eli with them. Da clapped him on the shoulder, pulling him closer than perhaps necessary, to lean his forehead on Eli's, and murmuring, "You're looking fine, son. I needed to see for myself."

"I am well, Da. Truly," Eli assured him, dragging him the rest of the way into a hug. The old man cleared his throat and pulled away, unaccustomed to the gesture.

"We expect you for dinner on Sunday, Eli," Emma chirped, giving him a peck on the cheek.

They left, and he returned his chair to the desk. "Perhaps with interruptions over, I can get some work done," he muttered.

FANNY CAME AWAKE slowly and blinked at the sunny room, brightly lit even though the curtains remained closed. Susan sat in a chair by the window, mending. She saw no sign of Eli, and the dread feeling she'd had the day before, waking alone by the trees, returned. She let her breathing steady and tried to sort her muddled thoughts.

You're in the earl's manor. The earl, your brother. Who is determined to care for you. She had hoped for assistance and gotten more than she'd bargained for. *Amy and Wil are here and safe. Somewhere.* She squeezed her eyes shut. *Eli is here, too. You'll see him in a while.*

She sat, drawing a smile from her maid, who tugged the bellpull. "They're waiting below stairs to bring you a breakfast tray," the girl said. "I left orders to send warm water, too."

"I would prefer to eat with the others," Fanny said.

"Goodness, ma'am. They ate two hours or more ago. The morning is mostly gone," Susan said, busying herself laying out clothing. "I had plenty of time to unpack your trunk yesterday while everyone fretted over you and Mr. Benson being missing."

"We weren't missing. We were making our way here. People fretted?"

Susan spoke over her shoulder, "The earl paced to those front windows all afternoon. Goodfellow sent two of the grooms out looking. He planned to mount a full-scale search party this morning if you hadn't turned up. The grooms returned last night two hours after you did."

Fanny shook her head. "They missed us—or we missed them."

"All's well that ends well, I say. You're where you belong. This one?" Susan asked, holding up a blue muslin gown, Fanny's favorite.

Fanny nodded, and both women were distracted by a scratch at the door. Susan pulled bedcurtains to shelter Fanny and opened the door to a footman carrying water. Another followed with a tray.

In the privacy of the bedcurtains, Fanny mulled the maid's words. *"Where you belong."* Fanny wasn't so sure Clarion Hall was where the forgotten bastard daughter belonged—the Willow had been comfortable enough—but the thought had been kindly meant.

The door clicked shut, and she slid out of bed, eager to start her day. An hour later, fed and dressed, she made her way to the nursery floor to reassure Amy and thank Wil again for his bravery. She found the schoolroom empty except for the tiny between-stairs maid, who had been assigned to tidy up. The girl told her they had gone to the stables to meet a newborn foal, suggesting Fanny could probably catch up with them.

The last thing she wanted to greet was another horse, however adorable. She retraced her steps and descended the grand staircase to the first floor. She found the earl in the breakfast room, lingering over coffee and reading the London papers, a sheet of foolscap for notes at his side.

He rose and inclined his head. "Miss Hancock, I am relieved to see you looking so well. May I offer you coffee? I understood that a tray was sent up for you."

"It was, indeed. Your excellent staff has seen to my every need."

He nodded, taking the quality of his servants for granted. He gestured to a seat.

She sat so he could, if for no other reason, but waved off a suggestion he order tea for her and accepted a cup of coffee to be polite. "I thought I might find Eli here."

The earl frowned, and she wondered if it was her use of Eli's Christian name. "Benson rises early. Certainly earlier than I do. I expect you would find him in the estate office, going about his business," he said.

She had no response for that, and good manners required that she not jump up and run to the estate office.

"Did you sleep well?" The earl appeared as awkward as Fanny felt. She realized they had had few opportunities to speak alone together.

"I did, indeed. Thank you, my lord. You've done so much for me. I understand from E—Mr. Benson that you've directed him to find a cottage that may suit the ducklings and me. You must know that is an enormous relief."

The earl inclined his head. "The Clarion estate is obliged to assist— to the extent we can. I relied on Benson to manage the financial decisions. But don't think of that now. As long as some madman is intent on abducting you, we are better served keeping you here at the hall, where we can manage security."

Fanny felt her brows rise. She hadn't considered the matter. She had expected a clean hand off of assistance, not an ongoing participation. Interference. Her confused feelings—longing for safety, yearning for family, desire for independence—unsettled her. "For now, perhaps. We won't trouble you for long," she said. She wondered what Eli thought.

They sipped coffee companionably. When the earl picked up his paper, she asked, "I see you take notes. Political matters coming to a head?"

Clarion's sad smile held his respect for her question. "No more than usual. Some of it is political talk. Mostly, however, I like to follow the economic news, the crimes, the public sentiment. I look for things Parliament should be addressing before they become crises."

"Wise." Her response seemed to please this rather stern man. She had to remind herself he was her brother. Moments later she finished her coffee, rose, and curtseyed. "I'll leave you to it."

"Enjoy your day, Miss Hancock, and please know you are welcome here as long as needed. We won't abandon you."

She left him, oddly touched, but paused at the door. "My lord…"

He glanced up at her.

"Forgive me if I'm being impertinent, but you've been so kind. Do you think you might call me Fanny as the others do?" She hadn't realized it mattered, but this dignified and distinguished man was as much her sibling as Rob and Maddy—as Wil and Amy, come to that. She didn't want to be Miss Hancock, an outsider here.

His startled expression softened into something else and finally into his sad smile. "Madelyn would have corrected me before now, Fanny," he said. He sighed. "I believe, that being the case, that you might call me David in private. Clarion in public, as Madelyn does."

"Thank you," she murmured, wiping moisture from her eyes as she made her way through the house. It took her two wrong turns and a helpful footman to find the corridor that led past the kitchens to the storerooms and the estate office. The door was firmly shut.

At her knock, a voice—his voice—called, "Enter."

Eli sat behind a massive desk, piles of papers in front of him, pen in hand. He rose when she entered. "Miss Hancock! Good morning. I wasn't expecting you."

Miss Hancock? Not you! He held himself rigid, with the desk like a shield between them.

"I—" She swallowed, coming to a halt. A niggle of suspicion grew. The earl was his employer, after all. *Has Clarion—David—expressed disapproval of our—what is our relationship? Friendship? What utter nonsense. It is for us to sort and none of his concern.*

"Please, sit. Do you need my assistance?" Eli asked. The efficient steward had returned, all business.

She sat, tamping down hurt. "I believe I need your opinion. My brother has suggested—more or less ordered—that I stay at Clarion Hall for safety and that we postpone the search for a cottage of my own. Do you agree with this dictate?"

Eli made a show of straightening the papers in front of him. "It is sound advice, Miss Hancock. You know Rob, Sir Robert"—he stumbled over the uncomfortable (and in Fanny's opinion, ludicrous) return to formality—"and his organization are investigating the string of abductions. As long as an obsessive madman wishes to add you to his victims, you are safest here."

Fanny's heart sank, but he looked directly at her and spoke more gently, "I do have some news. We have word from both courts. Chancery has agreed to forestall foreclosure on the shop pending the outcome of the petition regarding the personal estate of Horace Rundle. The ecclesiastical court received the earl's request that you be named administrator of Wil's inheritance. Unfortunately, they either misunderstood or ignored his preference and wished to name the earl himself as administrator. Clarion's note in the margin to me is, 'Kindly address this in Manchester.'"

"I can be ready to travel in the morning," Fanny responded, excitement growing.

"No." He glared at her.

"What do you mean, 'no'? It is my business to conduct, *Mr.* Benson." She glared right back. "I'm going with you or without you."

He surged to his feet. "Damn it, Fanny, I'm not having you on the road. We would need to take half the king's army to keep you safe. Have you learned nothing?"

She rose as well and leaned as far across his desk as she could. "'Fanny,' is it? Make up your mind!" she shouted. "And when were you put in charge of my safety?"

Anger. Frustration. Hurt. She saw them all cross his face. His features settled into a troubled mix, his aspect begging. "Fanny, I can't bear to go through it again. My heart almost died when they held up the coach. You cannot go to Manchester."

She stood up, her hands clenched in front of her. "Very well, Mr. Benson, solicitor and steward extraordinaire. Take yourself off to court on the earl's behalf. Correct their misunderstanding if you can. But know this—" She leaned both hands on his desk and pinned him with a look. "—what is between us is not finished. We will address it when you return."

They glared at each other across the expanse of his desk, but Eli couldn't sustain it. His eyes softened, and Fanny felt certain she could see his pulse pounding in his throat above the informal cravat he wore. It gave her hope.

CHAPTER THIRTY-ONE

THE EARL'S BUSINESS doomed Emma Corbin to disappointment as it often did. Eli did not attend his family's Sunday dinner. By the time they sat down to her lovingly prepared capon, Eli rode, hell-bent, along Manchester Road, well past his overnight stop, ignoring custom and law by traveling on the Sabbath.

Consultation with Goodfellow had concluded with a dictate to travel on horseback for speed and flexibility. Eli had agreed but argued he could manage on his own, every able-bodied guard needed at the hall. In the end, he'd accepted the company of Tommy Withers, the Clarion groom, who rode behind him, armed and avidly scanning the road, pleased to have a role. He wasn't needed.

They arrived in Manchester late in the afternoon, well before dark, and bespoke a room at a modest hotel, stabling their mounts for the duration. The courts wouldn't open until morning. Eli, torn among checking on the Hancock drapery, seeking out Holliday, and investigating Fanny's abduction, concluded none were likely to be fruitful on Sunday.

Still, he changed into his dockworker garb, determined to begin seeking an answer to one question that plagued him. Manchester had no true port for ocean-going vessels. How were the criminals transporting their hostages?

The Sunday law didn't ban taverns from serving food, and he determined to seek out a dockside eatery. Tommy, who had collapsed in whoops of laughter over Eli's appearance, followed along with no complaints about the walk, weapons tucked away on his person. There would be stories told in the Clarion servants' hall when they returned.

Eli had learned on the previous trip that goods came into Manchester via the Bridgewater Canal from Runcorn and the ports at Liverpool. Some—much fewer—still came via the Mersey and Irwell Navigation system. It seemed an unlikely candidate for the felonious activity in question, but the Irwell River was closer on a late Sunday afternoon. They passed a succession of quays and wharfs, empty of activity but surrounded by coal barges and other small vessels feeding the manufactories and commerce of Manchester. Soon enough they were engulfed in the sweltering heat of the Riverman's Heaven, a filthy, rat-infested public house steps from the river.

The bulk of people clustered around tables and sipping from chipped teacups at a rough bar gave every appearance of laborers, although Eli's innate caution told him rogues of all sorts were likely scattered among them.

He and Tommy ordered food, expecting little.

"Tea?" the server inquired.

"Is that the only choice?" Tommy asked. Eli suppressed a laugh.

"On Sunday? That or river water. Pick your poison."

The tea served in mugs was hot and strong, the food filling and surprisingly tasty. Eli wondered what might have been in the cups at the bar. *Contraband hidden in porcelain?*

He regaled a puzzled Tommy with talk of the London docks, spinning his informative afternoon into the implication of long experience. "Of course, there's work to be had here, if you're looking. Different and not as much but plenty of it. You'd make more in London, but then, the expense of living would eat it up." He cringed at the sound of his voice, convinced it marked him as an outsider at best, some sort of government agent at worst. It may have.

A gentleman—a term Eli applied loosely—in a stained shirt with a towel tied around his waist approached the table. He glanced around the room, pulled up a chair, and sat. "From London, did we hear?" he asked.

"I spent time on the docks there," Eli answered.

"Not much, I'll wager." The man pinned Eli with a pointed study of his person.

Lies never worked, or if they did, they died quickly. Eli decided the truth—some of it, at least—would serve him better. He inclined his head. "A brief but highly educational stint."

"And more with the river police?" the man asked, not trying to keep his voice down.

"I've met them. Also briefly. I'm not one of them," Eli swore.

Their visitor's gaze didn't waver. Neither did he attack them, for which Eli was grateful. "Here to add to your education?"

"Something like that," Eli said. "River traffic is different from the Port of London."

"That it is." The gaze remained steady.

Eli returned it.

"What is your question?" the man asked eventually.

"I'm wondering how a determined man—or group of men—might get goods out of Manchester and out to sea," Eli said.

That startled his interrogator. "Same as it comes—in boats and barges. Mostly materials in, finished goods out. Down to the ports in Liverpool and Birkenhead."

"What if the cargo was…questionable?" Eli asked.

A snort of laughter met that one. "Free trade? You're on the wrong end of that stick. It comes from the seaports, the inlets and coves, inland. Not the other way around."

Eli shook his head. "Not free trade. I know nothing of that. What if these persons don't want their cargo seen? There are bound to be inspectors on the quay."

Intrigued now, the man scratched his chin. "Stolen?"

"After a fashion." Eli watched the man consider the matter for a while before he leaned in and whispered, "Human."

His newfound source showed less shock than Eli expected. "It happens," the tavern keeper murmured. The man shook his head. "Lowest of the low, them. But you're right. It would be hard to hide along here. Too many eyes and ears. Men may be poor, may dodge a rule or two, but that? Not likely to be overlooked. At least by most."

"Can you say any particular organization is dodgier than the others?" Eli asked.

"Not that dodgy. No such business in the city." The tavern keeper glanced uneasily around the room. If any of those listening avidly disagreed or had information to add, none spoke up. The man put both hands on the table to push up.

"One more thing," Eli called. "If a man with funds had a ship of his own, one he didn't want the harbormaster peering into too closely, where might he find anchorage?" It had been the suggestion of the river police, and a good one.

The man shook his head. "Ocean goer won't get too far up the Mersey coming this way, and nowhere on the canal. Ships that size don't pass Runcorn. Might find dockage along the Irish Sea between Liverpool and the Dee. Along the Deeside, maybe." A sly grin came over his face. "Of course, a dockman would have known that," he said and he walked away.

Early Monday morning, Eli visited the chancery and verified the hold on foreclosure by the bank. He went next to the estate agent to show him proof and urge patience until such time as Miss Hancock received authority to sell on her brother's behalf. Finally, he rode to the Hancock drapery to simply inspect the state of the property, finding it in order. By midmorning he had also popped in on Abbot the greengrocer, who'd greeted Eli warmly and assured him the neighbors were keeping a sharp eye on "Miss Hancock's store."

The fly in the ointment irritating Eli's sense of right and his need for well-conducted business was the ecclesiastical court's refusal to give Fanny the writ of authority to sell Wil's property. To clarify that matter, he had to travel to the bishop's court in Chester, forty miles south, a task for another day.

The larger shadow preying on his mind drove him to seek out Holliday, Rob's contact in Manchester. No one had said, but the man appeared to be one of Rockford's contracts, if not an actual agent. Fanny couldn't act—couldn't, in fact, leave Clarion Hall—until they found the madman seeking her. If Rob and his contacts couldn't do that, nothing Eli did mattered.

Holliday, whose office turned out to be a coffee shop between the commercial district and the quays, greeted him warily. "Back in Manchester, Mr. Benson? I hope you and Sir Robert were able to get Miss Hancock safely to that earl of hers."

"That we did, Holliday. Have you made any progress in ferreting out the men behind her abduction?"

"No more than I reported to Sir Robert. We have Edwards in jail, awaiting transportation. His immediate superior—man name of Everhard—disappeared from Manchester. He must be lying low because no one has seen him since that night at the Happy Cock. If he surfaces, I'll nab him sure as can be."

"*Reported to Sir Robert.*" Rob hadn't told Eli that bit, and it rankled. Perhaps it didn't matter. "Everhard is the one you chased that night? The one we want is above him. Whoever is directing this has more power and reach than a local thug." *And is a lunatic.*

Holliday nodded genially. "We're working bottom-up, Benson. We find Everhard, we'll know who's behind him. It takes patience."

"That's it? You sit and wait for him to bob up from the sewer?" Eli explained what they knew about Fanny being targeted. He expounded his theories about the transportation of victims, and his queries along the quays.

Holliday's amusement poked at Eli's eroding temper. "We have men along the river, Benson. If Everhard appears, we'll know."

"But have you—"

"Leave the investigation to the professionals, Benson. We'll contact you when we know something. You stick to estate sales and court cases."

Eli glared impotently across the table for several seconds. Holliday had shut the door on further discussion. Eli stood and snatched up his valise, sorry he'd brought the damn thing that branded him for the solicitor he was. "I'll let you know what I find," he said.

Holliday didn't hide his growing amusement. "You do that."

⁂

AN UNEXPECTED VISIT from Emma Corbin to Clarion Hall lightened Fanny's day. Harris showed Eli's sister into Fanny's small sitting room, where she had been struggling to write. Emma bustled over to a seat, breathless from hurrying. "Too soon for word from Eli, I'll warrant, but we've heard from Rob."

"Clarion did as well. A courier came last night—likely the same one—and I expect Goodfellow will have received some pointed words as well."

"The corporal must have reported the attack on the road, because Rob is on his way to Ashmead."

Fanny nodded and smiled a bit. She'd grown rather fond of both her new brothers, but Rob was rather more comfortable a presence than Clarion. "It will be good to have him here."

"I hope he brings Lucy. Da longs to dandle Kit on his knee," Emma said.

"He must know I'm safe here at the hall!" Fanny said. *I'm practically a prisoner.* She dismissed the thought; they all meant well. "Did you hasten up here to tell me Rob is coming?" Fanny asked.

"No. Something else. Probably nothing but a worry in any case,"

Emma said.

"We seem to be plagued with those lately." Fanny wondered if the men weren't the only overprotective Bensons. "What is it, Emma?"

"Eunice Norton is a gossip, but she has sharp eyes. She doesn't miss much. Eunice overheard a stranger asking questions about the hall."

"That's the worry?" Fanny pursed her lips to keep from laughing.

"Don't dismiss it. We don't get many strangers going up and down the coaching road, asking questions!" Emma's grim expression told Fanny the concern ran deep.

"What do you mean, 'up and down'?"

"Eunice says that Bessie Griggs, the butcher's wife, told her something similar. Then this morning the man turned up at our stables, claiming his horse threw a shoe. Said he needed it right fast. Asked similar questions. My Ellis came to tell me to come up here to warn you."

Fanny pinched the skin at her throat, mulling that over. "What did this stranger look like? Was he quality?"

"You mean like peerage? No. Nothing like Clarion or Glenmoor. Dressed in black but good quality, Eunice said. Very tall. Black hair."

"It wasn't the Earl of Grimsley," Fanny murmured, immensely relieved. The earl—all blond, sleek elegance—who closely resembled her fictional hero, had fallen so short he had become the villain in her mind. Thank goodness he hadn't followed her to Ashmead.

Emma shrugged. "He rode off, and with luck, he left the area. He could be lurking, though. After what happened last year with that awful American, folks around here don't take anything for granted."

Fanny had heard the story of Maddy's stepsons and the boy being held as a hostage by a deranged American. She dismissed it as irrelevant to her situation. "Don't invent worries, Emma. Some random stranger passing through is no threat. People are bound to be curious about the major houses in a neighborhood."

"Still, I'll pass it on to Corporal Goodfellow while I'm here," Emma said.

Fanny didn't argue. "Did I hear your children have been invited for nursery tea?"

The rest of the conversation moved smoothly to children and their antics.

CHAPTER THIRTY-TWO

ECCLESIASTICAL MATTERS FOR Manchester belonged with the bishop of Chester, whose deanery lay near the ancient Cathedral of Christ in that city. Eli left his hotel early, Tommy Withers at his side, packed and ready to travel on to Ashmead as soon as he dealt with the matter of Fanny's right to serve as administrator for her brother.

Just after noon, he was shown to the canon of the cathedral parish who handled such matters.

"The church believes a young boy requires a man's judgment." The canon, a bony, harsh-faced specimen, spoke through his nose—no small feat, Eli thought, with that nose lifted so high in the air.

Eli's temper, already short after his interview with Holliday and another blasted day on horseback, stretched ominously tight and threatened to snap at the self-important cleric. Eli took a firm grip on it and challenged the canon. "You will see from his letter that the Earl of Clarion disagrees in this case. Miss Hancock is his sister, and he is well satisfied she can best handle the affairs of her younger brother. My employer demands that you see to it."

The canon stiffened. His clerical paternalism slipped briefly, revealing his ugly underbelly, but he picked his role up, wrapping his expression and posture in the cloak of ecclesiastical authority. "My dear Mr. Benson, the church finds that young women, particularly those of questionable birth, are prone to reprehensible influences." He sniffed. "The earl may well choose to delegate to his *half*-sister, but his oversight would be vital. We recommend he watch her affairs closely."

I'm not your dear anything. Any oversight would fall to Eli should Clarion choose to exercise it, but the very concept insulted Fanny's intelligence.

The canon sighed wearily and went on before Eli could respond, "The woman in question isn't even of age."

"As you see, the earl requests that she become administrator on the day she turns twenty-one, a matter of days now."

The canon looked as if he had bitten into a lemon.

Eli glared at the man. "I demand to speak to the bishop."

The canon's startled expression gratified. Apparently, the dolt was unaccustomed to challenges.

The canon's chin quivered in outrage. "You can appeal, certainly. I would be happy to carry—"

"Let me spell this out clearly. The Earl of Clarion demands an interview with the bishop. I am his steward and the legal representative who acts on his behalf." Eli clamped his jaw shut and glared with unwavering determination. In the end, he bullied his way to an appointment the next day.

He found Tommy with the horses. "We're staying over in Chester," he muttered.

Tommy accepted that with equanimity but hinted that food might be their next goal, since they'd broken their fast in the wee hours, in the dark.

They found a café across the square, where Eli glowered at the massive cathedral as if it was somehow to blame for his dispute with the church. A fine meat pie later, his mood improved and a memory surfaced. Hadn't it been built by a monastery in the eleventh century? Eight hundred years! The big stone pile had survived the dissolution of the monasteries and been promoted to cathedral. It had also survived the roundhead revolution and the Jacobite incursion that had bedeviled Manchester. His anger began to wane. The building was far finer than the men who staffed it. He ordered another pint of ale.

One small thought sparked to life and lightened his mood further, something the tavern keeper had suggested when Eli had asked where they might find dockage for undocumented private vessels. *"Along the Irish Sea between Liverpool and the Dee."* Chester abutted the River Dee near the place where it widened into the estuary. A ride along the river to the sea would fill his afternoon and might soothe his ruffled feathers. It would probably be a fruitless exercise, but it might help him regain enough control to avoid punching a bishop.

FANNY STOPPED IN the nursery one afternoon to find Reverend Styles, who had come to tutor Wil, sitting on a rickety chair sized for children. The hall's nursery needed some adult-sized chairs and more desks. She had also noticed that the large cloak closet could double for much-needed storage if they added shelves. She wandered below stairs and sought out Mrs. Harris. Surely the housekeeper knew what could be done about it.

She did. "Mr. Benson will see to it," the housekeeper said with a confident nod of her head." With that, the subject obviously closed.

Mr. Benson will see to it. The words grated on Fanny's nerves, sending her pacing up and down the maze of corridors that was Clarion Hall.

Harris had said roughly the same thing over dinner when the earl had asked him about wine supplies. In fact, Eli's name echoed through every day since their confrontation in his office, after which he'd left without a word.

She had been walking near the stable yard when Goodfellow had complained the stables needed attention due to the additional horses. The head groom had promised to write up a plan for Mr. Benson.

Tenants had come looking for Mr. Benson; the project to drain the lower fields required his attention. Reassured that he would return within the week, they'd gone away satisfied. Mr. Benson handled wages. Mr. Benson oversaw supply orders. Mr. Benson hired staff, ordered repairs to tenant cottages, and oversaw planning for harvest. At twenty-four, he had become indispensable.

In short, Clarion Hall depended on the man entirely. So did Fanny. *Wil's inheritance depends on him. I'll never see my cottage until Eli makes it happen.*

She came to a stop at the door to the estate office, hardly realizing that had been her destination. His office radiated his presence, from the tidy workspace on his desk to the attractive watercolors. The faint hint of his scent, all balsam and pine, lingered in the air. She plopped herself in his chair with a dash of defiance and breathed deeply.

Indispensable. Her very well-being seemed to hinge on Eli's presence. Her joy certainly did; she couldn't deny it. She needed and wanted Eli Benson.

Where is the wretch? How long can it take to complete the legal business?

Sun blessed Eli's decision to explore the Dee and its estuary.

He and Tommy had ridden out from Chester and into Wales on the north bank of the Dee to face a decision at Connah's Quay, where the river widened into the estuary. Should they continue along the north bank back into England to Parkgate or follow the southern shore through Wales?

Eli stood in his stirrups, gazing out at an empty mass of reeds and wetlands to the north. The road twisted due that direction and back away from the river at that point. Parkgate might be a candidate but equally likely could be a regulated port, and the route would most certainly be roundabout. He decided to follow the course to the south.

Decision made, he and Tommy found their way across the river.

Mazes of water tracks, natural and man-made, confusing and dotted with expanding industrial facilities, blessed them less than the weather had. They passed riverboats, barges, small crafts, and small quays, with no sign of anchorage for a rich man's yacht. They passed large stretches of land watered only at high tide. Frustration and the knowledge that nothing could be accomplished in Chester that day drove them on past first one fishing village and then another with no luck. They made only brief stops to rest and water their mounts.

Tommy suggested they turn back if they were to make it to Chester before dark, but Eli knew that the arrogant little canon had scheduled Eli's appointment for late the next day.

Eli had become a man obsessed. Visions of Fanny drove him. Fanny in the hands of the brutes behind the Happy Cock. Fanny shoved to the rail of the Great Pagoda. Fanny forced to shoot a man on the road. Fanny trembling in his arms after riding cross-country. Visions of her nearness, the press of her body to his, tormented him. The maniac behind her peril had to be found and stopped—thoroughly, completely, permanently.

They reached the Irish Sea at sunset. The publican in the fishing village of Prestatyn served a decent ale and food that was filling at least. The man offered little by way of information regarding private anchorage and suggested they return back toward Mostyn for overnight accommodations. Temptation to continue around the coast seized Eli, but Tommy reminded him they had to return to Chester in the morning.

Retracing their steps, they found Mostyn and the inn their publican had called "honest," an ancient-looking place that boasted a crowded tavern, one tiny bedroom to let, and a clean bed. Tommy sank into slumber as soon as he nestled on his side of the bed, his snoring regular and soft.

Eli lay awake. He felt a fool, lodging in a decrepit hostel in Wales while Fanny remained at Clarion Hall, unable to get on with her life. He stared at shadows on the ceiling and allowed visions of the woman he loved free rein. It wasn't as if he could keep her from his thoughts anyway.

Sleeplessness persisted until he threw his legs over the side and padded across the room. A multipaned window, wider than it was tall, hung on the wall, at eye level. He pulled back the shade and gazed out at moonlight on the water. The inn lay just past a spit of land that jutted out into the Dee estuary shimmering in the pale-blue light. He glanced at the road where it passed his location. Tomorrow he would confront the bishop, get the privileges Fanny wanted, and return to her.

What will you do after that, Benson?

His body, hot and reckless, rose to make one answer, while worry about his employer's response intruded. Would Clarion frown on his courtship of Fanny? Eli didn't know, but it wasn't Clarion's business. Eli no longer fretted that Fanny was an earl's daughter and above his touch. Rob's wise counsel had put a period to that nonsense. He recalled his brother's encouraging words about his position, and he knew himself well able to support a wife.

In the end, his heart urged him to its true desire. Memories of her response to his kisses filled him with hope stronger by far than any of those other considerations.

Put your love to the test—for what else could this madness be? Ask the woman to share your life and your bed.

The thought terrified him. He would almost rather confront the criminal behind her abduction than put his heart at risk.

Fear holds you back, then, Benson? Some hero he was, needing courage to propose to a woman. His mocking mind reminded him that he was hardly the hero of her dreams, but he didn't care. He had reason to hope she felt as he did. A smile tugged the side of his mouth. He would do it. Once he'd obtained what she wished for, he would pay his addresses.

At the thought, a light across the water winked at him, as if to celebrate. Or warn him. He scanned the water until he saw it blink again. When it did, shapes in the distance, outlined by the light of the moon, came into focus. A ship bobbed at anchor out there.

Eli dressed quickly in the dark. He returned to the window, his eyes going unerringly to the ship. How had he missed it in the daytime? He wouldn't mistake it again. He'd be there when the sun came up.

CHAPTER THIRTY-THREE

T HEY'D COME AT low tide. From Eli's vantage point in a rocky
formation surrounded by scrubby trees, mudflats extended on
both sides of the sloping peninsula. The ship—for it had indeed been a
ship he'd sighted the night before—lay at anchor in a small inlet, listing
a bit to the side in low water fifty feet away.

The sleek, two-masted vessel—a sloop, Eli thought—had been
built for speed, but in these waters, it would wait for high tide. He
narrowed his eyes, wondering whether it was waiting or hiding.

*Absurd, Benson. What makes you think this vessel has anything to do
with the pernicious trade in bodies?* Nothing. Not one clue, except there
was no good reason for such a ship to anchor in a place like this. At
very least it demonstrated that a seagoing vessel could avoid port
authorities and find a spot to—

Movement caught his eye, two men climbing out onto the deck.
They stepped out into full sun, and Eli stopped breathing. He recognized them both.

Bateson! He discerned Grimsley's associate without any doubt. Of
the earl he saw no sign, but given the conversation he had overheard
at Danburys' garden, he doubted Grimsley lurked below. He suspected the sloop—the entire operation—belonged to Bateson. The rogue,
head and shoulders taller than his companion, gesticulated angrily,
while the other man seemed to shrink in front of him. Shrinking was
no small task for the hulking brute Eli recognized from the Happy

Cock. Holliday hadn't described the man he sought, but Eli knew he had just stumbled on the missing Everhard.

Eli sank down against a rock, filled with elation. A vision of himself descending on Bateson like an avenging angel and clubbing the snake to the ground transfixed his imagination. He removed his pistol from the pack in which he carried it and checked that it was armed and dry.

"What are we going to do, Mr. Benson?" Tommy, who crouched next to him, attentive and waiting, asked, wide-eyed. Eli studied the young Clarion groom, fear and bravery in his eyes in equal amounts. The fire drained out of Eli. If he asked the boy to charge down the bank with him and attempt to take that ship, he'd likely get them both killed. They couldn't guess how many men were belowdecks, but a ship of that size required a somewhat large crew. Everhard alone could probably subdue both of them.

Sinking back to earth, Eli realized a glorious but ill-fated stab at heroism wouldn't do Fanny any good, either. He gazed at Tommy. "You are going to ride to Manchester—the faster, the better."

Eli pulled out his notebook, the ever-present weapon of a steward, and scribbled a message to Holliday. "Located Everhard. And ship." He described the situation including tides, named Bateson as the likely leader, folded the message, and added Holliday's direction.

He had no idea how long it would take Holliday to bring reinforcements, whether the ship would sail, tides permitting, or when such a tide might occur. He handed the message to Tommy and urged speed.

When the boy scurried off through the protection of the clump of trees, Eli scrambled to his feet for another look. Bateson now lounged against a railing, watching the sun rise high above the estuary, unconcerned. He didn't look like a man in a hurry. An hour later, Eli still studied the sloop when two roughly dressed crew members slipped over the side on a pully of some sort. They went to work on the side. Whether they were cleaning, repairing, or removing barnacles, Eli had no idea, but it appeared they weren't going anywhere soon.

He had done what he could do; he considered perhaps his place was to keep his appointment with the bishop. He might have left then, if a rough-looking seaman hadn't blocked his way.

"Watchin' Mr. Bateson's ship, are you?"

One man? Eli thought so. He didn't see any others. He stepped to his right, eyeing the cudgel in the man's hand. "What are you doing over here?" Eli accused in his most authoritarian tone.

The man blinked, enough to tell Eli he'd made a hit.

Eli took another step to his right. "I saw you over at the tavern last night." He hadn't actually; it was a stab in the dark.

A flash of guilt rewarded him.

"Bateson won't like that," Eli continued, taking a third step. The ruffian mirrored his actions, sliding to the left as though moving in a circle. The man's gaze darted around nervously. He didn't speak.

"What will he do to you for being late?" Eli pretended to glance at the ship but kept his attention on the man and his weapon. "They've already started work on the hull."

The ruffian turned to look at the ship, and Eli broke into a run, making for the hotel and his horse.

FANNY LIFTED HER pen and stared at the page in front of her.

The End, it said.

She dried it and added the last sheet to the rest of *The Elusive Earl* piled on her desk, her mood far from celebratory. She would make a fair copy, ready to send it off to a publisher, but she wasn't entirely certain she wanted to do that. The golden earl of her initial imagining had turned into a dark figure until the heroine had had to be rescued from his clutches by a mysterious man in black.

She glowered at the manuscript. Rubbish—or at least not her best work—and yet she feared it would just meet Minerva's preference for gothic gloom. They might especially like the part where the mysterious stranger finds the heroine lost in the dark forest, hiding her just before the evil earl arrives. A rueful smile touched Fanny's lips. That sort of adventure was more uncomfortable in reality than it sounded in fiction.

Fanny rose and stretched, twisting her back to and fro to loosen it. She had spent more time than not all week alone in her room, writing. What she needed was a good, long walk or a ride, if only she could convince Clarion or the others to allow it. She set out to find her brother, knowing he likely hid in his library this time of day, corresponding about parliamentary business. She found it empty.

Harris, quickly summoned, told her, "Sir Robert came over. He and the earl decided to take advantage of the day, to ride across the estate." Rob had been in Ashmead three days. With Lucy engaged in the business of overseeing Willowbrook, he had come to the hall every day. Now the two of them had gone for a ride. Without her.

Fanny hurried to her room, grateful Lucy had insisted on a riding habit. If they could take advantage of the weather, she could take advantage of their presence.

She strode through the kitchen garden, toward the path that led through trees to the stable yard.

A guard stationed at the path eyed her riding habit nervously. "Corporal Goodfellow said as how you were staying in the hall, Miss Hancock."

"Did Sir Robert and his lordship come this way?" she asked.

"Aye," the man said, uncertainty marring his expression.

"Excellent. I plan to join them." She darted past. The man followed her, obviously torn between stopping her, something his universe told him would be inappropriate, and allowing her to put herself in danger, something that might cost him his job.

Fanny bustled through the woods, to the stable yard just in time. Rob pulled his horse up, glanced at the guard and back to his sister. "Fanny, what is it?" he asked, brows drawn together.

Clarion, who rode slightly ahead, turned around and approached. Both men leaned forward on their saddles. "Is there a problem?" the earl asked.

"Yes," she said. "A big problem." She let that sink in before continuing, "My book is finished, and I have no one to share it with, and I'm in danger of collapsing..." Their identical frowns amused her. "...under the weight of boredom. I need exercise. If you are going for a ride, I'm going with you. Surely the two of you can protect me."

Clarion frowned, and Rob laughed. *So much alike and yet so different,* she thought, aware of her miraculous fortune to have them both in her life. They waited until a gentle mare was saddled and brought to her. Two armed grooms, summoned with a gesture, mounted up as well.

She rode quietly and listened attentively while they discussed estate management, Rob frequently quoting Lucy with pride. They rode Fanny past cultivated fields and tenant cottages, stopping to gossip with many. At one cottage, the earl dismounted to inspect the roof, making a note of the damage caused by a fallen tree. "Benson will see to it," he said.

Fanny gritted her teeth. She waited until they rode on to ask what was on the tip of her tongue. "When?"

"When what?" The earl asked.

"When will Mr. Benson deal with the roof?"

"I think what she means is, 'When will Eli be back?'" Rob said, swallowing a laugh. "If he isn't back in one more day, I'm going after him."

CHAPTER THIRTY-FOUR

Eli reached the inn where his horse waited, saddled and ready for travel, easily enough, but when he galloped, pistol at the ready, out of the stable yard, the bruiser who had confronted him came huffing across the road. One shot stopped the seaman in his tracks. Eli didn't halt to check if he'd hit him or merely startled him. He rode up the coast road like the demons of hell were on his heels. Perhaps they were.

Now you've alerted Bateson that someone spied on him. He'll be gone before Holliday reaches here. He cursed soundly as he rode. Eli had another problem. Should he follow Tommy to Holliday or keep his appointment with the thrice-damned bishop?

For the sake of speed, he kept to the main coast road until Connah's Quay, still undecided about his destination. He pulled up to consider his situation. He neither saw nor heard anyone chasing him. If he'd hit his pursuer, it might be a while before Bateson discovered the body and sent someone to stop Eli. They would be too late because Tommy Withers was well ahead of Eli. If he'd missed, the man would have used Eli's escape to cover his own absence from the ship, and they were probably after Eli.

Either way, that ship couldn't leave until the tide turned. Tommy would reach Holliday long before Eli could. If, as he hoped, Holliday set out immediately, Eli would accomplish nothing by following Tommy to Manchester. He didn't even know what route they might take. On the other hand, if Bateson captured Eli, it would complicate Holliday's task.

Eli decided to trust the groom and the tides, avoid capture, and go where his skills might do some actual good. He deviated from the main road, following country lanes and cantering across fields back to the river to cross by bridge at Chester, his mood grim and angry, spoiling for a fight.

God spare that bishop if he proves uncooperative.

TWO DAYS LATER, Fanny heard banging on the massive oak door, the formal entrance, an unheard-of breach of etiquette. It could only mean trouble. She ran to the stairs to see Harris, frowning deeply, go to answer it.

"I need to see the earl!"

Still on the stairs, she couldn't see who spoke, but Harris didn't hesitate. He stepped aside to let Tommy Withers enter, dirty, disheveled, and limp with exhaustion. She pressed a hand to her thudding heart.

Eli. Dear God, Eli. What has happened?

Harris didn't wait for an explanation. He dispatched a footman for the earl and urged the young groom to the bench by the door.

Fanny ran the rest of the way down, slipped on the parquet floor at the bottom, and righted herself to approach the young groom she knew had ridden off with Eli.

"Sorry to barge in, Miss Hancock, but I rode all the way from Mostyn. I only stopped to change horses and—"

Clarion arrived first, hurrying from his study. "Withers! What news do you have? Where is Benson?" the earl demanded, striding toward them.

Pounding footsteps made it clear the boy's arrival had been noticed. The nursery set leaned over the upper gallery, and every servant who could paused nearby to listen.

Tommy leapt to his feet and bowed. "Mr. Benson sends word, my lord."

All Fanny could think was, *Thank goodness. If he sends word, he is safe.* "Is he in this Mostyn place?"

Tommy glanced at her and back to Clarion, as if uncertain how to go on. "He was, ma'am. But they were on their way to Manchester."

"This is obviously a complicated tale. We'll hear it from the beginning, but first, is Benson safe?" the earl asked.

"As can be, my lord," the boy said.

Fanny sagged with relief.

"And I assume Sir Robert reached him?" the earl went on.

"Not until it was all over," Tommy said proudly.

All what? Eli went to deal with the sale of the store. What on earth went on? She glanced at Clarion.

The earl responded with one of his sad smiles. "Let's adjourn to the servant's dining room and get this young man some refreshments so he has the strength to tell us what I suspect is a long story."

Tommy reached into his shirt, pulled out a creased and crumpled piece of paper, and handed it to Clarion. "Thank you kindly, my lord, but I need to give you this first. I almost forgot."

Clarion glanced at it and gave it to Fanny with a wry lift of his eyebrow. The words were few and the message frustratingly short. *Business successfully completed. Please tell Miss Hancock we won. Also, she is now safe. Home in three days. Benson.*

She trailed after them to the servants' quarters, her emotions careening up and down. They had won. She assumed that meant she could administer Wil's affairs. But "Miss Hancock"? *And what does the wretch mean, I'm now safe? Drat it, Eli, what were you up to?*

The story took a while to sort out, Tommy being a man who wandered about in his telling. He began with some tale of dockside taverns that made little sense, and added colorful travelogue. For a boy who'd never left Ashmead, two cities, a major cathedral, canals, and an estuary full of birds had been revelatory.

The earl nudged him back to the main story repeatedly.

Yes, Mr. Benson went to court in Manchester and to an estate agent, too.

Yes, the store appeared fine.

No, he didn't know about the sale.

Chester because the bishop, and Mr. Benson was that angry with the priest. "But that were good because if they'd given him what he wanted, we'd have come home and Mr. Benson would never have ridden up the Deeside coast."

"Why did he?" Fanny asked.

"He had me looking for a place to hide a ship. One that could sail the ocean, not one of them little riverboats or canal barges. We didn't see one the first day."

Fanny glanced at the earl, who murmured, "Looking for how our villain transported his victims, I suspect. Smart."

Fanny shuddered.

"Found him!" Tommy crowed. "Ship and some queer cove he recognized. Name of Bateson. I thought Mr. Benson were going to have me charge down with him like pirates or something to take the ship. Looked like thunder, he did."

Bateson?! "But he didn't?" Fanny held her breath. *Surely Eli wouldn't charge in there on his own.*

"Sent me after Holliday. One mention of this other cove, Everhard, and Holliday gathered up a small army to pound on down there before they could escape. I rode along with them," Tommy said proudly.

"And Eli—Mr. Benson—stayed in Mostyn to wait?" Fanny asked. *Please tell me he did nothing foolish.*

Tommy laughed. "They almost got him." The boy launched into a vivid and undoubtedly embellished story of escape, pistols, and a desperate ride up the coast that Fanny found difficult to swallow. "Besides, he had an appointment with that bishop. He were bound and determined that man would do as he asked."

The earl—her brother—David gave Fanny the broadest grin she'd ever seen him allow. "That's the Eli Benson we know, calmly taking care of business while chaos reigns around him."

That did sound like the man she loved.

"Yep. Finished his business and rode back to Mostyn. Got there as Holliday was bringing the prisoners up from the ship. Sir Robert was with him—Mr. Benson, I mean." Before the earl or Fanny could ask, he went on, "They met up in Chester. Sir Robert said he knew Eli had business there."

That left only one question, the thing most important to Fanny. "When will he be home? I know he said three days, but will that be enough time? Can I count on it?"

Tommy shrugged. "Mr. Benson went back to Manchester with Holliday to give his testimony. He and Sir Robert should be here in three or four days. Maybe."

THE DAMNED PONY cart broke an axel. Eli had endured more terrifying crises on the road, more undignified upheaval, and more hours in bone-rattling motion in the past few months than in his entire life before. Da's cart on its side was the final calamity in a long line of them.

He'd left Manchester fifteen hours before, one day after he'd sent Tommy on the road. While Holliday had made Everhard spill his guts over Bateson's evil operation and Rob had dealt with magistrates, all Eli could think about was Fanny. He'd given his written testimony and caught the first mail coach south, the fastest way to get to her, determined to put his courage to the test by proposing to her.

The coach had changed horses every ten miles. For the first twenty or so, he'd worked on a speech he thought might do, rewording and analyzing the main points he would make to state his case. By the third stop, he'd known that for foolishness. He'd taken stock.

What, after all, do you have to offer, Benson, glorified clerk that you are? If it is a hero she wants... As the coach had rumbled over the peaks, he'd reviewed what he had read in her notes. Tall? No. Blond? Decidedly not. Rugged and well-muscled? He'd snorted. Commanding and decisive? Alas, no. *A man has to consider a situation before he acts.* Loyal? Yes. She wouldn't find a man more loyal, a man who would be at her side for his entire life. There was that.

But heroism couldn't be everything. What did a woman want in a husband? Steady income and a home for her children.

You may not be wealthy, Benson, but a steward is a man of stature. You won't fail her. You can provide.

As they'd passed through Ashbourne, fear had set in. *What does Fanny want really? A cottage where she can write. Space of her own. You can give her that, Benson.* But was it enough? He wouldn't know until he asked. He had to put his poor heart at risk and ask the woman.

When he'd disembarked at the Willow, Da, who had come out to greet the mail, had clapped Eli on the back, delighted by the surprise. Eli had asked to use the pony cart and promised to come back the next day for a good talk. "At least I'll try." On to the hall and Fanny he'd gone.

Trudging uphill one more time, leading his father's pony and carrying his valise, he felt a fool. A clerk that couldn't even manage a cart. He glared up at the imposing façade of Clarion Hall, Fanny's ancestral home.

What on earth makes you think you can provide for this glorious woman?

He walked on around to the stables, handed the pony to the grooms, dispatched someone to take care of the cart, followed the path through the trees, and dragged himself through the kitchen as was his custom.

"Mr. Benson! We weren't expecting you for a few more days," the cook exclaimed. He waved off greetings politely and made his way down the long corridor to the estate office. His domain. His tiny apartment, a mere room, lay above it. Meager enough to show for his life.

He opened the door and stared around him. Little light shown in that afternoon, but even in the dimness, it felt familiar. He had always gloried in this world, but now it felt merely comfortable. Comfortable but not enough. He shook his head, walked to the desk, and set down his valise. He froze.

Curled up in his chair, a shawl around her shoulders, dainty toes peeking out from her hem, Fanny slept. His unruly heart raced, and his idiot male organs rose in celebration.

What is that she has in her arms? He peered at it closely. She cradled a ledger book to her beautiful breasts. *My ledger?* He dared hope she meant to embrace its owner.

He indulged the urge to simply look at her, letting his gaze graze her toes, follow the line of her legs where they curled beneath her, hug her hip, and wander along her arm to that ledger—his ledger—lying where he longed to—

"Benson!"

At the earl's voice, Eli spun around, pulling his valise to his front to avoid embarrassment. "My lord." He inclined his head.

"We didn't expect you for another few days," Clarion said. "I gather you not only completed our business but captured the malefactors behind Miss Hancock's misfortunes."

"Eli?" Fanny's voice, thick with sleep, preceded the sound of a ledger being dropped on his desk.

"Fanny, what are you doing in Benson's chair?" The earl sounded puzzled. Eli had been, too, but his delight had outweighed it.

"I… I came in to write a note and fell asleep." Fanny's sheepish expression gave Eli's aching heart a nudge.

The earl beamed at her. "No need. Our Benson has returned early."

"I took the mail." As an explanation, Eli's words lacked substance.

"We'll want to hear everything. Come along to the family parlor. It is better lit this time of day." The earl leaned to John the footman hovering behind him and ordered tea sent up. Clarion set off, confident they would follow.

Fanny came around the desk. Eli dropped his valise, and a hand come up instinctively to pull her into his arms. Sense stopped him, and he got as far as her cheek, his trembling fingers touching it tenderly.

"You dropped your valise," she said, her eyes boring into his.

"You're safe," he murmured.

She blinked. "We heard. Come. Clarion expects you to tell us all." She took his hand and tugged him toward the door.

"Fanny?" Eli hardly recognized his own voice.

"Yes?"

"We need to talk."

She tilted her head up and smiled. "Yes," she said.

CHAPTER THIRTY-FIVE

FOR AN EXCRUCIATING hour, Fanny watched Eli report to the earl, beginning, of course, with his duties to the estate. While dealings with banks in London and courts in Manchester might not be the usual thing for a land steward, Eli, of course, had managed all to the earl's satisfaction.

Does David have any idea what a treasure he has? Watching the earl's face, she suspected he did.

Prodded, Eli admitted his suspicion of Bateson and some startling activity in London involving the river police. That led to a rather more comprehensible account of how he'd managed to locate Bateson, his yacht, his henchman, and more to the point, proof. The ridiculous man downplayed any hint of heroism on his part, referring merely to "logic."

The clock ticked on under the earl's questioning, and Fanny's spirits sagged only to be buoyed up every time Eli glanced her way, as if he was as anxious to be alone with her as she was him.

At last, Clarion set down his cup, smiled at Fanny, and said, "I think Fanny has been busy in your absence. Do you know she finished an entire novel?"

"Well done! We shall have to develop our business plan for it." Eli beamed at her. Her heart and mind were not on her writing, however.

"I thought perhaps, my lord, Mr. Benson might be more interested in my other project," she said.

Clarion held back a grin. "I see. Then I suggest the two of you take a ride and discuss it."

Did David just wink at me? Surely not.

She peered at Eli, whose face had a comical mix of confusion, elation, and...she wasn't sure what.

"Ride?" Eli asked in a strangled voice. "I thought you didn't like to ride."

"I've been practicing," Fanny said, to her brother's amusement. She suspected Eli had had his fill of riding and travel. He would have to endure a bit more, just for today. She had something to show him. She rose to her feet. "If you gentlemen will excuse me, I need to change. I'll meet Mr. Benson in the stables."

⟫⟫⟫⟪⟪⟪

"WHERE ARE WE going? The ride toward Willowbrook is more scenic." Visions of dismounting in the privacy of one of the clearings in the wood reminded him of their night by the forest. It would be a perfect setting for what he planned to say. Fanny, he feared, had other ideas.

"You'll see." The mysterious feminine smile she gave him heated his blood as much as it frustrated him.

He recognized their direction; he knew every corner of the estate. On a slight rise on the east end of the estate, they came to a house, the cottage he had ignored when he'd become steward, preferring not to rattle around it alone, saving the estate the fuss of restoring it, for it had been in disuse since the old earl had died and Clarion had fired the previous steward.

Fanny stopped at the bend in the lane to study the place. Eli saw little change. Overgrown with shrubs and vines, the fine stone shone golden in the sun. The shutters still needed paint and... He blinked. The door had been painted. A flame of hope flickered to life.

"Help me down," Fanny said.

He dismounted and came around, reaching up a hand. She put hers on his shoulders, forcing him to take her waist and lift her down. She slid down his front and stood so close her breath warmed his face for one fraught moment.

She leaned up and kissed his chin. "That's better. Now come." She pulled him by the hand, strode up to the door, and took a key from her reticule to unlock it.

He followed her inside and closed the door behind him. He'd be damned if he would worry about propriety now. When he turned back, she stood close, intense and expectant.

He caressed her cheek with one hand, inching closer, never taking his eyes from hers. She met his action by leaning toward him. His hand slid down to her neck, his thumb lifting her chin, and she tilted her head up for his kiss. He touched her mouth with his gently, once, twice, and again. She met him kiss for kiss.

Enough holding back!

He yanked her bonnet from her head and tossed it to the floor, his mouth never leaving hers, running his hands into her hair to dislodge it from its pins with one hand while the other went around her waist. He pulled her hard against him.

His tiny love stood on tiptoe to meet him, but he needed more. Eli broke off their kiss and lifted her, pressing her against the door with his body, chest to chest, his arousal pushed against her. Her mouth opened under his when he probed and deepened the kiss, and her hands slid around his neck to hold on and to play with the hair at his nape.

Long moments later, he struggled for breath and sanity returned. He moved back enough to let her slide along his length to the floor, laid his head on top of hers, and sighed.

Her words muffled against his chest, she said, "My goodness, Mr. Benson. Is that your idea of talk?"

Eli shook with laughter. He had forgotten everything he'd meant to say, but her response gave him hope. "Did I get ahead of myself again?"

She grinned up at him. When she pressed a hand into his chest, he moved back reluctantly.

"Come look around," she said, taking him by the hand. She cleared her throat. "This floor has a good-sized parlor and a dining room." She rattled off the words while she pulled him along, pointing out the kitchen, which according to her needed improvement.

He wondered why she had him touring the blasted place, one he already—"What's this?"

She had pulled him into a west-facing room. One he might have called the steward's private study, except the desk by the window looked more like a lady's. Unlike the rest of the house, this room had been cleaned, painted, and furnished.

She paused there, letting him absorb what he saw: a coverlet lay over the arm of a rocking chair, a small ottoman sat in front of it, a painting—one of Eli's own watercolors of the Afon—hung on one wall. Did she mean for him to move his office here? To work on that scrap of a desk? His eyes skittered back to it. A neat stack of papers lay on top. *Do you know she finished an entire novel?*

She squeezed his hand, and he peered down at her, certain his hundred questions must be in his eyes. She swallowed. "My office," she whispered. "My writing place."

"The earl has offered you the steward's cottage?" he asked, searching her face for the meaning of life.

She huffed impatiently and gave his arm a yank, tugging him to the stairs. He swore the words she muttered were "slow top."

At the top of the stairs, she retrieved her hand and began to point. "That room for Amy. That for Wil, or we can make one in the attic if we need it. The one in the corner for a nursery, and this one—"

Nursery? His mouth went dry, and his mind went blank.

She dragged him through the door to a larger suite of two rooms.

"This one is—"

"Yours," he said, the imp urging him to tease being more comfortable than the realization that overwhelmed him.

She punched his arm. Hard. "Ours, you lackwit."

He tenderly cupped her chin, rubbing her neck with this thumb. "Ours. Is this a proposal, then? I rather hoped to do it myself."

The green Caulfield eyes filled with moisture, and she blinked them away, pursing her lips together. "Then you should speak up, Eli Benson. I've been waiting."

He leaned his forehead against hers. "Miss Frances Hancock, would you consider my poor self a suitable husband? I know I'm a simple clerk and not the hero of your dreams, but I offer—"

She reared back to glower at him. "You are not a simple anything, Eli. You are the brilliant fixer who cares for us all. You are..." She peered at him intently and breathed, "You are everything to me."

He pulled her hard against him and squeezed his eyes shut. "And you, my beloved, are everything to me."

She tugged his head down to kiss him.

"Is that yes?" he asked, smiling against her mouth.

Her response became muffled in a kiss, but he thought she said yes. That and "nodcock." He gave himself over to the kisses his dearest seemed to want. He kissed her until it wasn't enough, and he glanced around the empty room.

When he lifted her to a windowsill so her face was even with his, she spread her knees to pull him closer, and he joyfully took advantage, beginning the love play that would last their lifetime. He spared a glance out the window over her shoulder as he slid her gown up over her knees and pressed his aroused member up against her, but he saw no one. Only the passing sheep would be scandalized when he kissed his way down her neck while he tugged her gown down to expose her beautiful breasts to his heated gaze and suckled, drawing moans of pleasure from his beloved.

She rocked against him, incoherently begging for more. Eli took her mouth in his and slid his hand between them, his fingers finding her moist heat, caressing gently and then more firmly.

When the last spasm of pleasure shook Fanny and she sagged against his shoulder, disheveled and replete, Eli Benson felt more powerful than he ever had in his life. He kissed the top of her head and asked what she had just mumbled.

"Words aren't everything," she replied.

He held her there, unwilling to move, willing the discomfort of his own arousal to subside, glad that no words were needed. He kissed her hair again. "There is one problem with this house," he said at last.

She sat up then and began to fiddle with her bodice. He planted a quick kiss on her breast before she could go on. She gave him a playful smack and continued tying it up to cover herself. "What problem?" she asked, peering around.

"There is no bed," he said, enjoying the sight when her hand stilled, delighted by her rosy cheeks.

Still perched on the windowsill, she put a dainty finger under his chin and pulled his gaze up to hers. "Ah. There will be a bed," she said. "Mr. Benson will see to it."

He kissed her again. What else could he do? They rode back to the hall long after dark.

EPILOGUE

FANNY, ROUND WITH child and wrapped in a shawl, sat at her desk eighteen months later, lifted her pen, and watched a rare snowstorm cover the land around the Steward's Rest. They had named their house so because it was their own destination at journey's end. It was theirs to name. Though the earl could not make the cottage and twenty-odd acres around it truly his gift, because it was entailed, he'd had documents drawn up to make it theirs for the lifetime of Fanny and their children. The Clarion tenants called it Benson's Harbor and joked about his missing boat.

She smiled at the lone figure riding up to the house, hat pulled down over his head, scarf wrapped tightly around his face to fend off the wind. Eli came early today, an unusual event, one she planned to enjoy.

She rose and walked to the kitchen. "Tea, Mrs. D. And some bread and butter. Mr. Benson is early today."

"We have Chelsea buns from the Willow," Mrs. D., or Mrs. Dalton, replied. She was both housekeeper and cook and happily went by the shortened name.

"I thought I did them in! Yes, please. Chelsea buns," Fanny said.

"Your office, ma'am?" Mrs. D. asked.

"The upstairs sitting room, please," Fanny replied, drawing a knowing smile from her housekeeper.

He would be a while seeing to the horse, she thought, climbing the stairs.

"Eli's home, Fanny," Amy chirped, coming from her room. "Have you ordered tea?"

"I have, indeed." Fanny put an arm around Amy's shoulders and brought her with her into the sitting room.

Soon enough boots sounded on the stairs and Clarion Hall's indispensable steward swept a cold wind and the smell of snow into the little room. Fanny's heart filled, her world complete.

"I come with tea," he said, laying the tray on the table in front of Fanny. "And news."

"Big news?" Amy asked, reaching for a bun, catching herself, and sitting back to wait for Fanny to pour.

"We'll see how big. I haven't opened the mail yet." Eli pulled two letters from his pocket.

He handed the first to Amy, for it was addressed to Mr. and Mrs. Eli Benson and Amy in Wil's distinctive hand. He had been boarding at the Latin school in Risley since Michaelmas, having declined the earl's offer to seek a scholarship to Eton for him. Eli had been torn, but Wil's decision had satisfied Fanny. He would be more comfortable there, do well, and find his own way.

Amy read aloud the usual brief note to let them know he was fine, describe an adventure rambling in the countryside with the other fellows to prove it, and remind Fanny to take good care now that "you know." That last made Amy's cheeks pink.

"What is the other?" Amy demanded.

Fanny put down her tea. Eli's sober expression gave her pause. The letter he handed her was from A. K. Newman and Company, Publisher. She opened it quickly, and her hand flew to her throat. "Oh, Eli. They want it. They're going to publish *The Steward's Revenge*." His joy multiplied hers. "And he wants to know how soon I can send him another."

"What are you calling the new one, Fanny?" Amy asked.

"*The Gambler's Downfall*," she said.

Amy brushed crumbs from her hands. "I will leave you two to celebrate in peace. I'm still working through the mathematics propositions Eli gave me on Sunday." Ever since Eli had discovered the girl's gift for numbers, there'd been no stopping her.

She closed the door with a snick, and Fanny met the gleam in Eli's eyes.

He took her hand to help her rise, searched her face, and smiled at what he saw there. He ran one tender hand down her rounded belly. "How is the little fellow?"

"He is fit and fine. So is his mother."

The heat in Eli's eyes flamed higher. He locked the door and led her to the adjoining bedroom. "It's a good thing this house acquired a comfortable bed," he said, his lips against her neck. It was an old joke between them.

"It's a good thing Mr. Benson saw to it," she murmured, returning his kiss. "He sees to everything."

And he did.

Author's Note

Eli and Fanny were a joy to write. I already knew him to be loyal, bright, and a master of ferreting out details. In the course of three books, he has grown into the role of land steward, a formidable position for one so young, but Eli has proven himself to the earl many times over.

While researching this story, I discovered that land stewards were highly educated, professional men, not servants. A landowner would place his steward above his lawyer or doctor in the hierarchy of professionals.

Contemporary handbooks urged landowners to compensate their stewards well if they wished them to avoid the temptation to abuse power—and a steward had enormous power. He oversaw rents, hiring, purchasing, and so on, as I described. "Mr. Benson will see to it" is precisely the sort of role they had. They were generally very well paid, making twice or even three times as much as a butler, who was the senior servant and ran the household. A steward also customarily received a house as part of his compensation.

My hero lucked out in one regard. More than one book advised against hiring a provincial solicitor, as Eli was at the beginning of book one. They were believed to be too narrow in their thinking and not up to a grand agricultural enterprise. Such a point was made of it that I suspect it was a common practice with well-known pitfalls. Clarion, however, had a treasure in Eli Benson.

How authentic is the danger to Fanny? Barbary slavery was very real. Human beings had great value in the slave markets of the North African coast. One author has estimated 1.25 million Europeans were enslaved in the Barbary markets. Other authors challenge his methodology. In any case, it is well below the twelve million Africans believed to have been enslaved and shipped to the Americas. On the other hand, Christians and Europeans weren't their only targets. Plenty of Africans and Muslims were also captured and sold, so that number swells.

What were they used for? First and foremost, ransom. Ransom money was a growing concern, and ransom charities abounded on the European side of the Mediterranean. I made use of that activity in *Dangerous Weakness*. If no ransom was forthcoming, they could be sold. Men by and large were used for hard labor, the worst being as rowers on the galleys. Women might be laborers also, but yes, comely young women had great value as sexual slaves or concubines. They were luxury items for wealthy households and sold for much higher prices.

Most people think of high-seas piracy when they think of the Barbary pirates, but they were coastal raiders as well. Land raids occurred along the Icelandic, Irish, Scottish, and English coasts to capture people to be sold. The most notorious case was a raid on Baltimore, Ireland, during which 107 people were carried off. The raiders were known to be in those waters, and it isn't far-fetched to imagine they might have business dealings with smugglers and other criminals along the same coasts, as I suggest in this story. After all, if large sums of money are involved, crime flourishes.

Would red hair have added value to a captive? I found no evidence of it, but why not? Blond hair certainly did, and red is a rarity. Just 1–2 percent of the human race has red hair. Even Ireland, which has the highest percentage, boasts only about 10 percent of the population with ginger hair, by most estimates. As to northern England, I put the best guess I found into Rob's words: "I have reason to know that not more than five or six people out of a hundred in this part of the world have hair the color of mine. Even fewer are female, young, and attractive."

Add a bit of obsession, and yes, Fanny could feasibly have been a particularly valuable target.

One more thing. Beta readers asked if Clarion would have his own book. If you are one asking the same, take heart. He is *The Upright Son*, and his story comes next. Look for it in May or June 2022.

About the Author

Award winning author of family centered romance set in the Regency and Victorian eras, Caroline Warfield has been many things (even a nun), but above all she is a romantic. Someone who begins life as an army brat develops a wide view of life, and a love for travel. Now settled in the urban wilds of eastern Pennsylvania, she reckons she is on at least her third act. When she isn't off seeking adventures with her Beloved or her grandson down the block, she works happily in an office surrounded by windows where she lets her characters lead her to even more adventures in England and the far-flung corners of the British Empire. She nudges them to explore the riskiest territory of all, the human heart, because love is worth the risk.

Website: www.carolinewarfield.com
Amazon Author: amazon.com/Caroline-Warfield/e/B00N9PZZZS
Good Reads: bit.ly/1C5blTm
Facebook: facebook.com/groups/WarfieldFellowTravelers
Twitter: twitter.com/CaroWarfield
Email: warfieldcaro@gmail.com
Newsletter: carolinewarfield.com/newsletter
BookBub: bookbub.com/authors/caroline-warfield
You Tube: youtube.com/channel/UCycyfKdNnZlueqo8MlgWyWQ

Printed in Great Britain
by Amazon

81509207R00153